Daisy smiled, happy that Bass was pleased.

Ollie moved past him and apologized. "Sorry, Bass. I must've left the back door open this morning. Only way Butler coulda got in the kitchen. I'll make sure he don't cause ya no more problems. 'Least for today."

"I'm grateful it was only a goat. I heard somebody downstairs and thought I'd better check since I assumed I was still alone. But I couldn't get down here fast enough to stop the initial damage. As you can see, he fought hard in the parlor until I got him roped and cornered behind the table."

Bass brushed a hand through his dark hair, powdering it with even more flour. "But it was worth it, getting to hear your mama laugh like that."

"You laugh pretty well yourself." Daisy returned the compliment as his eyes studied her directly.

"That's on my daddy list. Likes to laugh," Ollie reminded. "Ya remember, don'tcha, Mama?"

"Yes, love. I remember." Able to look Mama straight in the eye was on there, t~~~

Bass was begi~~~ ~~~st's requirements.

And Daisy was ~~~ ~~~at.

She wanted hi~~~

* * *

DeWanna Pace is a *New York Times* and *USA TODAY* bestselling author who lives in Texas with her husband and pets. She has published two dozen novels and anthologies, several of which have been chosen as book-club selections by Doubleday, Rhapsody, Book-of-the-Month, *Woman's Day* and The Literary Guild. DeWanna combines her faith with her love of humor and historical romance. Let her show you the ways a heart can love.

Books by DeWanna Pace

Love Inspired Historical

The Daddy List

The Daddy List

DeWANNA PACE

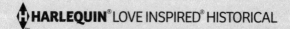

HARLEQUIN® LOVE INSPIRED® HISTORICAL

Recycling programs
for this product may
not exist in your area.

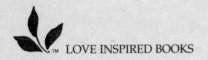 LOVE INSPIRED BOOKS

ISBN-13: 978-0-373-28305-7

The Daddy List

Copyright © 2015 by DeWanna Pace

www.Harlequin.com

Printed in U.S.A.

In all thy ways acknowledge Him
and He shall direct thy paths.
—*Proverbs* 3:6

This book is dedicated to:
Jodi Thomas, Linda Broday,
Phyliss Miranda and Gail Fortune.
Thanks for the years, the tears and the persistence
that made this dream come true.

Most of all, thank the Lord for leading me to
Shana Asaro and the crew at Love Inspired Books.
I'll forever feel blessed.

Chapter One

Spring, 1868

Keeping her promise would wear Daisy Trumbo out before this was all over with, but keep it she would. With long strides she hurried down the planked sidewalk that led from the mercantile, where she'd been stocking up on supplies. According to a handful of outraged citizens, her seven-year-old daughter was over at the bank holding men hostage with a gun.

Daisy had agreed to consider every man her child chose to interview in the quest to gain a new father, but holding them prisoner until each passed or failed inspection was simply taking her newfound mission too far.

Where in this wild stretch of Texas had Ollie gotten her hands on a gun?

Daisy broke into a run, the hem of her skirt threatening to tangle with her long legs. If she managed to trip she'd leave these widow's weeds in the dust so fast she'd show up in nothing but her bloomers. That would give her neighbors something to talk about.

She reached her destination without mishap. From

the number of horses hitched outside the establishment, the banker had an unusual amount of customers this morning. Saturday often brought cowhands into town to collect their pay and waste it in the saloons. She'd been so busy at the mercantile she hadn't noticed if the overland stage had already arrived and brought in more visitors to High Plains. Just how many hostages were involved? she wondered.

"Protect my child from herself, Lord," Daisy whispered as she forced down panic. No need to burst through the door and startle anyone. That might get someone hurt. Instead, Daisy dusted her skirt, adjusted her bonnet and squarely braced her shoulders for the trouble ahead. Her fingers shook as she reached for the doorknob.

She was tall enough to see above the curtains that covered the door and front windows. From the sight of raised palms, her daughter still had the weapon aimed at somebody.

Please make these men the forgiving sort, Daisy prayed.

"Hand that gun to the banker immediately, Olivia Jane Trumbo," she ordered, opening the door, "or you're going to get a good talking-to all the way ho—" She stumbled as the door swung open faster than she had pushed it.

A dark-haired, blue-eyed woman stood there, blocking Daisy's way and flicking open a lace fan held in one hand. Two more steps corrected the awkward momentum that almost spilled Daisy, giving her a whiff of fragrance that smelled like a spring breeze dancing through a meadow of wildflowers. A pleasant surprise amid the stuffiness of too many warm bodies gathered in one place.

"Your name, please?" asked the lady in a cultured voice sounding younger than her appearance. Dressed in a tea gown the blue of her eyes, her hair swept up in some fancy do, she seemed overdressed for a simple visit to the bank. "That little hoodlum told me not to let anyone in here but her mother."

"That would be me," Daisy informed her, wishing she had taken a little more time with her appearance this morning, "and she's no hoodlum. Olivia just sometimes goes about things different from most folks."

This was as much her fault as Ollie's. She'd wanted Ollie to be older before she learned about the death of her father, but Ollie had started asking questions about Knox several months ago. Someone had obviously opened the subject of his death up for discussion. Her child finally asked why she still wore widow's weeds since Old Miz Jenkins said the proper mourning period should be only two years, not three. Daisy simply replied that the material was still sturdy and they didn't need to be wasteful.

Since finding out about her daddy, Ollie had a burr under her saddle, insisting she didn't want to be hugged on too much. Daisy tended to give her daughter time on her own so she wouldn't feel overprotected or smothered with attention. Too much time this morning had allowed the seven-year-old to get her hands on a gun and arrive at this crazy hostage scheme.

"Olivia Jane, where did you get that gun?" Daisy demanded.

"Better step aside and let her in," Ollie warned, nodding her honey-colored head. "She used my gettin'-in-trouble name."

Daisy moved past the beautiful lady and around some baggage next to the door.

"Did you say her last name is Trumbo? Were the two of you related to Knox Trumbo?" asked the stern-faced man who stood by himself to the left of the teller's cage. He started to edge closer, his forehead furrowed as his gaze swept Daisy from hem to bonnet.

On a different day, she might have taken the time to study him closer, admiring his good grooming and such, but all she could do was concentrate on reaching her daughter's side rather than answering him.

"They're his widow and child," informed the banker behind the teller's cage. "Daisy and Olivia."

Ollie waved the gun at the woman with the fan. "Don't move any closer, mister, or I might accidentally hurt your lady friend here. It won't take Mama but a minute to make up her mind about all you fellas then I'll let'cha go. If she likes you, you can talk to her plenty in a minute."

The seven-year-old's head rose then fell as she took in the sight of him from hat to boot tip. "She's got a real fondness for clean people, though. I should know. I got dirty bathwater to prove it all the time." Ollie nodded toward the cowboys standing to the right of the cage. "And since you're the only fella wearing Sunday clean, 'cept Sam, you got a pretty good chance out of all of ya to get on my list. Sam don't count, though. He's the banker. He's *got* to dress good."

Daisy cringed at her daughter's outspokenness.

The clean-looking man didn't back up the few steps he'd gained but seemed willing to wait her out. Cautious, Daisy decided. A wise man.

"Take a quick look, Mama, then I'll be ready for some sense." Ollie's gaze locked with Daisy's and confirmed that she understood totally the kind of talking-to she was about to get from her mother.

Daisy realized Ollie was deliberately avoiding an answer about the gun, so she went ahead and studied the well-groomed stranger long enough to make sure he meant no harm to Ollie. He dressed like a businessman and clearly spent more of his hours indoors than out, but broad shoulders and his muscular frame appeared strong enough to handle himself if someone wronged him. She hoped to end this situation before anything such as that took place.

"The sooner you and your daughter are finished, ma'am—" his voice held a timbre deep and resonant, making her wonder from what part of the country it had been cultivated "—the sooner my sister can return to my side and we can go about our business."

That put a whole new light on his intentions. Daisy couldn't fault him for wanting to protect his own. She respected such a man and would have shown him a friendlier disposition if they weren't in such tense circumstances.

"I'm sure these fine gentlemen mean me no harm at all," cooed his sister, flashing the cowboys a smile and fanning her face. "Please, take your time, Mrs. Trumbo."

Ollie's hands started to shake just from the sheer weight of the gun. Daisy faced the lineup of cowhands, deciding it best to get on with her daughter's ploy so this could be ended as quickly as possible. Though one or two cowboys focused intently on Ollie, none appeared too worried about their safety. A red-haired cowhand in the front of the line was actually grinning.

"How about me?" the banker asked. "Can I move now that your mother's here, Ollie?" Sweat stained his thinning hairline and darkened his shirt near the armpits.

Daisy didn't give Ollie time to answer. "You go about

your business, Sam. We apologize for this and promise it won't happen again, will it, Olivia?"

Ollie's twin braids swung back and forth as she shook her head. "I better not promise, Mama, 'cause I might be lying. Sometimes I do that 'fore I know what comes over me. Old Miz Jenkins says that's 'cause I'm young and still got a bunch'a sins to sow. I don't know what that means, but when she says it everybody around her pew gives her an 'Amen, sister.' You don't want me breaking one of them commandments if I can help it, do ya?"

"I most certainly do not." Daisy frowned, though several of the cowhands laughed and she noticed a grin flash across the brother's face.

She should have been happy most were taking this with such good humor, but Daisy couldn't until she had control of the gun.

Ollie took a deep breath and finished her discussion with Banker Cardwell. "Besides, you don't have to worry no more anyway, Sam. Mama said all your whiskers would give her burns if you was a kissing kind of man. And you know that's one of them things on my list. A new daddy's got to be good at kissin' Mama, and I don't want it hurtin' her none when he does it."

She seemed to remember where she should be targeting and adjusted her aim. The tiny crooked last finger she'd inherited from her daddy's side of the family stuck out as if she were balancing a teacup. "Just gonna see if any of these fellas over here will do."

"First time I've ever been held at gunpoint to prove I'm a good kisser," one of the cowboys joked.

Heat blazed in Daisy's cheeks as she dismissed him and her daughter's demand, instantly moving on to the three men who had been hanging around High Plains on weekends the past month. She had heard they were helping out at the old Rafford place during branding season. The others were probably looking for work. Dressed in work shirts, bandannas, vests and chaps to cover their denims, they didn't appear any different than most cowboys who rode the circuit of ranches come spring.

Despite Ollie's earlier comments about the more finely dressed man, most of the cowboys had shaved and cleaned up before riding into town. That showed respect, one of the requirements Daisy had added to her daughter's list. She appreciated a respectful man of clean ways who traveled a good path. As she tried to do herself, though she failed at times.

If she ever did choose to remarry, not that she thought she actually would, the man must honor all of God's ways and love her and Ollie as his own. He must put no one else but God before them. She would offer her heart to no one less. She would give Ollie no less than the best of fathers this time. Until that ever came about, she intended to be and provide everything her daughter needed. No matter how hard the struggle.

Daisy moved on to the cowboys' faces and whether or not they could stare her straight in the eyes. Every one of them looked away before she finished, a couple of them edging their hats down low as if not wanting to be seen too closely. That made no points with her. Anyone she allowed to enter her and Ollie's lives she needed to trust, and eyes spoke volumes about a person.

The rest of the men's features ranged from passably pleasing to make-you-look-twice, but she put little value in appearances these days. Each of them would be a suitable match to some woman in the world somewhere, just not her.

Daisy supposed she should have never told Ollie that Knox had been the handsomest man in the county when she'd married him. Her daughter now believed having uncommon good looks was an important requirement for a would-be daddy. As Daisy had learned the hard way, a man needed something more than pleasant features to be a good husband or a father. He needed a heart filled with sincere love and kindness and a soul full of truth. She'd discovered too late that Knox had fallen short of that expectation and she hadn't known how to help him improve.

Ollie knew only that her father had the reputation of a hero. What purpose would it serve to let her or others believe any different of him? It would only hurt Ollie in the end. Daisy decided it was better to keep the sad truth hidden away in her own heart than to crush Ollie's.

Though she allowed Ollie to have her fun with the future-daddy list, Daisy doubted any man could ever really measure up and be able to heal the depth of that hurt in Knox and disappointment in herself. Instead, she set about proving to herself and every other member of the Trumbo clan in this community that she could make a decent living for her and Ollie and didn't need anyone else to make them happy or earn their keep.

"Let these men go, Olivia," Daisy said quietly, her tone filled with the pain of memories. "We've delayed them long enough."

Ollie shrugged. "I wasn't much stuck on none of 'em, either, Mama. Not a one knows a thing about threading your machine or making a shoe, so they won't be no help with the biz'ness. They just shoo cows and keep 'em rounded up. How 'bout their eyes? Any of them got that special look you want?"

The cowboy in front thumbed back his hat and

winked at Daisy. He had one of the priorities Ollie had written on the list. *Taller than Mama.* A lot of men fell short of matching Daisy's height. Six feet in widow-black daunted more men than it didn't.

"You got a real rooter-tooter on your hands there, Widow." The winker's grin broadened. "I might be willing to stick around to change your opinion." His voice lowered into a husky tone that implied more than Daisy needed or wanted to know about the kind of man he was.

The lady with the fan tapped Daisy with it and gave a low throaty laugh. "I wouldn't turn that one down, ma'am. He looks like quite a charmer."

"Leave the dear widow to her business, Petula," warned her brother, his gaze locking with his sister's. "I've already told you, we won't be here long enough to make any proper acquaintances."

Petula's lower lip pouted. Daisy took note of the undercurrent of emotion layering his tone and his stoic expression. His features were similar to but more angular than his flirting sister's. His eyes, though, were incomparable to any others she'd ever seen. The blue-violet of the lake water in her back pasture after a spring thaw, they were layered with fathoms so clear nothing could be hidden in their depths. The kind of eyes that one might trust, she wondered, unsettled that they had stirred such a curiosity within her.

Daisy quickly pushed the question aside. He was someone just passing through. She'd had enough of trying to trust a man to settle down. To make herself important enough in his life he would prefer to stay.

The expression that now thinned the stranger's lips and chiseled his jaw held no softness, no gentleness, only command for his sister's obedience. He didn't appear a man to be taken lightly.

"*Proper* wasn't exactly on your sister's mind, mister," the winker dared.

"What are you implying?" demanded Petula's protector, his legs firmly planting themselves apart. Massive fists rose to defend his sister's honor. "Ladies, please step out of the way."

His knuckles looked scarred and broken, certainly not the hands of a duded-up gentleman. This would not be his first fight or the first defense of Petula, Daisy noted.

Time to get this under control.

"Excuse them, sir," she apologized for the cowboy's rudeness, hoping to play peacemaker, "you're new to these parts. Men around here love a good Saturday fight just so they can sit in church the next morning and have something to ask forgiveness for. Don't you, fellows?"

She hoped she could make the defender see reason and not let this escalate into a brawl. "They sometimes deliberately rile somebody just to get a rise out of them. It's a source for bragging rights so they can confess the most amount of wrongdoing and need for redemption come Sunday. That lets them enjoy the women who want to sit beside them and tame the bad boys." She shrugged. "Just a Texan's way of courting, so to speak."

"Yeah, that's what we're doing—" Winker elbowed the cowhand next to him "—courting. What you gonna do about it, partner?"

Bass Parker didn't want to fight and wasn't sure if he could take them all on, but he'd go down trying if forced. Maybe the mouthy winker would be man enough to meet him one-on-one instead of making this a brawl.

He appreciated the widow's attempt to defuse the situation, but he wasn't about to let the man's coarse implications stand without letting him know of his disapproval.

Defending Petula's honor had become a habit Bass hoped wouldn't follow them West, but it seemed to be a daily occurrence now. Long before their parents' deaths, he made a vow he would look after his younger sister and see her raised right. But the more men Petula met, the more determined she was to flirt. The more situations and comments like this could not be left unchallenged.

It might be a thrill to her to have men pursue her, but he feared Petula would take her need to experience what she thought was love one step too far someday and get into more trouble than the scandal she'd left behind or his defense of her could handle.

Bass hoped to find them a place to call home where she would want to straighten up her wayward thinking and become the lady he knew she could be. They both needed to put their troubled pasts behind them and find a way to turn their lives around for the better.

If only he hadn't decided to stop in and try to make things right with Widow Trumbo one last time before heading on to California. The money he'd sent her years ago remained untouched in the High Plains Bank, despite several failed attempts in writing to persuade her to use it for a memorial for Knox. He'd expected continued resistance but not with this woman calling herself Knox Trumbo's widow. She looked nothing like the woman Knox had introduced to him as his wife after signing the papers of conscription.

"I said, what are you gonna do about it, partner?" Challenge echoed deeper in the redhead's voice. "Just stand there and think about it or actually do something before you moss over?"

"If you insist. Let the ladies be on their way and we'll finish this." Bass prepared himself for the inevitable. "Petula, take our bags and wait for me at the livery."

"But—" Petula argued.

"Listen carefully. Do exactly as I say and you won't get hurt." Bass's attention remained on his challengers but his words targeted the widow now. "Ma'am, it's wise if you do the same. Take your little one and leave, please."

The widow grabbed the gun away from her distracted daughter and moved in front of the child. "Mister, put your fists down. Nobody's going to fight anybody. I apologize for everything that's happened or been said." She aimed the gun at each man including Bass. "We all say things when we're on the edge and don't mean them."

Her amber-colored eyes widened with apology. "I've let my daughter go too far with this. It's about to cause more trouble than she meant it to, isn't it, Ollie?"

Ollie peeked around the widow's skirt. "I guess so, but that sure looked like it was gonna be a great fight."

The tyke's humor caused a few chuckles, and Widow Trumbo's efforts to quell the tension was admirable, but Bass didn't drop his fists.

Ollie pointed a small finger at the rest of the cowboys in line. "Anyways, I learned plenty about these ones before ya got here, Mama. So I wrote one or two on my maybe-daddy list."

Bass had wondered what purpose drove the little scamp's hostage taking and now he understood. She wanted a new father. His gut twisted with knowing that, if this little girl was truly Knox's child, and Banker

Cardwell indicated she was, then *he* played a part in why she'd lost her daddy and needed a new one. He had to find a way to get her out of here safely and make it up to her and her mother somehow.

"They said they ain't rich men but always got enough to get by on," Ollie continued as if the grown-ups weren't on the edge of battle. "So it won't cost us nothin' to feed 'em. And when I told them you like to run, Mama, they said they admired a woman who knows how to do that good. But him—" she stared at Bass "—I ain't had time to ask him nothin'. He don't say much. Figured I'd leave him for last."

"Looks like he don't *do* much, either." With a flash of a hand, the winking cowboy drew a pistol from the holster strapped low around his right thigh. The other cowboys did the same and all aimed with deadly intent at the widow and her daughter. "Think a pair of fists are big enough to stop all of us, do you, dude?"

Bass tried to think fast. He couldn't fight them all, but he might get most of the men down before anyone got off a shot. *Down. That's it. Get the women down first.* He prayed Petula would listen to him this one time.

The widow pointed the gun directly at the winking cowboy, who seemed bent on a fight. "Stop badgering him."

She had courage. Bass welcomed her bravery, but knew it might get her killed.

"Or you'll do what, Widow? Take on all of us?"

"Mama, don't try to shoot." Apology filled Ollie's face. "That gun's empty on account of I didn't find no bullets in Daddy's old trunk. I was just foolin' all y'all."

"Hope you're telling your mama the truth, little missy. Pardon me if I don't trust you." Winker's weapon still aimed at the widow. "Just slide that gun this way,

Mama. Do what I say…" His attention focused on Bass for a second. "And we'll keep this easy."

Bass made no move. He needed the perfect moment. Maybe the widow would provide it.

The redhead nodded at the banker. "Open that safe and hand me what's in there. Don't make any quick moves while you're at it, either. Best keep your hands where I can see them or the kid'll be nothing but a memory or maybe a funny story I'll tell miles down the road. Who would've thought we'd be held up pulling our own bank robbery? And with an empty gun, no less."

Bass hoped the widow was no fool. The man's laughter was as serious as a hanging verdict. If she did what she was told it might give him the opportunity he needed. He waited, holding his breath, praying she showed the level head she appeared to have.

Slowly, she bent and slid the pistol across the room toward the winking cowboy's feet.

"Drop now!" Bass shouted at the women, diving as the gun slid. Momentum carried his body straight into the leader, sending him and several cowhands falling like unstrung fence posts. Out of the corner of his eye, he saw Petula collapse, either in reaction to his shouted order or in a dead faint. He made the mistake of turning slightly enough to check and see if the widow and the little girl had done the same. Both still stood.

Only one way to protect them now. His fists connected with flesh, echoing loud punches over the room.

Lord, let me prove myself more than the coward people think of me. Help me save my sister…

And give me time to set things right with the widow and her child.

Chapter Two

Someone got off a shot. Another.

Instinctively, Daisy turned, threw her body over Ollie's and rolled, pinning her daughter beneath her. A shotgun blast layered the air with the acrid smell of gun smoke, splattering a hole in the wall and raining slivers of wood everywhere.

Sam! Daisy remembered the shotgun behind the counter. He must have fired a round. She dared to look, but someone returned fire. The banker fell backward out of sight. Daisy screamed as her eyes slammed shut, praying he was still alive.

"Trouble at the bank!" yelled a voice outside, though it moved away from them instead of toward. "Somebody get the sheriff."

The sound of flesh punching flesh, grunts and bodies scuffling continued as Petula's brother tried to subdue the robbers with only his fists. Daisy prayed fast and hard for the brave stranger, asking God to protect the man who defended them.

"Get out of here now," Winker ordered, his voice full of pain amid the bone-crunching blows. "Grab the money and ride!"

Another shot fired. The punches stopped. Daisy's eyes flashed open, fearful of the fistfighter's fate. A need to remember him, his face, his eyes, the trust she'd questioned earlier seemed important now to bring into focus. She willed him not to die though his slumped-over figure did not move.

A frantic scraping of boots and spurs sounded the retreat amid another hail of bullets. Daisy braced herself for the impact of hot lead, her hands frantically trying to protect Olivia from being hit. *Help me, Lord. Keep her safe.* Her prayer kept pace with her pulse. *Don't let me lose her, too.*

Another volley of traded shots shattered glass from the door and windows, then a thunderous pounding of hooves eased into a silence so quick Daisy could hear her heart beating as if it was lodged in her ears. Her blood raced like the Guadalupe River at flood tide, her tongue drying as if it was a slab of jerky, leaving her unable to speak.

Daisy waited for someone to enter the bank. Anyone to assure her the shooting was over, the robbers away and the townsmen who had shot back still outside and alive. She needed to check on Sam and the two strangers, but she was afraid to move away from Ollie yet.

No one entered.

"Is everyone all right?" she asked, finding nerve enough to speak and needing to hear each voice in return.

"They shot him. They shot my brother," screamed Petula. She crawled over to him as his frock coat darkened with the spread of blood.

"Don't cry, Pet," their rescuer whispered, motioning his sister to stay away. "Don't come closer. I'll be all right." He crumpled and passed out.

"Get some h-help, Daisy," Sam pleaded from behind the counter.

"I'm so relieved." Daisy released a long breath of air, realizing both men still lived. "I thought you might have been... Just hang on, Sam. I'll get Doc."

"He's in town. Maybe at his office or M-Meg's." Sam paused and took a few breaths. "Sounds like her brother needs help quicker than I do. See if anyone else is hurt." Pain filled his voice despite his words. "I...I can hold on."

"You sure?" She wanted to check and see for herself.

"Do what you've got to do, Daisy. Quick."

"Yeah, let me up, Mama. I can't breathe."

Daisy stood and helped her daughter stand. She examined Ollie for any sign of injury and found only minor scrapes from flying glass and splinters caused by the shotgun blast. Filled with relief, she lifted Ollie and hugged her so tightly the child complained again.

"That's enough, Mama. You keep squeezin' me and I'm gonna be a goner for sure."

"It's never enough, honey. Never." Daisy pulled back and studied the tiny face one more time. She had to keep Ollie safe. This time. Every time. "You sure you're not hurt anywhere?"

She frowned. "Just where you hugged me."

Daisy set her down and stared squarely into eyes that mirrored her own. "Then do you think you can go find Doc for us? That way I can stay here and help do what I can until he gets here."

"My *brother*," Petula stressed, kneeling beside him to rest his head in her lap. At the sight of his wound, her words became shrill. "Hurry, he's all I have." She brushed her hand across his brow and glanced up at

Daisy, her eyes glazed with worry. "Make him stop bleeding."

"We'll get help," Daisy assured her then hesitated. Memories of the outraged citizens who told her about the hostage-taking rushed in to caution her. Someone outside might think she or Ollie had started the shooting. What if they decided to shoot first and then ask questions? She couldn't take that chance. "Stay here, Ollie. Let me make sure it's safe for you to go."

Daisy exited the bank and froze, waiting, looking. She had lost her husband to violence as he bled out on some needless battlefield where the opposing forces didn't know a cease-fire had been called and the war ended. Tears she hadn't shed when he died suddenly blurred the images before her now.

She hadn't been there and couldn't have helped Knox, but their longtime friendship and practical marriage demanded that she love Ollie enough for the both of them and keep her safe always.

That single clear thought stemmed the flow of Daisy's tears and shook her out of her frozen panic.

A crowd began to run this way and that, shouting words so fast that Daisy couldn't determine who said what. Someone lay in the street wounded. Another man slumped over a water trough near the livery.

The blacksmith, a bald giant of a man who often fished with Olivia, reached Daisy first.

"Oh, Bear, I'm so glad it's you." Relief rushed through her. "We need help. There's been a robbery. People are hurt." She brushed the tears from her face, her voice breaking as she added, "O-Ollie's inside."

Bear bolted past Daisy only to come to an abrupt halt when a tiny voice said, "No, I ain't, Mama."

Daisy swung around to find Ollie reaching up to tug on her skirt.

"You scared the hide off me, Widow." Bear's exhaled breaths looked as if he was pumping his bellows hard at the smithy. His brown gaze swept over his fishing partner from braids to kid boots. "I thought Tadpole had caught her last catfish."

"What are you doing out here, honey?" Daisy frowned. "I told you to wait inside until I was sure it was safe."

"But I heard ya cryin', Mama. Are ya hurt?" Concern darkened Ollie's eyes. "Ya didn't give me time to see if ya got hurt."

Daisy bent and hugged her. She hadn't even considered Ollie's worry for her. Of course the poor baby feared losing another parent. "I'm fine, sweetheart, but I'd feel much better if you'll stay with Bear until I've finished here."

Daisy offered an apology to the blacksmith for scaring him then added, "I don't know where her uncles are today. I think they've gone boar hunting. Do you mind if she goes with you to get the—"

Bear didn't let Daisy finish the question. He grabbed the seven-year-old and lifted her onto his shoulders. "Don't worry about Tadpole. We'll find the sheriff then me and my missus will take care of her." He motioned up the street. "Doc's headed this way. He just came around the corner of the mercantile with some men." His attention refocused on Daisy. "You sure you don't want me to stay instead? Let you and Ollie go on home?"

"I'm sure. There's a lady inside. Her brother's hurt, and she's been through a lot. I think she needs another woman with her right now. Since this is our fault, I must stay." Images of the violence threatened to return, but

Daisy willed them away. "Ollie doesn't need to see any more of this."

"Ahh, Mama. I can take it." Ollie tried to sound tough. "Besides, that stranger's talkin' again. Says he needs you to come see to his sister. She's white as Old Bessie's milk and bawling like a calf that can't find her mama."

"Go on." Daisy shooed them away. "She's probably just scared. I'll check on her."

She watched her daughter's honey-colored braids bounce against her back as the burly blacksmith trotted down the street. Assured that Ollie had a chaperone who wouldn't let her get back into harm's way, Daisy returned to the wounded inside.

"Where is everybody?" Petula glanced up from fanning her brother. Fear and anger mixed to darken the blue of her eyes against her ashen face. "Didn't you bring someone? He's going to bleed to death."

"Now, Pet, she's doing all she can." His voice sounded weaker with each word. "I'm not the only one hurt."

Daisy hurried and bent down beside him, staring at the fistfighter's face. Pale and splattered with blood, she couldn't tell if it was from the wound in his shoulder or from something more. She took off her bonnet and pressed it over the shoulder trying to stem the flow. "Are you hurt anywhere else, sir?"

"Just t-there," he informed, staring at her as if he wanted to say more but didn't have the strength.

There was serious enough, she thought as she noticed his uninjured arm reaching out to his sister, patting her hand to reassure her. He seemed a truly caring soul, his love for his sibling stronger than his obvious pain.

Daisy felt herself invisibly adding his qualities to Ollie's list, then realized her foolishness. If he didn't get better help soon he'd be no part of any list. He would bleed out on this floor. Daisy's heart beat faster with another fervent prayer that he would survive. She needed to be able to thank him for saving her and Olivia's lives.

"Doc and a group of men are just a few businesses away." She smiled trying to assure him that all would be well and the situation was firmly in hand. "They should be here any second."

"Just promise me," he said, as his breaths became shallow and he looked as if he might lose consciousness again, "make sure my sister is taken care of. She doesn't handle things like this well. Hopefully your banker is hearing this. Cardwell, make sure she gets paid well for her efforts."

"I h-hear you."

The way he said "sister" filled Daisy with compassion. Daisy nodded. "I promise, but I need no money."

The words barely left her mouth before Doc Thomas appeared, followed closely behind by others who carried a stretcher.

"This man's shot in the shoulder. He's lost a lot of blood," Daisy informed the physician. "He's breathing but it's shallow."

She pointed toward the teller's cage. "Sam's behind there badly hurt, no matter what he says otherwise. I heard it in his voice." She explained that the banker wouldn't let her take time to examine him.

"You two men watch over Sam 'til I check on this one," instructed Doc Thomas, a reed-thin man with spectacles who looked older than his forty-some-odd years.

He motioned for two others to come closer as he pulled white cloth from his medicine bag and bent to examine the fistfighter. He laid Daisy's bonnet aside, studied the wound and placed the clean cloth over it. "'Fraid that goes to the scrap bin, Widow, but it helped. Good thinking."

He stood and gave his assistants instructions. "Carry this man to my office and somebody make sure you keep this over the wound until I get there."

"But he can't wait. He's going to die if you don't take care of him now. *Here.*" Petula's fear rose with each word.

"He belongs to you?" Doc asked.

Petula nodded, her voice breaking, "He's m-my only kin. My brother."

"Are you hurt?"

She shook her head. "Just sick to my stomach."

He handed her another cloth. "Then keep this pressed down hard on his shoulder while those two men carry him. Keep changing it with new bandages until I get there. That'll stem the flow. You'll find clean cloths stacked on my shelves."

She shook her head again and moved her hands away as if he were asking her to grab a snake.

"The sight of blood makes me sick. I might faint. I can't press hard enough anyway."

Impatience etched Doc's face, making him look even older. He shoved the bandages into Daisy's hand. "Widow Trumbo, will you help?"

The wounded stranger's blue eyes opened for a moment only to close as quickly as he lost his words. "I need—"

Daisy wanted to stay and help Sam, but she couldn't leave this man's care to his hysterical sister. She owed him that much. "I'll do my best, Doctor."

She pressed the cloth firmly against the darkest part of the bloodstained shoulder. The stranger flinched, groaning from the pressure. His body reacted and tried to jerk away from her touch.

"Keep him still," Doc Thomas ordered. "The more he moves, the more he bleeds."

"Please, sir, don't move," she whispered in his ear, hoping he was conscious enough to hear her. Daisy motioned the men to lift him onto the stretcher while she attempted to distract him. "I'm sure it hurts, but it won't take us long to carry you if you'll stay as still as you can. Your sister's coming with us."

Petula finally stood and moved away from her brother.

Daisy's words seemed to reach him through the pain. "I…I'll try. Thank you for watching over her."

His body tightened as if he was bracing himself to endure the pressure. Daisy's eyes riveted on Doc's. "He's ready to move. You'll let me know about Sam first thing?"

"Quick as I can. Got to see how bad the men outside are shot up."

Daisy wanted to shut away the image of the body lying over the trough, but she had to keep focused on the bandage so she wouldn't slip off the wound. She said a quick prayer for the townsman and stood in unison as the assistants rose with a firm hold on the stretcher and patient. Her unusual height equaled the men's, easing the problem of adjusting their balance. "Are you coming with us, miss?" she asked the squeamish sister.

When she didn't answer, Daisy used the woman's Christian name. "Petula, I think you want to come with me."

Petula blinked, looked at her hands then began to scrub them. She walked toward the door, muttering, "Mother's going to be so angry. I'm not supposed to get dirty."

Sympathy filled Daisy. The poor thing was dazed with worry. When they reached the unhinged, bullet-ridden door, Petula faltered. She stopped sniffling and her knees bent suddenly.

"What's wrong?" Concern echoed in her brother's tone. "I don't hear my sister."

Just about the time Daisy thought Petula might faint, the young woman reached for two heavy-looking valises next to the door. "She's fine, sir." Daisy felt compelled to reassure him. "Just picking up what must be your baggage."

"Too heavy for her," he gasped, trying to lift his head and shoulders as if he meant to get off the stretcher.

A considerate soul, Daisy noted.

"Got a handle on things in here?" asked a man who poked his head around the door, his piercing coffee-colored gaze intent upon studying each person. "Need any help?"

"Got it all in hand," Doc said, "but I'd appreciate you making sure everybody's got help outside, Teague."

"Already done and the sheriff's taken a posse and set out after the gang."

Daisy wasn't surprised to find Teague checking on things now. He had the fierce look of a predator, with eyes squinted by long days in the sun. Broad shoulders were cloaked in a worn duster, his legs stretching long from denim to boots that had seen better days. He looked like a man accustomed to riding hard trails, but he'd been hanging around High Plains lately.

All Daisy knew of him was that he was kind to Ollie and made a point of getting her home if she strayed too far.

"Could you help me carry my bags?" Petula seemed suddenly coherent enough to ask for assistance.

"You headed to Doc's with them?" He linked one arm with hers and grabbed the baggage.

"Who's that?" asked their patient, his body tensing.

"Someone who just wants to help." Daisy tried to calm him. "Don't worry."

Doc Thomas's office was around the corner from the mercantile and only took a few minutes for the men to carry him there. Daisy managed to hold the cloth steady on its target, but the real effort came from keeping the curious crowd away from the procession. By now, most in town knew of the robbery and wanted to help in some way. She suggested they check with Doc or secure the bank for Sam.

Doc's office door was never locked. Teague set the baggage down just inside the entryway while Petula dismissed the parlor that had been made into a waiting room and disappeared into a hallway of doors. A few seconds later, she poked her head around the corner and motioned them all forward.

"In here," she said, "there are a couple of beds in this room."

Getting through the doorways proved harrowing since Daisy didn't dare take her hand off their patient's shoulder. She barely managed to squeeze through, bumping her elbow hard enough to leave a bruise. Daisy just managed to keep the pressure on the wound while they got him settled on the bed.

Only then did she notice the quality of her patient's slightly worn but well-tooled boots, something her livelihood as a shoemaker made priority on most first meetings with strangers. He obviously appreciated skilled handiwork but wasn't afraid to put some wear on it, either. A man of means but a working man no less. Her interest in getting to know more about him sparked.

One assistant interrupted her thoughts. "We've got to get this stretcher back to Doc, so we're going to leave you ladies and that other fella with him for now. We'll be back as soon as we can."

She nodded and checked on her patient. His eyes opened again to stare at Daisy, their blue-violet depths coherent despite the pain.

"We made it?"

"Yes, you did well." She needed him to remain still and relaxed. "And so has your sister. Teague," she said as she nodded at the baggage handler, "how about keeping this pressed down for me while I look for clean cloth?"

"No problem." Teague didn't hesitate and moved up to accommodate her.

"I can hold it myself." Her patient's hand reached up to wave him away.

"You're going in and out too frequently." Daisy gently grabbed his hand and pushed it back down. "I'll hear no argument."

"Sounds like she's got her apron tied, friend. She means business," Teague warned. "Best just lie still."

Daisy gathered her will and braced herself for the challenge ahead. "Petula, help me get him cleaned up and the wound dressed as best we can before Doc returns. That will help speed things up."

Helplessness darted over Petula's face and she scrubbed her hands again. "I've never doctored anyone before."

"I'm not asking you to. Doc will take out the bullet. Do you think you can put a pot of water on to boil in the kitchen?" His sister certainly didn't have the same consideration her brother offered.

"He doesn't have servants?"

Servants? Petula revealed more about them in that one question than if Daisy had spent the past few hours interviewing them for the list. They were people of means. "Doc doesn't. It's up to us. You'll need to help, too." Daisy added a stiff, "Please."

"I'm afraid I've pampered my sister, ma'am," her brother apologized. "Really, it's no problem to wait until the doctor arrives."

"It is a problem and we're not waiting if I have to do this by myself." Daisy rarely allowed her temper to flare, but the events of the day had worn down her best behavior.

Petula headed into the hallway, reluctance in every footfall. "Can someone show me how to heat the stove?"

"I'll show her so you can stay here with him," Teague offered. "It shouldn't take long if Doc's already got wood chopped."

Petula turned, accepting his offer with a breath of relief that ended in a smile. "Thank you, sir. I always heard you Texans were such gentlemen."

"Make sure you help and not hinder Mr.—" warned her brother.

"Teague," the man finally introduced himself properly to all. "Just Teague."

Daisy didn't have time to comprehend the meaning behind the two men's locked gazes that followed, but then she'd never really understood most men all that well anyway. Petula, on the other hand, had the look Daisy clearly understood.

"Tell you what, Teague," she said. "You get his coat and shirt off while I'm grabbing fresh cloth, then I'll send you and Petula to deal with the stove."

Minutes later Daisy returned to find her patient's upper garments lying in a bloody heap on the floor, but the yellow duster Teague had worn now acted as a sheet to offer the man some modesty. Ollie's friend had handled someone wounded before.

"Send some of these back now, damp, please." She handed Teague several cloths. "I know they won't be hot yet. Just heat the water as quickly as you can."

Daisy managed to hold the blood at bay until Petula showed up, gripping a pan with pot holders.

"The stove was hot. Your doctor must have made a pot of coffee not long ago because the pot was still warm and he already had a kettle heating up with water in it. We put another one on to boil, but it'll take a few minutes. At least this one's a little warm."

She set the pan down on a small table that separated the two beds and dipped a cloth into the water and wrung it out for Daisy.

"Keep those coming," Daisy instructed, hoping if she kept Petula's hands busy the distraught sister might stay composed. Daisy accepted the cloth and warned her patient, "This is going to hurt a little more. Are you ready?"

"Yes," he whispered, the word a slow hiss.

When Daisy made the first stroke, he nearly jumped off the cot.

Petula started crying.

The blood kept coming.

Time after time Daisy exchanged cloths.

"I'm all right, sis. No need to cry." No criticism filled her brother's voice, his tone soft and reassuring. "It hurts, but it'll get better, don't worry."

Respect for the man's endurance and kindness grew by the minute. Daisy marveled how he managed to maintain his composure under the circumstances. She didn't know if she could have done the same.

Teague returned with the other kettle just as Doc arrived with Sam in tow. Bandages wrapped the banker's entire chest and one stretched across his forehead and left eye. His mustache and whiskers looked half shorn off as if a bullet had razor-creased its way across his face.

Daisy barely caught a glimpse of the rise and fall of his chest before having to turn back to her own patient. She pressed yet another cloth against the wound. "Is Sam all right?"

Doc Thomas stood beside her now that they'd settled the banker on the second cot. "Hurting but sedated for the time being. Bruised a couple of ribs, and he won't be blowing any bugles for a while. Nearly got one eye shot out, as you can see. You ready for me to take over here?"

"Gladly." She rolled her shoulders, setting off a sharp reminder that her elbow had been bruised. If he'd been much longer, she would have done her best to dig out the bullet, but doctoring was not a talent she had any bragging rights to. And considering everyone else's wounds, she had no right to complain about a bruise.

"The widow's done a great job, Doctor," her patient rasped.

"Good, I see you're conscious. That's helpful." Looking down the bridge of his nose through the ever-sliding spectacles, Doc Thomas examined all Daisy had done. "Mighty fine work, Widow. Couldn't have done better myself. Now let's see the exit wound."

He pushed the glasses up again. "You strong enough to sit up, son?"

He nodded, but Teague lent a hand.

Daisy caught the first glimpse of her rescuer's back. No wonder he was losing so much blood. She'd been so worried about stemming the flow in front that she never considered the bullet might have exited. Had Teague noticed it when he removed the shirt and coat? Surely he would have told her if he had. Trying to handle him and take off the clothing at the same time must have blocked the sight.

"You two new to town?" Doc Thomas probed the wound. "I haven't seen you around here before."

"Fresh off the stage," gasped the fistfighter as he flinched.

Petula stood in one corner so she couldn't see her brother's grimaces. "We haven't even gotten a room yet."

"No relatives here in town?" Doc Thomas poured some kind of liquid on two cloths and pressed them against both wounds. "Hold him still, Teague. That's going to burn like fire, but it'll stop much of the bleeding."

"No relatives," Petula finally answered.

"Just passing through," her brother whispered through gritted teeth.

"That's a shame." Doc frowned, grabbing instruments to sew stitches. "I was hoping you had a place you could settle in for a few days to recuperate. You're going to need to gain some strength before you do much else, and certainly no traveling for a while."

He reached up and pushed his spectacles higher before dabbing the exit wound dry and beginning to stitch. "Trouble is, the boardinghouse and hotel are stocked full of people in town for the race tomorrow, so I doubt there's a room to rent anywhere. Guess you can stay here in this bed for a couple of days, but I can't promise your sister much more of a place to sleep other than the davenport out in the waiting room. I can't stick around and wait on you hand and foot 'cause I've got more shot up like Sam here and no telling what kind of ruckus the crowd will stir up tomorrow."

Daisy realized he was deliberately being long-winded to distract their patient.

Doc finished one side and switched to the other.

Petula spoke up. "But I don't know how to take care of—"

"You won't have to." Daisy flared but quickly decided that would serve no purpose. The privileged young woman didn't know how or didn't want to know how a lot of things were done.

This situation was all hers and Ollie's doing anyway. If she hadn't left Ollie alone long enough to get a gun and hold hostages, this man would not have been shot. He and his sister wouldn't have to be concerned about needing a place for him to recover or someone to watch over him.

Only one thing would make it right.

"You and your brother are welcome to stay at my house," Daisy offered, setting her shoulders to the task ahead. "I've been expecting my sisters for a visit, but they've missed the last two stages so I've got extra rooms for now. It's the least we owe you for the trouble we've caused. My cook and I will help take care of your brother."

"Really?" Relief eased Petula's expression. "We'd be so grateful, wouldn't we, Bass?"

Bass? An ominous feeling raced over Daisy like a storm threatening blue-fired lightning in the sky. Surely, no two men in the world shared the same dastardly name or could possibly show up here to unsettle her.

Life couldn't be that cruel, could it?

"Extremely grateful—" Bass nodded then seemed to

think better of the painful motion "—since we stopped here just to meet with you, Widow Trumbo."

It's *him*, Daisy's heart thundered as the storm of reality swept through her. *Bass Parker* had come to High Plains.

And she'd just invited the man she blamed for taking Knox away from Ollie to stay in their home.

Chapter Three

Bass Parker struggled through the pain forcing himself awake. Strange images swarmed in his brain making no sense. *A small girl with a gun. A tall woman with eyes the color of warm honey and hair the shade of ripening wheat. Dressed in black.*

His mind began to surrender to sleep again, but Bass shook his head trying to ward off the darkness threatening to engulf him once more. *Petula, not safe! His fists connecting with another man's body. Gunfire. Bank robbers! The child and her mother. He must protect the innocents.*

Bass bolted upright as reality rushed through him. He groaned and grabbed his left shoulder, praying the burning would subside as quickly as it had blazed. The sight of his half-bandaged body assured him he had somehow survived the shoot-out, but where was Pet? Was she hurt?

He concentrated harder. Vague images of her holding his hand, riding in the back of a wagon with his head in her lap, the sound of her voice thanking someone named Teague for coming with them to the ranch, all reassured Bass that Petula was alive. But had she managed to stay out of trouble? That was the question.

Taking stock of his surroundings, Bass found himself in someone's home and the comfort of a bed. An armoire took up most of one wall in the room and a table and chair set next to the four-poster, offering a lamp for reading. No fancy lace curtains or doilies adorned the room that contained only practical, functional furnishings.

The sheets were clean and the patchwork quilt comfortable but frayed. He'd apparently kicked the quilt off due to the oppressive heat, but whoever attended him was kind enough to leave open a window to bring in a breeze. His host was certainly thoughtful.

He strained to remember who that might be.

You can stay with us.

The widow's generous words came back to him. He'd been stunned by her offer. Surprised at the gentle care she'd given him in tending his wound until the doctor arrived. He hadn't expected such charity from the woman who had avoided even written contact with him previously.

Despite being shot, he adjusted his feelings about stopping at High Plains instead of just sending money and messages by way of Banker Cardwell as he'd done before.

He was especially glad he'd come since the banker and the doctor both confirmed Daisy as Knox's true widow. He needed to find out just how long the widow had known each of them and why in '60 Knox had introduced another woman as his wife. He hoped Knox Trumbo would not prove himself to be anything other than the hero Bass thought him, but if this was truly the man's wife and child, there was a mystery to be solved in the matter.

Bass pushed aside the sheet that barely covered him. He wore no shirt, most likely to allow for changing the bandages easier.

But bloomers? Whose idea of a joke was this?

"Petula, I'm awake," he announced strongly. "Come here, please. I need you." He knew full well she wouldn't have dared be any part of changing his clothes. Or any other man's, despite the scandal that followed her from one end of the country to the other.

"I'm comin' in. You nekkid, Mr. Parker?" asked an oddly familiar voice from beyond the door.

When he remembered the light-toned, Southern accent, Bass scrambled to grab the sheet and quilt. He wouldn't put anything past a little girl who toted a gun easily, empty or not. "I'm covered. Will you tell my sister that I need to speak with her, please?"

"Can't." Olivia Trumbo opened the door, carrying paper, a book and a pencil. "She's off in the barn with Teague. It's just you and me and Mama and Myrtle in the house right now. They're fixin' you somethin' to eat and they'll be up here in a minute."

She grabbed the chair at the small reading table and scooted it next to the bed. Plopping herself down, Olivia rested the book on her lap and the papers on top of it, then stared him square in the eye. "Ya ready?"

"For what?" Bass pulled the quilt up a little higher despite the heat. How could a child feel so intimidating?

Because she's capable of holding men hostage. He felt as if he had his back against the wall and couldn't make a move without shocking him or her.

The little Trumbo's amber eyes disappeared into her

upper eyelashes, as if she were asking God to intervene for her.

"For my questions," she said with a sigh of impatience. "I told ya at the bank, I wanted to ask ya some questions. But things got a little wicked and I had to wait. Now I got to catch ya while I can or Mama will make me leave ya alone 'til ya get better. Who knows how long that'll be?"

"Why is my sister in the barn with that man?"

"I'm supposed to be asking the questions, not you." The child's eyebrows knitted together.

"Answer that and I'll answer a question for you."

She hesitated then nodded. "Okay, Mama always says fair is fair. Your sister is learnin' how to muck out a stall so Teague can keep him and his horse there. She only wanted to watch, but he told her she had to help if she was goin' out there instead of helpin' Mama. Said he's gonna stick around here for a while to make sure Mama don't need him to help with ya or anythin'."

"Who is Teague?" Bass wondered if the man just offered his presence as a measure of protection or had other motivations for wanting to stay. Petula didn't need to make male acquaintances here in High Plains until he could get back on his feet to chaperone her.

"Uh-uh. It's my turn." Olivia glanced down at her paper and readied her pencil. "How tall are ya countin' them fancy boots?"

Bass reluctantly gave in to her stubbornness. "Six feet without. I never measured what I am with them on."

"Mama would say about this much more, I'd guess." She stretched her thumb and forefinger vertically.

Bass estimated. "About three inches?"

She nodded. "Yeah. She makes boots and stuff, so she'd know. That might do. How much money ya got?"

"Whoa there, that's two questions for my one, and a man usually doesn't disclose…*tell*…that kind of information about himself to a stranger."

She put the book and paper on the edge of his bed and stuck the pencil through one of her braids to rest on her ear. The child stood and offered him her left hand. "You can call me Ollie. Now we ain't strangers no more."

Offering his hand, Bass leaned over and shook hers. "Bass Parker. Glad to meet you, miss. You can call me Bass."

"Oh yeah," she said when their hands released. She grabbed one edge of her overalls and curtsied. "I forgot. Mama said I have to do this when I meet somebody, but I like a good old handshake myself, don't you?"

"I think mamas always know best."

"Figured ya'd say that. So how 'bout it?" She grabbed her writing instruments then resumed the interview. "How much money do ya have, Bass?"

Persistent little soul. "Enough to pay for meals and board while we're staying here."

The child scratched down words then answered his second question. "Teague's one of my pals. He comes and goes, but mostly he notices things. I watch him watchin' other people. He does that real good. Says he likes to keep his eye out for bad men, so I think he must be some kinda special marshal or somethin'. He's letting the sheriff chase the robbers this time. Somethin' about jury's-friction, whatever that is. I figure he's gonna make sure the town's safe during the races tomorrow while the sheriff and the posse's gone."

Ollie leaned in a little closer as though she was sharing a secret. "When I ask him about being a lawman, he says he won't tell me I'm right and he ain't bashful about telling me when I'm wrong. I'm sticking with it 'til I find out for sure, so he'll see how smart I am, even if I'm only seven and a half. I got him on my for-sure list for Mama, though, if he's a good man. And he seems pretty good so far." She exhaled a long breath. "Whew! I ought to get two questions for that big ol' answer."

"So Teague is interested in your mother?" Not Petula, Bass was glad to know that. About the widow? She'd grieved more time than most did. He respected her for that. Showed love and devotion. Something Bass respected above all else.

Ollie shrugged. "He likes Mama just fine, but there ain't no sparkin' goin' on. You know that kissy kind of stuff. Now, how 'bout you? Are ya good at kissin' and do you think you're handsome?"

Bass acted as if he was rubbing his chin in thought but he needed his hand to hide a grin. "I can answer the one and the other is none of your business, Little Friend."

Her eyes rounded in surprise.

"I don't discuss kissing with anyone but whoever I'm kissing and, as far as my looks go, I am not anywhere near as handsome as your daddy was."

Her mouth gaped. "You knew my daddy? You seen him in real live person?"

Her astonishment hit Bass in the gut. He hadn't realized Ollie had never seen her father.

Still, it made sense. Daisy must have been with child when he met Knox. Knox died after the war ended, killed in a battle by men who didn't know a cease-fire had been agreed upon. He must have never made it to his new home in High Plains during his years of conscription. Never held his child in his arms.

Bass's guilt worsened, twisted something deep in his heart. He owed Daisy Trumbo and Ollie much more than he realized. If only he hadn't hired Knox, giving him the money to take his place in the war. Reasons that seemed so strong then didn't measure up to the price the Trumbos had paid. No wonder the widow refused his help and his money. She obviously considered him, not the war, the reason Knox had lost his life. The reason Ollie had never met her father.

Full of remorse, Bass struggled to find appropriate words. Finally, he whispered, "Your daddy was a truly heroic man, Ollie. Handsome and gallant to the ladies, brave and a leader to his men. Knox won many battles. I followed all his victories in the papers, wrote him letters to say how proud I was of him. That's one of the reasons I'm here. I want to help your mother if she'll let me."

By doing so, he could put his guilt about the whole matter behind him and lead him and his sister to a better place. A happier path.

"Then you was his friend?"

"I'd like to think so." Bass looked around the room, studying the furnishings. The widow had a right to be living much better than this. He could help make that happen if she'd just let him. "Do you know if there's a stone marker on your father's grave yet?"

"There's a perfectly good wooden cross posted," announced Daisy Trumbo, entering the room with a tea service, "and fresh flowers when the weather allows."

Tall and thin, she reminded him of a stalk of wheat standing defiant to the wind, exuding a strong silent will that he suspected couldn't be buffeted easily.

"I help clean up the grave real good every time, don't I, Mama?" Ollie glanced up from her chair.

"You sure do, honey."

Behind the widow, carrying another tray, followed

a woman whose body was as round as it was tall. Gray hair streaked through her temples and in the chignon pinned atop her head, making her dark hair look salted. Her green eyes could have cut him, they appeared so sharp in color.

"Your money's still in the bank where you sent it."

The rotund woman answered what he'd really wanted to know from the widow, challenging him with a lift of double chins.

Bass waited until his hostess set her tray on the table and actually looked at him before shifting his gaze toward the interfering woman. "Is this your cook?"

"I'm Myrtle," the angry-looking woman spoke for herself. "Cook and most everything else around here, mister. Particularly, friend and protector to the Trumbos. Daisy's already told me what I need to know about you."

Bass introduced himself properly anyway to both women since he'd never really officially met Daisy. "We stopped in town wanting to visit with you, Mrs. Trumbo, before continuing on to California, where we've sent our things. I hope you'll change your mind about accepting the money or at least allow me to erect a memorial to Knox in the town square. I'm sure you'd like to see that he has a more permanent marker for his grave. I won't feel I've done him justice until I take that worry off your mind."

"You should have thought about that when you hired him to take your place fighting." The cook glared at Bass. "She didn't want your coward's money then, she sure doesn't now."

"Now, Myrtie." Daisy held up one palm as if to ward off her cook's fierce defense. "Why don't you set your tray down and go about your duties. I'll feed our guest so he'll get some rest and be able to get on his way sooner."

That was the politest way Bass had ever been told neither he nor his money were welcome, but he was determined to put his guilt at rest. To convince her that she should accept his offerings. His stomach rumbled as he got a whiff of something that smelled wonderful.

"Drink this first." Daisy poured from the tea service and handed him a cup, squarely meeting his gaze. "Verbena tea with a touch of mint will strengthen you faster. That's the point here, Mr. Parker. I owe you for saving my and Ollie's lives earlier, but that's where this ends. I want nothing else from you than for you to get well and continue on down the road."

"Clear enough." He took a sip of the tea. She intended to continue fighting his good intentions. He wouldn't allow that. He couldn't go on to California with no closure about Knox. He must somehow make her understand he felt it a duty he owed them and he didn't leave duties undone. As soon as a room at the hotel or boardinghouse became available, he'd thank her for her caregiving and find another way to convince her to take the money she should have accepted long ago.

But first he needed to find out what had happened to his clothes. "May I ask who put these bloomers on me and why?"

She hesitated and looked uncomfortable for a moment. "We left your belongings at Doc's office and my supplies at the mercantile to be quicker. I had to pick up Ollie and we thought it best to get you here as soon as possible and settled in, then go back and load everything else. Teague will help me fetch them in a—"

"Stop spit and sputtering about those bloomers, Parker." Myrtle's fists rounded on her hips now that her hands were free of the tray. "That handsome drink of water out there and me managed to put those on ya. Bloomers was all we had handy. You best be glad Daisy had an old pair and she's so tall. Otherwise, you'd be wearing mine."

Ollie giggled.

The widow shooed Ollie out of the chair and took her place. "Why don't you and Myrtle go see about those poor chickens or they're going to lay sour eggs. You can ask him more questions tomorrow after he's good and rested."

"Ahh, Mama," Ollie grumbled. "He was tellin' me all about Daddy. He said he met him."

The widow's body stiffened and long golden lashes closed over her eyes. It took her a second, but she finally spoke quietly. "After you get your chores done, Ollie, I want you to take a bath and scrub yourself good. Don't worry about the bathwater. I'll pour it out later."

"But I took one last night, Mama. Can't I skip one?" Ollie complained.

"I won't have you running around at the race tomorrow looking like a dust storm. You know what your uncles will say."

"Uncle Maddox will dunk me in the horse trough and pin me to a clothesline, but that's kinda fun sometimes."

"They'll be out here afterward trying to tell me how to raise you, that's what." The widow exhaled a breath, obviously attempting to keep calm. "I'd like to skip at least one gathering without them knocking on my door afterward to tell me what I'm doing wrong with you, please."

"Best come on now, before you get yourself in a heap of trouble," Myrtle warned, taking Ollie in tow and heading out the door, deliberately raising her voice but looking over her shoulder at Bass. "Ain't you learned when your mama's about to blow her top at somebody and doesn't want you to see it? Let's go ruffle some chicken feathers."

Bass waited for the yelling to begin, but instead Widow Trumbo stared quietly at his cup.

"Are you finished with your tea? Would you like some more?"

He handed it back to her, aware something had changed in her but he couldn't define what. "No, thank you. It tasted as good as it smelled, though."

She stood and took a cover off a bowl on the other tray, grabbed it and a spoon then sat back down. "This is stew. Are you ready to eat now?"

Her words were neither friendly nor stiff, just precise and efficient to the task. Bass wondered if this was the quiet that came before her storm.

He blinked at her unwavering gaze. A yawn filled him, though he tried to squelch it. "I'm suddenly feeling a little sleepy again, although I am hungry. I'm not sure I won't spill it."

"I intend to feed you." She leaned over to offer him a spoonful of stew. "Doc gave us something to put in the tea to make you rest. Take a bite. You need to eat as much as you can."

Bass accepted the spoonful and enjoyed the beef, particularly the broth. He appreciated her treating him with such kindness, though he suspected she was doing her best to hold her temper in check.

She lifted another scoop after he finished the first. "I make one demand of you while you're in my home, Mr. Parker." The authority in her voice brooked no argument. "You and your sister are not to talk to my child about Knox without my permission. I, alone, will tell her what she needs to know about him."

Petula knew so little of Knox, she would be no threat in the matter. Bass sipped the second spoonful as he mulled over why Widow Trumbo might want him to keep such information secret from her daughter. Did it have anything to do with the other woman he'd thought was Knox's wife? Did Daisy know about her?

"Mama," Ollie hollered from downstairs. "All the uncles just rode up. Uncle Maddox looks madder than a rooster run out of the chicken coop."

"Tell him I'll be right down." Daisy stood and offered Bass the bowl. "You'll have to finish this without my help."

Bass shook his head. "I don't want any more. Please put it on the tray before you go."

Her cheeks paled, though her back stiffened once again as she braced herself to face this new turn of events.

The widow had quite a day so far. A daughter who'd held hostages, surviving a shoot-out, saving his life and now nursing someone she clearly didn't want in her home. Rarely had he seen such grace under pressure.

Bass thought he should ease her mind before she went downstairs to face the new trouble that had come calling. "Mrs. Trumbo...*Daisy*...I give you my word. I won't talk with Ollie anymore about Knox unless you say it's all right."

"I'll hold you to it, then, *Mr. Parker*." Her hand trembled as she set down the bowl, rattling the porcelain against the tray. "But you may not have to concern yourself with it after today. Her uncles may take her away from me if they found out you're here."

Chapter Four

Daisy stepped aside as her brothers-in-law carried the Parkers' baggage inside the house without bothering to knock or offer a greeting.

All three claimed the broad shoulders and considerable height of the Trumbo clan, but the doors of this house had been built to accommodate the comings and goings of Viking-sized kin. The only real differences in the three sandy-bearded men's appearance were the angle of their broken noses and the length of their tied-back hair. From the looks of things, one of them had enjoyed a recent fight. She supposed she'd hear about it in church tomorrow.

Maddox, the oldest and tallest of the trio, shifted his gray eyes upstairs then glared at her looking like a wolf studying its next supper. "Doc says these belong to a couple'a boarders you took in. Figured we'd save you a trip and bring out these and the supplies you left. Where do you want 'em?"

"Just set the baggage by the coatrack, please. I'll carry them up later. And thanks for being so thoughtful. I was just about to head into town and pick up everything." Daisy's pulse did double time as she maneuvered her body to block the Trumbos from heading upstairs. What else had they learned about today's events?

"Myrtle will want the supplies in the root cellar and salt shed like usual."

Maddox nodded at his brothers. "Y'all drop what you got and I'll do the rest in here. See that you make Myrtle happy with the storing then find out where Ollie ran off to and fetch her inside. Meet me upstairs after you're done."

They dropped their load and the door shut abruptly behind them.

Daisy stepped backward and stood on the first stair, blocking the way, trying to appear calm and in control. It wouldn't be fair to subject her patient to Maddox's fury until he was stronger.

The fact that Maddox wanted Ollie present didn't bode well, and Daisy wasn't all that sure why she felt so compelled to protect Bass. She ought to just turn him over to her in-laws, but keeping her word had to be honored. "I'm sure Doc Thomas told you what happened. My guest is hurt and needs some rest. I can deliver their belongings to them later."

"We heard one was a man. I'm going to look him over some. Make sure I don't need to run him off now." Maddox moved up and stood there waiting for her to let him pass with the baggage under each arm. "Got any reason why I shouldn't?"

Maddox would go up whether she liked it or not. A sigh of resignation escaped Daisy as she finally relented and stepped aside, allowing him to take the stairs two at a time. All she could do was pray that he would control himself in dealing with Bass Parker. He was already injured enough.

* * *

Any thought of dozing fled from Bass as a giant of a man barreled into the bedroom and dropped baggage on the floor without ceremony. If the stranger meant him any harm all he'd have to do was pull off the covers. Bass would have died of pure embarrassment being caught in a pair of pantaloons to defend himself. The giant didn't need to offer any introduction. Clearly this must be one of Knox's brothers. The resemblance to Knox was jarring.

"You Parker?" A scowl hardened his features into stoned angles as he towered over the side of the bed.

Bass tried to clear his head from the tea-laced medicine he'd drunk to make him sleep. Though at a disadvantage since he was unable to stand in Trumbo's presence, Bass leaned forward, offered a hand and answered the question. "I am and you must be one of the Trumbos."

To his surprise, the man accepted and returned the handshake. Not knowing how the brothers felt toward him and his role in Knox's conscription, he half expected to be flipped out of the bed and his skull crushed.

"Maddox," the giant introduced himself. "Oldest. Grissom and Jonas will be up here in a minute."

"I see the resemblance." Knox's facial features had served him long whereas this brother's had obviously been adjusted occasionally, yet there was no denying the kinship. Bass could sense someone standing behind Maddox and noticed the black hem of Daisy's skirt, but the breadth of her in-law consumed the space and didn't allow a better view of her.

"Heard what you done for Ollie and Daisy. Much obliged for that but don't much care for you staying here. We want you gone once the crowd clears."

Silence ticked by as Bass studied Maddox's fixed gaze and knew the man would tolerate no compromise on the subject.

Bass nodded. "I hear you. I'll get a room elsewhere as soon as one opens up. And so that you know, my sister and I will be no burden while we're here. I'll pay our board and keep."

"If Knox hadn't took money to stand in for you, you'd be six feet under by now for getting him killed," Maddox assured him, "but fighting's in our blood and he always wore restless boots. He was headed to war anyway. Just happened to be your thousand dollars that got him there."

"I'd like to offer more than that if Daisy or you and your brothers would let me."

Quickly explaining his purpose for being in High Plains, Bass hoped Maddox might see reason where Daisy had not concerning the memorial.

"Just how much money we talking about?" Maddox swung around to eye his sister-in-law before turning back to Bass.

When Bass told him, Maddox shot around quickly, his voice thundering across the room at Daisy. "You mean you had that kinda money all this time and done nothing but plant a few flowers around my brother's grave? Taken up all that fancy footracing and shoemaking to prove you can feed my niece a decent meal? Let her run around in clothes not fit to use for tote sacks? Done all that so people won't know how much you don't need Knox and probably never did? He deserves to be remembered, Daisy, no matter his failings, and Ollie needs more."

Regret filled Bass. He hadn't meant to break open an old wound between Daisy and her brother-in-law.

Though her face paled, Daisy's gaze dared to lift to Maddox's as she defended herself. "I see to it Ollie and her clothes, which she loves to wear, by the way, are clean and warm. That she's fed before any of us eat. I don't give her everything she wants, but she gets all she needs. No, I've never touched a penny of Mr. Parker's money. If it's still in the bank then *he* kept it there, not me. I've never even seen it. Check with Sam Cardwell if you don't believe me."

"Plan to first thing tomorrow if he's up to it."

"But if you think that I didn't accept or use it because I wanted to dishonor Knox in any way," Daisy responded, anger darkening her eyes to burnished gold, "you're sadly mistaken. I wish every day since he died that he could be here to watch Ollie grow up. That I could have been enough to keep him settled in one place. I'll go to my grave making sure Knox is held in honor by this town, but I'm not going to take anyone's blood money to do it with."

Knox may have been the one who'd gone to war, but Daisy Trumbo apparently had waged her own here. Bass decided she could be a formidable opponent and he definitely needed to tread cautiously about his plans to honor Knox or help her any other way.

She took a deep breath and continued, "And, if there's any way I can stop that money from being used, Maddox, neither will you or your brothers."

Her anger focused on Bass, including him into her vow. "What you all don't understand is that this is Ollie's and my right, not yours, to see that he's remembered well. Until Ollie is old enough to truly understand the sacrifice her father gave, it's going to be our decision when and how we honor him. Can I make that any clearer?"

Bass knew he'd been sorely put in his place, but silence claimed the Trumbos as if battle lines were being drawn again. The two headstrong people had challenged each other's will before. He remembered Daisy had feared openly that her in-laws might take Ollie from her upon their arrival, but here she was standing her ground with the giant of a man.

Admiration for her grew and Bass sensed that she was holding herself together as best she could on what she felt was right.

She needed a friend. Someone to support her decision. Maybe she would accept his friendship and that, in turn, would eventually help her accept the money. He'd already separated Ollie from her father. Bass didn't want to cause a rift among the in-laws.

"How about if I just leave the funds in Ollie's name and she does with it what she wants when she reaches the point you think best?" Bass suggested, trying to ease the tension and let her know he was on her side.

"The money is not the real issue here, Mr. Parker," Daisy insisted. "My brother-in-law doesn't think I'm capable of caring for my own child. I've done just fine without anyone else's help and I'll continue to do that until I have no further breath in my body."

An undercurrent of words were being spoken and Bass realized Maddox resented that Daisy had proven herself worthy so far of being both mother and father to Ollie. What lay behind such resentment?

"She's a handful, that's for certain," Bass defended Daisy again, feeling that the scamp would be a challenge for anyone to handle. A whole room of men and women had failed miserably earlier this morning.

"Hey, Uncle Maddox! Uncle Jonas said you want to

see me." Ollie came running into the room and skidded to a halt, interrupting the adults' serious discussion.

Maddox's palm shot out and ruffled Ollie's hair setting the braids to bouncing. He swept her up into his arms and let her straddle his right shoulder. "You being good?"

Ollie seemed to weigh her answer carefully. "Uh, good as I get most times."

Maddox chuckled and Bass was grateful the child's words cooled the tempers that had been simmering moments ago.

"You got plenty to eat?" Maddox's gaze swept over her as if examining her for good measure.

"Yep. Too much sometimes. Mama always says to clean my plate and not waste stuff, but I get Butler to help me if I can't."

"Butler?" Maddox frowned. "You still keeping that goat in the house?"

"Not since he ate Myrtle's darnin'. She made me turn him loose in the barn a couple of days back. Says he needs to butt heads with somebody else but her. All he does is knock himself silly."

"Is your mama doing right by you?" Maddox faced her mother.

Ollie didn't hesitate, not looking threatened at all by Daisy's intense expression. "She's huggin' on me a lot and I don't like it much, but she could've taken a switch to me this mornin' and she didn't. Old Miz Jenkins will prob'ly pray about me tomorrow for sure." Ollie proceeded to tell him about holding the men hostage.

Maddox chuckled as he set her down and bent on one knee to search her eyes. "Ya little wildcat. Guess ya can't help yourself. Ya got your daddy's fire in ya, don'tcha? You'd tell me if ya ever wanted to come live with me and your uncles instead, wouldn't ya?"

"Maybe. Maybe not." She shrugged one shoulder. "Y'all snore a bunch."

Maddox snorted, wrinkling his nose into a twisted angle. She giggled. "See what I mean? Mama don't snore like that. She snuggles me up when the lightnin' comes. You uncles just snore it all away. I'm gonna stay with Mama, if that's okay with you and God."

Maddox tucked a thumb up under Ollie's chin and raised it. "What's God got to do with this, Little Britches?"

"He didn't let Daddy stay with Mama. I'm just hopin' He'll hurry up and let me find her someone to hug on in case He don't let me stay with her, too."

Daisy's heart tightened as if someone had struck her with a mallet. She never dreamed that the reason Ollie wanted to find a new daddy was because she feared leaving her mama alone. She'd assumed Ollie was tired of being smothered with affection and wanted it focused on someone else. At first, her interviewing and list-making seemed endearingly funny and sometimes frustrating, but now Daisy felt only selfish and unworthy of her daughter's true concern. Ollie had lost a father and feared losing her as well to her uncles' decisions.

"You're not going anywhere, Ollie." Daisy crossed the room to stand beside her. "So there's no need to worry about that, is there, Uncle Maddox?"

Daisy stared at Maddox, hoping that her voice sounded more certain than she felt, praying it held no hint of begging. Surely he could see that Ollie needed the security of all she'd known, of a mother's love, of living with someone who would never let her father's name be dishonored. Even by the truth.

"I'll chew on it for a while. No need to pick more bone for now."

"What does 'zat mean?" Ollie looked puzzled.

Bass Parker chimed in. "That means he needs some time to make up his mind. Right, Mr. Trumbo?"

"If you're gonna sleep under my brother's roof you might as well call me Maddox." Maddox rose to his six feet five inches of height. "And you're right. I'll hold off 'til you move to town. By then I'll know more what I'm going to do about you and why you're here. Ain't decided if I'm gonna tolerate it yet. Can't speak for the boys. They'll decide for themselves."

He held out his bear-paw-sized palm. "It's been a waste of good boar-hunting weather meeting you, Parker. I can see by your knuckles you got more than good manners in ya and you can see by my nose I ain't squeamish about shifting bones. So I hope we get through this without having to trade blows. We'll be checking in on ya and making sure you're healing good. People'll get to gossiping and such if ya take too much time mending, being you're under Daisy's roof, ya know what I mean?"

Bass started to speak but Daisy interrupted him. "He's hurt in the shoulder, Maddox. His ears are just fine. And don't be threatening him if you want him out of here as soon as possible. The more he's hurt, the longer he'll have to stay."

Her defense filled Bass with gratitude and more than a measure of surprise.

Ollie leaned over the side of the bed and took a good look at his knuckles. Her eyes softened as she studied him. "I better pray good and hard for ya tomorrow at church, Bass. Nobody, but nobody's ever whupped Uncle Maddox. It would be the best fight ever, though, but you'd get hurt for sure."

Maddox roared with laughter just as his brothers came running up the stairs and entered the already crowded room.

Jonas, the youngest of the three brothers, closest to Daisy's age of twenty-four, ripped a bandanna from around his neck and handed it to Maddox. "What's got ya gushing?"

Grabbing the bandanna and wiping his eyes, he also blew his crooked nose before handing the bandanna back to Jonas. Daisy almost withered with embarrassment right there on her planked flooring.

Maddox told his brothers what Ollie had said to set him to laughing so hard he'd cried.

Grissom, whose nose had fresh purple-and-yellowish hues that now wound into a second curve, looked down his odd-shaped snout. "I thought we came up here to kick him into the hereafter."

Despite the fact that Bass looked as if he was struggling to stay awake, he spoke up and informed the newly arrived brothers what all had been said, discussed and judgment passed on concerning his reason for being here. He focused the conversation on himself, targeting the possible threats only at him and not at her custody of Ollie.

Daisy really took in the sight of her dark-haired patient. Though weak and obviously tiring more each moment that passed, his blue eyes were full of kindness and unspoken defense of her. A wounded knight in tarnished armor. Yet he guarded her. Though reluctant to admit it to herself, she appreciated him doing so and finally accepted something from Bass Parker gratefully.

"Maddox here said he'd give me time to heal my shoulder before he decides whether or not to adjust my nose," Bass finished. "I hope you two gentlemen will do the same."

"Maddox? All that true?" Grissom exhaled a long breath that revealed he had been holding in a readiness to add his fists to a fight.

"True as boogers on bandannas," Ollie announced before Maddox could reply.

Male laughter erupted in the room.

"Lord help us, child." Daisy tried to keep a straight face. She didn't know whether to laugh or be exasperated yet again. She wasn't even sure if she meant keeping her in-laws at bay or getting her daughter raised. "Are any of us up to this challenge?"

Ollie pointed to their houseguest and leaned in to whisper to Daisy only. "Don't worry, Mama. I'll keep my eye on everybody. And I won't let them hurt Bass, 'least 'til I make sure he ain't the daddy I been askin' God to send me."

Chapter Five

Bass woke Sunday morning sore but feeling better. The house was quiet and he wasn't sure if anyone else was awake. He liked this time of day when he could review the previous day and set a goal for making this one work well for him.

But yesterday had been eventful. Of all the things that occurred, the one conclusion that came from it was to focus on getting to know Daisy Trumbo better so she'd let him fulfill his obligation. Let him make up for his role in Knox not coming home. What little she'd shared of herself so far intrigued him, and he had to admit he was grateful to have met the real woman to whom he owed the obligation.

He knew the Trumbo brothers were a huge challenge, and she faced them with great courage. He admired her bravery and liked that she stood her ground with them concerning her rights to keep and raise Ollie. Bass envied having a parent who was able to love that much. Negative thoughts concerning his own mother and father threatened to seep inside his musings, but he pushed them away. That was troubled water already crossed and no amount of wading through the memories would do anything but drown him in sorrow.

Focusing again on what he'd discovered about Daisy, he smiled at her stubborn spunk, her readiness to defend even him and the kindness of her heart. She'd been able to put aside what she disliked about him and was still willing to help him recover. Daisy was fair and just. It had been such a long time since he'd met anyone like her.

He even found her oddly striking in appearance and that surprised him most. Tall, slim, hair the color of harvest wheat, eyes the color of what? He wasn't sure he had ever seen anything worth their comparison. He'd have to think about it awhile. For now, maybe he'd settle on the amber of the crystal chandelier that graced one of the mansions he'd visited in Biloxi on Plantation Row.

She just didn't fit the description of any woman he'd ever shown any interest in before. His occasional choice of dinner companion, more often than not, was a dark-haired beauty of shorter stature and quick wit. Not that he'd had all that many social engagements.

From the time he was a boy he'd seen his parents use love as a weapon to turn on each other, so he didn't want to love like that. Bass told himself if he hardened his heart then no one could hurt him and he would never anchor anyone down who wanted what he couldn't and didn't know how to give. He planned to focus solely on doing his duty and raising his sister. He would never allow his heart to love.

A rooster crowed shaking Bass from his reverie. He decided to see how much movement he could endure, hoping his injury would at least allow him to get out of these bloomers and dressed for the day.

Bass threw back the covers and sat up. Someone had

redressed his wound last night and he had been too sedated to remember who. He'd have to be sure and thank Myrtle or even if it was the man named Teague.

The thought of the stranger and Petula spending time out in the barn yesterday urged Bass's feet to shift over the side of the bed.

Too quick a movement. He steadied himself a moment before looking for the baggage that Maddox had dropped near the armoire. His own was still there. Petula must have taken hers sometime after the Trumbo men left.

He wanted to get dressed so he could discuss matters with her, and he'd feel much better doing that downstairs in the parlor. No matter how shaky he seemed, staying abed would never give him back his strength. He might not be able to travel far, but he'd heal quicker upright.

Bass stood, testing the strength in his legs. Though wobbly, he garnered his will to manage a slow walk across the room. An attempt to lift his baggage proved more than a little troublesome. The weight bit into his injured shoulder and forced him to simply take out the garments he needed and leave the rest alone to unpack when he felt more stable.

The walk back to the bed and exchanging the bloomers for trousers tired him. Bass gratefully sat on the edge of the bed again to catch his breath a moment before fastening the buttons on his shirt. His fingers trembled as he began the effort. Too much, too soon, he guessed. The doctor was right. He wouldn't get far down the road like this.

A knock on the bedroom door surprised him. Someone else was awake. His fingers fumbled with the remaining buttons as he acknowledged, "Yes?"

"Mr. Parker, I heard you milling around. Please don't

overdo it today. We'll be in town much of the morning, and I'm going to have to count on you to pretty much take care of yourself while we're gone. Myrtle and I will have your breakfast ready in a few minutes. I hope you like buttered flapjacks."

Daisy's voice sounded excited, not at all tired from yesterday's events. He did enjoy flapjacks and hadn't eaten homemade ones in a long time. "Sounds wonderful. Thank you."

"I'll see to it that your sister's awake and ready if she wants to go to church with the rest of us. I'm sure she'll enjoy the gathering for the races. She'll have an opportunity to meet some of the other young women in town."

The races were today, he recalled. Something obviously important to the widow. Though he didn't much care that Pet would be able to meet the young men as well, he knew he must start trusting his sister at some point. If he held her at too tight a rein, she would rebel. He couldn't blame her for that. He'd done the same with their parents' expectations of him, hadn't he?

His mother and father had reminded him constantly that he was the reason they didn't reach their goals or failed. He didn't want Pet to end up feeling unworthy of being happy, as their criticism had often made him feel. Bass refused to become *that* hard-hearted or let Pet become the same.

Perhaps it was time to be a little lenient with Pet.

Time to dust off his own prayers and hope for the best.

Everyone would be gone for quite a while this morning, probably even the afternoon. That would give him plenty of time to properly groom himself without anyone trying to help. Maybe he could even manage to get his own breakfast and save them effort.

"Don't trouble yourself for my sake," Bass replied, looking forward to being alone. "I'll see to my own care, Widow Trumbo. Go on with what you need to do to be on your way."

"Hey, Bass," a childlike voice added followed by a second knock. "Can I come in?"

He hurriedly finished the last button on his shirt. What did the little minx want now? "I'm dressed now. You may come in."

A whispered argument echoed from the other side of the door before they finally opened it and entered.

Ollie stood there all decked out in a calico dress and Mary Jane shoes spit polished to a glossy black shine. Her blond hair had been brushed and tied back with a ribbon the color of bluebonnets in fresh bloom.

Daisy looked equally as becoming, outfitted in a lovely gray dress with lavender piping and buttons. A social acceptance of color to bring into play after at least two years of grieving, Bass remembered from his own experience after they'd lost their parents. Petula had hated wearing black and wanted to get to the lavender stage as quickly as possible.

This was probably Daisy's Sunday best.

Her long braid had been pinned into a coil, making him assume she'd probably done that to keep her hair out of her face as she raced. In a dress?

He'd never really thought about how women raced. He knew it was all the rage back East for them to show their ability for sport as equally as men did, but apparently the trend had reached farther West. It didn't quite seem fair that they were forced to participate with disadvantages men didn't suffer.

Embarrassed that he'd just sat there staring at each of

his hostesses, he needed to say something. "My, don't you both look nice."

Ollie took a seat in the chair beside him and frowned at her mother. "I look scrubbed, ya mean."

"Olivia Jane, what do you do when someone gives you a compliment?"

"Oh yeah." She stood abruptly, grabbed a hunk of calico at her hip and curtsied. "Thanks, Bass. I guess I…what do you big fellas call it? Cut mustard?"

"*Muster.* And you certainly do." He imagined the lovely lady she would make someday if she ever allowed any boy to court her. Probably as lovely as her mother.

The child's gaze swept from him to Daisy.

"Well, what about you, Mama?" she challenged. "He said ya look nice, too. What'choo gonna do about it?"

Daisy's cheeks reddened as she bobbed quickly. "Thank you, Mr. Parker. That was kind of you to say so."

It gave Bass an opening to finally express some of what he'd been thinking. "My pleasure, indeed, Mrs. Trumbo."

Ollie sighed and wrinkled her nose. "Y'all just call each other Bass and Daisy, okay? Them long ol' names make me tired. Why don't y'all shake hands like me and Bass did, then y'all can be friends?"

Bass offered his first and Daisy slowly shared hers in return.

"Bass." She squeezed gently in acknowledgment.

"Daisy." He did the same with a sense of gladness. Another step in breaking the ice that might allow them to warm into friendship. He truly wanted to become her friend, someone she trusted. The urge to help her pulsed even stronger in his blood like a log heading into a fast current. "I hope you do well with your races."

"Thank you." Her hand lingered for a moment before slipping slowly from his.

When she turned and headed for the door, he fought the compulsion to tell her he would join her and the others at the breakfast table. To lengthen this truce between them. To spend more time talking with her about something of interest only to her. To learn anything she'd allow him to know that would give him a clue how he might best proceed with his plans concerning her and Ollie.

Daisy had set up strongly in his thoughts since he'd met her, allowing an old dream to resurface. Could such a woman like the widow actually turn his heart from stone? Could any woman for that matter?

Bass had prayed that such a woman might enter his life and teach him how to love, but the prayers went unanswered. Now so long denied, he scoffed at the idea. He'd known Daisy hours, not days. She despised him and wanted him gone. She'd made that clear. He willed the dream away, presuming he'd simply found some of her qualities fitting for the kind of woman that might have appealed to him had he made a list similar to Ollie's.

Before he could get his thoughts back in line and offer to join the Trumbos for breakfast, Daisy turned and told Ollie, "Finish your business with Bass so we can let him rest and be on our way. Time's wasting."

There would be no lingering at breakfast. Bass focused on Ollie. "What business?"

Ollie left her chair, grabbed his hand and pulled him downward. "Can you get on your knees?"

She took to hers at the side of his bed. He joined her, even though it was mighty painful.

"Put your hands like this." She pressed her palms together in front of her.

Bass did the same. Since his prayers went unan-swered, he hadn't been on his knees in a long time and suspected the discomfort was from more than being shot.

"Now bow your head, brother." Ollie bumped her shoulder against him and winked. "That's what they say in my church."

Bass bowed his head and closed his eyes, anticipating what was about to be said. Another doozy of enlighten-ment, he supposed.

"Old Lord, me and Bass have come callin' on Ya. We need Your help real bad."

Bass stole a glance at her.

"And forgive him, Old Lord, for peepin'. Mama says we gotta conscience-trate when we pray. He might not know no better, just like me sometimes."

His eye slammed shut.

"Ya see, Old Lord, my mama's got it in her head that Bass needs the preacher to come callin' and to say some kind of healin' words over him. 'Fact, I heard her tell Myrtie what she's gonna do since he can't go to town with us is bring church back to him."

Her voice got squeakier. "Gonna bring the preacher and some folks so he can get to know 'em! This is just too much for me, Old Sir."

She sighed heavily. "I barely do good in one service, much less two, in the same day. Ya said somethin' like if two of us ask, then that'll get it done. So we're askin' and there's two of us here. I counted. I knew Mama'd be mad if she heard me askin' Ya, but I figured my *friend*—" she opened her eyes to stare pleadingly at Bass "—wouldn't mind. He ain't ready to meet some of these folks around here, and You and me both know it. And I ain't ready for too much more preachin', if Ya don't mind. I'll prob'ly forget some of it."

Knowing he wasn't prepared to meet others who might disapprove of his reasons for being in Daisy's home, in any part of her life, and now in a truce with her, Bass whispered, "Amen to that."

Tired from church services, the race and the level of interest stirred up by the leather wares she sold and took orders for after the race, Daisy almost wished she hadn't asked Preacher Thistlewaite and the others to visit Bass this evening.

She needed to get started on making the shoes and boots as soon as possible. Most wanted them when they came back to see the final race at the end of the month and that would take a good deal of time to meet the deadline. What had she been thinking?

She could have just waited until Bass was strong enough to attend regular services himself, but she owed him this kindness until he felt better. Christian duty required her to treat him as she would have wanted to be treated under the same circumstances.

Daisy steered the team toward home, glad that it took only about fifteen minutes from town. Fortunately, Teague had rounded up Ollie out of the crowd and got her, Myrtle and Petula settled on the wagon before heading off to make sure the horde of visitors dispersed in a friendly manner.

Seemed he'd gotten news the sheriff and the posse were on their way back empty-handed, so he was going to stick around until they returned and keep things on an even keel.

Petula finally broke her silence that had lingered on the ride home. "Sorry you didn't win the race."

Daisy shrugged. "Second place allows me to be in the next round, so that's all right with me. As long as I place in the top five each time, I've got a real chance to win the big purse in the last one. That's when all the finalists compete against each other."

"Bass will be sorry he missed this. He'll want to see you run when he's better and can watch." Petula fanned herself and offered a compliment. "He's always admired women who aren't afraid of showing all they're capable of. If he ever marries he'll choose someone like that. Not that I think he will. He's pretty much set on not taking a bride. Me? I plan to marry a man who'll make me respect him and want nothing else but to be his wife. No man I can wrap up in knots, that's for sure."

Marriage? Not now, maybe never again. Daisy didn't dwell on the subject, though it was hard not to because of Ollie's constant interviewing for her daddy list. But she had to admit she was looking forward to seeing Bass Parker this afternoon. Oddly enough, she couldn't wait to share with him the good news about placing second. Even if the well-wishes came from a man she had every reason to dislike, he seemed to truly wish her the best and having someone other than her family anticipate her doing well had added to her joy in placing.

"Do you think Teague will return anytime soon?" Speculation filled Petula's tone. "Or do you guess he'll stay in town for days?"

So Petula had set her bonnet for him. The young beauty had enjoyed several men's attention today, but she seemed bent on keeping an eye focused on Teague. That Petula had settled on chasing one man should ease Bass's mind a little. But Daisy hoped Petula knew the challenge she was taking on in winning the heart of a man such as Teague.

"I'm not sure how long he'll be gone," Daisy admitted, "but he said he'll return to help with your brother. I've never known him not to keep his word. Then again, I don't know all that much about him."

"He'll come back," Ollie spoke up. "He left some things like his bedroll in the barn, remember?"

Bedroll in the barn? "Butler!" Daisy, the cook and Ollie shouted in unison, nearly causing Petula to tumble across the wagonbed.

"Hang on," Daisy warned and flicked the reins, hurrying the team into a faster gait. "Let's hope that goat hasn't chewed Teague out of more than just his bedroll."

Once they got there, everything seemed to be fine in the barn. Nothing was amiss except Butler. He was nowhere to be found.

Inside the house proved an entirely different matter.

Daisy and her troupe walked into the parlor and everything looked as though a battle had taken place. Chairs were tumbled on their sides. A curtain was missing over one of the windows. The handwoven rug that once lay in front of the settee was now folded on its side halfway up the stairs. Pieces of some white powdery substance mixed with hay scattered a path from parlor to kitchen.

Dread enveloped Daisy, remembering the pending threat of last night. She tried to recall if she'd seen her brothers-in-law at church or in the crowd at the races. Jonas and Grissom, yes. Maddox, no.

"Better run upstairs and make sure Bass is all right, Petula," Daisy insisted, wanting to get her out of the way if she found Bass in this mess somewhere. "Myrtle, you check the kitchen. Ollie, you stay right where you are so I can keep you in my sight. It won't take us but a minute to make sure everything's okay."

"Mama, I didn't do it. I was with you all the time, remember?"

Daisy nodded, more to reassure her than anything else. "I know you were, honey. I'm sure there's a logical explanation for all of this." *And I hope it wasn't Maddox. Please be all right, Bass.*

"Bass?" Petula yelled as she made her way cautiously upstairs, taking slow steps, clearly afraid of what she might find. "Can you hear me? If you do, yell out."

"I'm in the kitchen, trying to clean up this mess."

His voice, though aggravated, sounded like a blessing.

Daisy exhaled a deep breath, allowing her heartbeat to slow from its rapid pace.

At least he was conscious.

All four females rushed to the kitchen.

There before Daisy stood her patient dressed in flour-coated nankeen pants. An as-yet-tied apron covered the blue chambray shirt that matched his eyes. Holding a broomstick in hand, he looked a sight with the white powder dusted across the floor, the table and him.

In front of the table on its side with ladder-back chairs to block both ends, lay a tote sack that had been chewed open.

A loud "Nah-ah-ah-ah" sounded from behind the overturned table informing Daisy of just who had instigated the damage. The goat!

The black, brown, white and gray billy looked at her as if he was saying, "Not me," chewing some of the flour dusting his mouth and long tongue.

Butler wore the missing curtain as a collar. Bass must have tried to rope the goat first before cornering him. The man whose fists took on a gang of bank robbers had done his best not to harm the animal while capturing him. Bass looked so helpless yet endearing that Daisy's heart filled with a sense of respect about his efforts to make things right.

He blew a strand of hair dipping down into one eye and it sent flour dusting the eyebrow above.

She blinked once, twice, laughter bubbling up inside her. She tried to quell it. But Daisy just couldn't help it. Out exited, free and without any finesse whatsoever, a snort of a giggle.

That set everyone to laughing, particularly Bass.

His deep, full-throated laughter filled her with pure joy. She allowed it to envelop her like a warm ray of sunshine, easing the tension of all that had happened yesterday, all the feelings about Knox that Bass had resurrected since his arrival, all the fear and concerns of having him in her home now. They were simply people enjoying a moment of shared humor and the joy of it, the innocence and newness of becoming more than strangers.

Daisy wished this sense of friendship was something she could trust. She missed sharing herself in such a simple way. But experience had taught her to be guarded against such innocence. That she should never again be so gullible about giving more than she received, of being someone's easy, too trusting companion.

"Here, let me take that from you." Myrtle waddled up and grabbed the broom from Bass. "You look like you're about done in. Don't want to set that shoulder to bleeding again. Take a seat somewhere. I need to get this cleaned up and food cooking anyway. Folks'll be here before you know it and some of them will stay for supper."

"I'll help," he insisted. "I made this mess."

Daisy shook her head and motioned him into the parlor. "Let me set the furniture back in its place and I'll have a chair ready for you in a minute. Petula, how about you and Ollie grab a rope and tie Butler up in the barn. Make sure he isn't anywhere near Teague's belongings. I don't want him running around the place while the preacher's here. Let's hope I've got another set of curtains washed. That one will smell too much like goat now."

Petula didn't hesitate, which caused her brother's eyes to widen. "That must've been some kind of church service this morning," he complimented.

Daisy smiled, happy that he was pleased.

Ollie moved past him and apologized. "Sorry, Bass. I must've left the back door open this morning. Only way Butler could'a got in the kitchen. Me and Pet'll make sure he don't cause ya no more problems. 'Least for today."

"I'm grateful it was only a goat. I heard somebody downstairs and thought I'd better check since I assumed I was still alone. But I couldn't get down here fast enough to stop the initial damage. As you can see, he fought hard in the parlor until I got him roped and cornered behind the table."

Bass brushed a hand through his dark hair, powdering it with even more flour. "But it was worth it, getting to hear your mama laugh like that."

"You laugh pretty well yourself." Daisy returned the compliment as his eyes studied her directly.

"That's on my daddy list. Likes to laugh," Ollie reminded. "Ya remember, don'tcha, Mama?"

"Yes, love. I remember." Able to look Mama straight in the eye was on there, too.

Bass was beginning to qualify for a lot of the list's requirements.

And Daisy wasn't sure if she was prepared for that. She wanted him gone, didn't she?

Chapter Six

Bass did his best to keep from nodding off as the stout, lion-maned preacher finished his sermon, but no one else in the crowded, hot parlor appeared distracted from the redhead's resonant voice and earnest subject. Bass decided his lack of attention must be because he'd overextended himself when corralling Butler and changing clothes yet again before company arrived. Too much activity too soon had worn him out. It might take another day or two before he regained his true strength.

But he couldn't have begged off from attending the service since Daisy had gone to so much trouble to arrange it for his sake. All he wanted now was for the gathering to be done and to finish whatever remaining expectations Daisy required of him this evening before heading up to his room. His mind was full with trying to remember each person's name in the meet and greet that occurred before Preacher Thistlewaite began the sermon.

Bass had decided already that they would stay here in High Plains longer than just giving him time to get well. At first opportunity, he would notify his lawyer to put things on hold until he made up his mind whether or not to establish his and Pet's new home and barrel-making factory in San Francisco or make this town their permanent residence.

He needed more time to learn what Daisy wanted for her own future, and decide how he could best go about making sure he helped her achieve her goals. He may have felt a sense of duty to her because of Knox, but now he had more reason to help her. She was a decent person, full of kindness for others and obviously loved by her community. She deserved someone to be kind to her.

The fact that he even dared consider the thought of changing his initial plans to take his business and his sister as far west as possible said a lot about how much fulfilling his sense of duty to her and Ollie meant to him. After all, their furnishings were already packed up and waiting for their arrival. Not to mention, the farther west they chose to settle, the more likely Petula's reputation could be protected.

If he elected to linger in Texas was it possible Petula might be satisfied to stay in this small town? She loved big cities and High Plains offered few attractions for her. He glanced around to locate his sister. She did seem oddly happy here more than anyplace they'd been so far.

On the settee, Daisy sat on one side of him, Ollie on the other and Petula in a chair next to Ollie. A choice he appreciated given that a few in the crowd would have made him feel uncomfortable sharing the seating arrangements.

He studied the strangers in the chairs that formed a half circle opposite the preacher. For much of the sermon, some of the congregation stared at Bass as though he might sprout horns. Had Daisy's cook informed them of his identity or did most form an early opinion of him on their own?

From the downturned lines of Esther Sue Jenkins's mouth, the elderly woman clearly didn't approve of him. He hadn't really talked to her all that much, so he could only assume she didn't appreciate him being in Daisy's and Ollie's company.

As if she could read his thoughts, Ollie leaned over and whispered, "Don't mind Old Miz Jenkins. She's lookin' mean at'cha 'cause she don't like nobody but her own self. Ask anybody."

"Shh," the thin, Roman-nosed woman demanded, pressing a gloved forefinger against her lips.

"Olivia." Daisy leaned over to look past Bass just enough so the one word made Ollie clam up.

Bass gently patted Ollie's hand and silently mouthed, *I'm sorry.*

Ollie beamed up at him then turned and stuck out her tongue at the woman who'd passed judgment on her.

He tried not to chuckle.

Daisy elbowed him in the side. "Don't encourage her."

Bass found amusement in Daisy's expression, not real criticism. He smiled at her and shrugged, pleased that she smiled back before returning her attention to Thistlewaite. She had a sense of humor it seemed.

"And so, my friends, I thank you for gathering on this special come-to-meeting in welcoming the Parkers, Bass and Petula, to our community. We pray his healing is fast and their stay with us is a blessed one, even if it's short."

A few "Amens" echoed across the room.

"Now, before concluding our services, are there any announcements we need to make? I ask you," he said, looking directly at Esther Sue, "to please be brief due to the infirmity of our new brethren and the lateness of the hour. We would all like to get home before sundown, please."

The woman stood and started to say something but Maddox cleared his throat, drawing attention to himself. "I got something what's got to be said, Preacher. Pardon me, Miz Jenkins, but I want to get it said first, if you can hold your bonnet a minute."

Bass and Daisy turned at the same time, both staring at the towering Trumbo standing near the doorway to the kitchen. He must have slipped in the back door without them noticing. His brothers stood beside him. From the gasps across the parlor, Bass suspected the men didn't visit spiritual gatherings on a frequent basis.

Noticing Daisy tense up at the sight of her in-laws, Bass placed his hand over hers. She instantly slid it away, but not before he realized she trembled slightly. Her chin lifted and her shoulders set straighter. He sensed her bracing herself as she'd done last night, obviously unnerved by what Maddox might say or do now.

Whatever his words, if they affected Daisy and she didn't like them, Bass decided to help her any way she'd let him to deal with the circumstances. He wouldn't let anyone bully her into something she didn't want to do.

Mrs. Jenkins slowly sat, her mouth turned down in disapproval. "Then get on with it, Maddox. You know I have quite a lot to say about what's going on here. An unmarried man residing in this house, no matter what the reason, is unseemly. I've told you what needs to be done."

So this is about me. Bass wondered if the Trumbos had changed their minds and came to give him the boot, but it sounded as if more might be involved in the decision. Poor Daisy, everyone telling her how to run her household.

"You know why I've opened my home to him." Daisy stood and spoke to the whole crowd, ending by squarely facing the older woman. "He's been nothing but a perfect gentleman. A respectful guest. An eager-to-get-well patient."

She could have just kicked me out and ended all of this. Bass appreciated her defense of him. He wanted to do the same for her. "Widow Trumbo has been a wonderful example of your community's kindness to strangers. All of you have shown me and my sister such a gracious welcome. Taken us in as if we were family. In fact, you've been so considerate that we may elect to make High Plains our home rather than go on to California."

There, he'd said it aloud, committing himself to the choice.

Daisy looked as shocked as Mrs. Jenkins.

Petula didn't utter a single word of complaint, which he hadn't expected. Maybe she liked High Plains as much as he suspected.

Ollie bobbed in her seat, squealing, "Now that's tellin' 'em, Bass."

Maddox moved closer and stood next to Daisy, wrapping one arm around her. "Well, that sounds mighty fine, Mr. Parker. Maybe you'll be around for the wedding."

"What wedding?" Daisy and Bass echoed in unison.

An unsettling feeling swept over Bass, and he found himself wishing away Maddox's next words. *Don't let him say it.* But then why did it matter if he did?

It mattered because he didn't want Daisy feeling threatened in any way.

"Mine and Daisy's, of course. Miz Jenkins there came clear out to my ranch and read me that story about taking on your brother's wife when he dies. She argued a good point and I been thinking about it pretty strong. I want Ollie to have a decent life and plenty of meals. I figure I can provide that sure as anyone, so I figure Daisy's about to quit her mourning. Guess since she's ready to shed her black," Maddox said, his eyes sweeping over Daisy's lavender-and-gray dress, "then I'm ready to hitch up with her and ease her burdens."

"I'm not marrying you." Daisy jerked away from his arm and sank into her seat. The crowd buzzed with the news and her stubbornness.

Maddox bent beside her, resting on the back of his spurs. "Ah now, Daiz, ya know ya like me well enough. We get along just fine. It's best for Ollie Girl, there, and that's all that matters."

"I like you. I don't love you. At least, not in the way a woman should. A woman wants to choose the man she marries. To know how important she is to him."

"Not everyone marries for love, Widow Trumbo," Mrs. Jenkins reminded. "And he has an obligation to take care of you on behalf of Knox. It's the very reason I told him so."

Daisy shook her head and ignored the instigator. "You owe me nothing, Maddox. I will take nothing. Promise nothing."

She then stared at Bass, her amber eyes full of a quiet desperation that asked him to help in some way.

This was exactly the opportunity he'd been waiting for. She needed him. Maybe if he stalled, or rather stalled Maddox, this could be the start of her trusting him and letting him in closer. Maybe she'd finally allow him to make amends for Knox not coming home.

"Why don't you give her some time?" Bass began, an idea forming that might also work into his own plans. "After all, a woman needs to be courted properly."

Others agreed that his suggestion sounded fair and worth consideration.

Daisy's desperation seemed to ease slightly. Bass smiled, partly to reassure her, mostly because he needed to set things in motion. Maybe he could curry her favor during Maddox's courting time. If Daisy wouldn't take his money, then perhaps he might offer marriage himself and then half his money could be hers to do with what she wanted. She would become wealthy and not have to struggle. He could fulfill his responsibility to them. Then they could both move forward with putting the past behind them.

It wasn't as if she'd be depriving him of true love. He didn't expect that of her. He would gain someone to be hostess in his home and show Petula how to be a lady. Ollie would get a new daddy as she hoped. Sounded like a good business venture if nothing else and a credible way to repay the obligation. Nobody would get hurt, and he would never challenge her in regard to how she raised Ollie. Everybody would come out winners.

But how to go about gaining her favor when she didn't want to like him in the first place?

The first step he'd take is get a good look at Ollie's daddy list. See what Daisy appreciated in a man and might demand from a suitor. He knew some of the requirements already just from the questions Ollie had asked.

Bass realized Maddox had yet to agree to allow her time to decide. He looked past Daisy and demanded, "Will you court her awhile?"

Maddox remained silent for a moment then nodded.

"A month ought to be fittin' and proper. I need to get brandin' underway and clear out some of our gear to the bunkhouse if we're gonna take in wimmen. I guess Myrtle's welcome to come with you, Daisy, being she's such a fine cook."

"Thanks a bunch, Maddox. I'll spiff up my hot pepper jelly recipe for you fellas." Myrtle's sarcastic voice echoed how thrilled she was at the prospect. "But if she accepts your hand, you men ought to live over here. This house is better built and rides out the winter a lot warmer than your place."

"Right'cha are. I helped build it so I ought'a know, but I like being farther down the creek. The boars favor there and I get better hunting prospects. We'll settle up on the issue after we're hitched."

"A month won't do," Daisy insisted. "My sisters are coming to visit while my parents are away on a trip. Our family home is being renovated and they want the girls out of the way. Snow and Willow should be here any day now. The races will take up most of my time and I have all my shoe orders. I don't have time to court anyone at the moment. I don't have time to be married, in fact."

Maddox shrugged. "Mighty inconvenient for me, too, but we'll get it done and make it work somehow. Could be a good thing your sisters are coming. They'll be here just in time for the I-dos."

"I promise you, I don't. I won't. And I'm perfectly happy being your brother's widow."

"'Zat why your daughter's taking a bead on every prospect come to town? Don't sound to me like she's happy about it none." Maddox reached over and ruffled Ollie's hair, setting her bluebonnet-colored ribbon off-kilter. "How 'bout it, Little Britches, ya reckon you'd like me for a daddy?"

Ollie shook her head. "Naw, I already told'ja what's all wrong with ya, Uncle Mad. 'Sides, what would I call ya? Uncle Daddy?"

Her question ended any further discussion and sent everyone on their way home to speculate whose will would prove stronger, Maddox's, Daisy's or Esther Sue Jenkins's.

Truth be told, Bass wondered if any man would be good enough to earn Ollie's respect or loving enough to heal whatever hurt rooted Daisy's heart in the past.

If he ever truly courted her and proposed to her, he almost wished he could offer Daisy something more than security. But the best he could offer her was friendship and a pledge to always treat her kind and with respect. Maybe she would accept that being enough to live the rest of her life by. It certainly seemed a decent prospect for him.

For now he'd just keep quiet and take advantage of Maddox's willingness to give Daisy time. Maybe something better than proposing to her would come to mind.

The dishes were all washed, the chairs returned to their normal places, Ollie's splinters from the bank wall finally removed and the house quiet. Daisy's mind had been too unsettled to sleep, so after helping Myrtle set things right again she'd worked on the first of her shoe orders, cutting the soles from the leather. But exhaustion from the full day set in and she knew it was best to stop so she wouldn't make an error. Leather was too costly to hurry the construction.

After a quick glance at Ollie in the bed they now shared, Daisy decided some tea sounded good before heading there herself. She grabbed a lit lamp so she could check one more time on Bass and make sure he had finally gone to sleep. He'd asked Ollie for something to read and the child had begged to spend some time reading to him.

She thought it kind of him to say he enjoyed listening to her, and the child had taken a hankering to spending time with him. Daisy suspected Ollie was probably interviewing him further and he was indulging her. She could only guess what all they'd discussed.

Despite her anger with him, she liked Bass. Found that she felt at ease in his company when he didn't pester her about funding a memorial. It made her angry that someone like Esther Sue Jenkins could put evil thoughts in people's minds about a person she knew nothing of. Bass didn't deserve such judgment. There was an innate goodness about him that would not allow him to step over any line she asked him not to cross.

He'd shown Ollie a great deal of patience.

And he'd helped with Maddox.

She'd unconsciously reached out to him for guidance, and he'd offered an answer. Maybe for only a brief time but no less a solution. She would simply keep so busy Maddox would have no time to court her. That might offer enough time to sway him until he rid himself of this crazy notion or found someone else to take as a bride. She did want each Trumbo brother to find love someday. She just didn't expect Maddox to seek a union with *her*.

As Daisy walked toward her former room, she noticed the light shining beneath the door. Could Bass still be awake?

She rapped gently on the door.

No answer.

"Bass, are you feeling all right?"

Papers rustled. "Oh, sorry. Still reading. Have I disturbed you?"

"No, I'm going down to get some tea. Would you like a cup or something more to eat?"

"Tea sounds nice, if you'll join me, that is."

She thought about Mrs. Jenkins for a moment then decided she wouldn't let the woman rule her kindness. "Of course. I'll be right back."

Halfway down the stairs, she heard a door shut and footsteps behind her. She glanced back to find him following, dressed as he'd been at the service, not as she'd expected this late.

She realized why he still wore his day clothes and felt she owed him an apology. "I'm so sorry. We got busy with cleaning up, we totally forgot to check and see if you needed your bandages changed."

"No problem. It's not as good as you or Myrtle would have done, but I managed. Changed them before everyone arrived. They'll be fine until tomorrow. Thought we'd have tea down here. Wouldn't want to set anyone's tongues to wagging, would we?"

She suspected he didn't want her feeling awkward no matter how innocent their sharing tea proved, and it made her appreciate his thoughtfulness.

He walked with her to the kitchen and started to grab some wood. "I'll stoke the stove and get—"

"No need, it's still hot. I left it warming because I like a late-night cup of something before I finally go to sleep. The tea's done. Just take a seat and I'll get the cups. But thanks for offering."

He sat at the table and pulled a chair out for her. "Tell me about your work. About making shoes."

"All right, give me a moment." Daisy gathered the cups and saucers, set them on the table and grabbed the teakettle. After filling each cup with the aromatic brew, she offered him sugar and cream, which he declined.

Plain and simple, she noted, returning the kettle then sitting adjacent to him. He might dress fancy, but he had easy ways. Another thing she liked about Bass if she was listing such things.

"There's not much to tell, really," she began, finally relaxing. "I cut pieces from leather, sew uppers to lowers and that makes shoes. Occasionally I add battens to help keep mud and moisture off so the shoes can last longer."

"I noticed you and Myrtle and Ollie all wear shoes that have right and left formations. Do you make those?"

"It's the good thing about any business you have. At least you never run out of that one particular supply. Yes, I make ours. Most cobblers just sew one uniform shape for both feet, but the McKay allows me to sew both right and left patterns."

She noticed his puzzled expression. "Oh, I guess I ought to explain. A McKay is a new type of sewing machine. I was blessed enough to get one when Knox sent me some money and told me to buy something useful for myself. I thought it would help me make a living and it has. The machine speeds up my production immensely. I cut my patterns and then finish sewing on the McKay."

"I'd like to watch you make a pair sometime."

"I'm sure you have better things to do, Mr. Parker."

"We're at Bass, remember? And I have nothing better to do than get well. So, unless you want me to be totally bored while I'm healing, I hope you'll allow me a bit of curiosity."

"Very well, maybe I can arrange a time for you to watch."

Each took a sip of their tea at the same moment, studying each other over their cup rims. The flame of the lamp above its wick flickered light and shadow along the walls. A sense that she and Bass were on the edge of sharing something more than a companionable evening together enveloped Daisy and she wondered if she dare trust the dance of shadows in his gaze.

Chapter Seven

Morning dawned with a sense that the house thrived with activity. Sun shone brightly through the windows making Bass wonder if he had overslept. He had wanted to get up early and familiarize himself with every part of Daisy's normal routine, but he'd stayed up too late reviewing the notes Ollie kindly shared with him.

Her daddy list was extensive and full of aspects about possible suitors he'd never really considered before. Did women really delve that deep into a man's personality before making a choice?

If he ultimately decided to court her, the layers of worth he needed to grow might take more than a month and lots more than his twenty-seven years on this earth had taught him so far. She'd already shown she was not a woman easily swayed.

He'd dreamed half the night of peeling away the skin of an onion, then shaking out his clothes. Like removing bad habits he thought she might not approve of. He couldn't remember ever wanting to do that for anyone. Bass assumed the dream meant she would challenge him to be at his best.

Dressing as quickly as his injury allowed, he made

his bed then headed downstairs to make himself available to her for the day. Surely one good shoulder and hand could be used for something. That could be a small beginning in the right direction.

Finding his sister eating breakfast while the cook washed dishes, Bass discovered Daisy and Ollie gathering odd supplies to pack in a basket. They'd already eaten.

"Good morning," he announced, taking in the sight of Daisy dressed in a light brown dress with no frills and a row of buttons down the front. When she turned to acknowledge his entrance, he thought the hue particularly brought out golden streaks of ripened wheat in her blond hair. The more he looked at her, the prettier she seemed. "How are you all this fine sunny day?"

"Better than we deserve, and you? I must say, you finally look rested."

Daisy's reply sounded positive even though from someone else it might have been a half complaint. Bass eyed the basket curiously. "Couldn't feel better, matter of fact. What, may I ask, are you two packing?"

Ollie grabbed a small pail from inside one of the lower cabinets and stored it in the basket. "Got the little one, Mama. Want me to fetch the scissors an' a knife?"

"I'll get those. Why don't you go wash your face and grab a sweater? Now, don't give me that pout. You know how the wind can kick up without a moment's notice, so we'll at least wrap it around your overalls so you'll have it with you. I'll finish up here and then we'll be on our way. I plan to do some more sewing this afternoon so we won't be gone that long."

"Where are you going?" Bass wondered aloud then thought maybe he should have minded his own business. It sounded as if he fit nowhere in her plans.

"Out to the cemetery," Petula said around a mouthful of biscuits and gravy, "to clean it up. They do that on Monday mornings if the weather's pretty enough."

"Knox's grave?" Bass had wanted to pay his respects and hoped this might give him an opportunity to do so. Not to mention the time it would give him with Daisy.

He knew the widow studied him now, waiting to see if either he or his sister would break the promise he'd given about not discussing Knox with Ollie. He said no more.

"Sure," Ollie answered his original question, easing the moment of silence. "Daddy and some of our other gone-befores are out there. I like to keep it all cleaned up and pretty for them."

He dared to test Daisy's trust in him. "May I go with you?"

"Can he, Mama?" Hope filled Ollie's cherubic expression. "He can help me with Butler if that ol' billy gives me any fits."

She swung around to explain. "Mama said Butler's got to spend a couple of days out in the pasture since he's been so rowdy lately. I think it's gonna make him real mad and I might need you to help me catch him again if he decides to buck me off. I ride him out there 'cause I can't keep up with Mama's steps."

"Are you up to a walk?" Daisy pointed at Bass's injured shoulder. "It might do you good to get some fresh air."

"A walk, yes. A horse or a wagon? Maybe another day or two."

"Don't count me in." Petula lay down her fork and dabbed her lips with a cloth. "I'll find something to keep me busy around here."

"Like doing her own dishes," the cook recommended, "straightening up her bed and hanging up her clothes."

"Do that first, Pet. Afterward, I'm sure you'll find something to keep yourself entertained." He was so eager to join Daisy that he hadn't given his sister a second thought. That was a first. "Your friend Teague is not back yet, is he?"

Petula's expression soured. "Not yet. He's still in town, I suppose, waiting on the sheriff."

"Any ranch hands about?"

Daisy shook her head, setting the long braid hanging down her back to swaying. "If we need help we always rely on the uncles."

Bass knew she understood the reasoning behind his questions and appreciated her quick reassurance. The fact that it would just be the cook and his sister at the house made him more willing to give Pet looser rein. "Then, by all means, Petula. Enjoy your day and I will, too."

"I guess we're set." Daisy grabbed a biscuit out of a pan on the top of the stove and stuffed it with two pieces of bacon. Pouring a cup of milk from a pitcher sitting on the table, she handed both biscuit and cup to Bass. "You need to eat something. I'll finish up packing and Ollie can go get her sweater and Butler. If you don't mind eating while we walk it will help us hurry along."

"No problem at all." He watched her add more biscuits, bacon and some cheese to the gathered items and suspected it was for his benefit. She took a red checkered cloth and spread it over the basket, tucking it in so the contents wouldn't spill during their journey.

"Follow me." Ollie headed toward the back door of the kitchen. "I'll be the leader."

"First, you'll get your sweater like I told you," Daisy reminded, grabbing the basket, "then you can be leader."

"Aww, Mama, I done put one on Butler and he wasn't too happy about it. I knew ya was gonna make me wear one so I tied it around his neck."

She disappeared out the door as Daisy complained that it might not be the nicest-smelling sweater if she had to wear it home.

Bass offered his good arm to Daisy, allowing her to link hers with his. "I take it we'll be walking upwind of her and the goat?"

"Most definitely."

As they began their first outing together, his chuckle mingled with the sweet sound of her amusement.

Hopefully, the day would prove even more promising and he'd get to learn more about Daisy than her daughter's list provided.

Daisy discovered it was easy to talk to Bass. He seemed sincerely interested in all she'd done to the ranch to make it a decent home for Ollie. Keeping the place in good shape took a lot of work, especially since her shoe business required her attention in order to earn a better living. Making improvements on the land came second.

One day she would earn a small stipend from her parents, as would all her siblings, and her mother and father had offered it when she'd lost Knox. But she had needed to prove to herself that she could stand on her own with no one's help and asked them not to make an exception in her case. She would wait like the others to receive her inheritance and she prayed that wouldn't be for years to come.

She also didn't care to ask her brothers-in-law for help unless there seemed no other way. Maybe some would consider her reluctance pride, but the true source of her unwillingness was that she felt she owed Knox and Ollie her best effort first.

To her great pleasure, Bass kept in step with her along the way and didn't slow his pace for her sake. It felt good to walk with a man who didn't seem intimated by her height and stride.

"There it is," she announced, raising the basket a little higher to motion downslope. "Look just to the right above the lake at the stand of trees. That's our private cemetery."

"Hey, Mama," Ollie shouted behind them. "Butler's smelled the mint. He's gettin' a little bouncy. W-whoa, buddy. I can't. Hold. On. Bass, help!"

Just as a streak of brown, white, gray and black attempted to gallop past them, Bass's arm unlinked from Daisy's and grabbed Ollie from her precarious perch, jerking her toward him. The momentum sent him backward, bumping Daisy, setting all three of them on a downward roll, like tangled tumbleweeds chasing each other.

"Ouch."

"Watch out!"

"You're gonna squash me!"

Seconds ticked by in echoes of pain until, finally, the hill leveled out near the bank of the lake and the rolling came to an abrupt halt.

Daisy spit out sand and grass, shakily raising her face from the ground where she lay. "Ollie? Bass?"

"Made it, Mama." Ollie sat up and dusted off her overalls. "Oohwee, that was pretty wicked."

"Bass? You okay?" Daisy tried to brush hair from her eyes. Strands of it had pulled away from her braid and now hung like drooping willow branches blocking a clear view of his location.

"Over here," he muttered. "You can bury me right here if I die. No need to tote me up there. I'm not moving for a minute or two."

She finally spotted him a few feet upslope. He lay on his back with all four limbs sprawled, pointing in different directions.

Ollie ran over and looked down at him. "Take a deep breath, Bass. It'll make ya feel better. Did me."

"Sounds like a good idea." Bass inhaled deeply and let out a long stream of breath, then repeated the process a couple more times. Finally, he managed to sit up.

By then, Daisy had gotten to her feet and untangled her skirt hem enough to allow her to cross the distance and check on him. "How's your shoulder?"

"Which one?" He reached and touched the original injury, wincing. "Hurting like nobody's business, but it doesn't seem to be bleeding through."

Her eyes examined him closer. "And the other?"

"Bruised, I'd guess, but nothing's broken that I can tell."

"That's a blessing. It could have been a lot worse," she worried aloud. She could have had to bury yet another man she had mixed-up feelings about.

What was she feeling about Bass anyway? He was becoming something more than just a what? A foe? Could she allow him to become a friend?

"Hey, y'all—" Ollie pointed "—look at Butler. He's chompin' that ol' mint. It must be real good. So dark it looks like somebody washed it."

Daisy watched the goat gnawing voraciously on the patches of mint already greening up for spring, dark emerald shoots of fragrant herb that covered the rise leading to the graves.

Myrtle liked Daisy to bring some of the mint home each time they visited here to use in her stews and teas, but she didn't have the heart to tell her cook how distasteful she found the task. The fact that it grew only here near Knox's grave made her feel nauseous when she took a bite of anything that contained the mint. She almost hoped Butler would eat the ground bare.

Time was wasting and they needed to be about their business. Daisy pointed to the upturned basket behind them. "Why don't I see what I can salvage of our things and you and Ollie go ahead on to the cemetery," she suggested. "Take it slow 'til we see if you'll be steady on your feet, Bass. No running or chasing that goat, Ollie. I'll be right behind you."

Ollie offered Bass a hand up and, to Daisy's relief, he stood without any obvious additional injury. Maybe having the breath knocked out of him and a tumble wouldn't set his recovery back too much.

She retraced their steps and grabbed the basket. The biscuits and bacon would have to be left for birds or Butler if he ever moved away from the mint. She could dip the half-moon of cheese in the lake and clean it off with the checkered towel.

A quick search found the scattered utensils. Small wonder no one had been stabbed by the scissors or knife as they'd been flung into the air. The last thing she found was the mason jar of tea she'd brought and the drinking cups. How the glass jar had managed not to break she would never know, but Daisy was grateful.

By the time she gathered everything and stopped at the lake a moment to wash her hands then clean the cheese and wrap it in the cloth, Bass and Ollie were already sitting on the bench she'd built inside the fenced-in cemetery. Bass obviously had tired making his way there and needed to rest.

Maybe he was hurting more than he let on.

She hurried to join them. Once there, she studied him further. His face was paler than before and he still hadn't completely calmed his breath. "You aren't feeling well."

"I will be. Just give me a moment."

"I been askin' him some more questions, Mama, and he's been talkin'."

"Let those questions rest for now, Ollie, and we'll get busy with the cleanup. What do you say?"

"Can I do Daddy's first?"

"Certainly. Pick up all the twigs and leaves and put them in the pail. Don't touch the scissors or knife for now. I'm going to get Bass something to drink, then I'll be over to help you."

Daisy handed Ollie what she needed and set about pouring Bass tea. When she finally offered him a cup, his hand seemed steadier. Their fingers touched and her eyes immediately met his.

The color of them was stunning. As blue as the spring-thawed water below. She remembered they were the first thing she'd noticed about him when he was nothing but a stranger to her in the bank.

"Thank you," he said quietly and sipped the tea, his gaze still riveted on hers.

"You're welcome." Her pulse sped up and beat strong as it did when she raced.

"I don't mean just for the tea. For taking us into your home when you didn't have to. For understanding that I came here with only the best intentions concerning Knox. And for allowing me the opportunity to become your friend, I hope. I've rarely been shown such kindness."

"Why?" Daisy sat down beside him on the bench, curious about his past other than his dealings with Knox.

"It's a long story, full of self-pity, some would say. Self-preservation, I prefer to believe."

"You've been hurt by someone you love, haven't you?" She heard it in his harsh defense. She felt it in her bones. She sensed it because she, too, had suffered the same.

"What's love?" Bass stared, as if looking into the distance. "An impossible longing to be someone's everything only to discover you mean nothing at all? No matter how hard you try, you aren't enough? You're a burden not a blessing to them? You can never be or do enough to make a difference? So you harden yourself from caring. Quit even trying to give anything of yourself to anyone. You learn to simply exist."

His words hit too close. Hadn't that been what she'd done since marrying Knox? She'd quit trying long before she lost him. Nothing she did had been enough, so she'd simply existed, accepting her role and what she'd dealt herself.

"There's Petula," Daisy reminded, trying to show him he had love within him somewhere.

"And your precious Ollie," Bass acknowledged. "That's our saving grace, isn't it? We have them to show us that we're still capable of caring, whether or not we choose to love. But part of that's duty, too."

His gaze looked in the distance. "I wanted to believe there's a love so great, so overwhelming that it comes from a place beyond reason, beyond doubt, and has no motivation other than to please and give. I prayed there was such a thing as limitless love and all I had to do to be worthy of it was to offer the same to someone else. But that prayer's gone unanswered and I won't ever be satisfied with simply enough."

No one had ever expressed how she felt about love, and Bass amazed her with his words and understanding. He knew the pain of feeling inadequate. She knew now why she felt so compelled to defend him to others though she nursed her own anger with him. She recognized the depth of hurt he suffered and couldn't be a part of adding to it.

Watching Ollie brush away the duff from her father's grave, Daisy recalled her daughter's nightly prayers and her dedication to maintaining the daddy list. Ollie believed there was hope. Daisy yearned to have her child's faith that life could offer as much as one asked from it.

"You know, Bass. You said a minute ago that you're unable to give of yourself anymore, yet here you are with the best piece of advice I've ever received and it was straight from your heart. We're older and wiser. We know the pitfalls. So, why don't both of us take courage to seek life at its best? Under our terms. Who knows, it just might be the greatest thing that will ever happen to us, God willing."

"And if He's not?"

"I think we've got to trust the path He's put us on and see where it leads us."

Chapter Eight

The visit to the cemetery had been everything Bass hoped it would be. They'd worked together side by side cleaning the graves and enjoyed a picnic, talking about anything and everything. After he'd opened up to Daisy concerning why he'd closed himself off to marrying, he had been afraid he'd frightened her off with his brooding. Instead, she'd understood and pointed out to him that courage was called for now and to put aside what had held him back for so long.

On their walk back, he found himself thinking about what she'd said.

The fact that she'd understood his hurt made him wish he could have taken away her pain. Knox had been so heroic on the field of action, that until Bass realized the woman he thought was Daisy proved to be someone else, he had no clue Knox was anything less than an honorable man.

How much had Daisy suffered at her husband's hands? Did Daisy know of the other woman? Bass hoped not and promised himself never to bring the subject up to her unless she demanded the conversation. Even then he didn't know how much he would tell her.

Some hurt was too deep and served no purpose in drawing attention to it.

As for himself, Bass didn't know if he could ever forgive his parents. They'd never wanted children and made it clear that he and Pet were burdens to bear and must live up to the social expectations of being a Parker.

The accident that had taken his parents' lives had ended the cold interactions with them, but his and Pet's hearts remained shackled by lack of experience with true affection. He'd surprised himself by mourning the life he could have had with his parents had things been different, but he quickly steeled himself against the pain so he could show Pet how to survive it all.

But had they really? Daisy reminded him this morning it was time to take courage and seek more from life, not just endure it. Maybe the thoughts he'd had concerning courting her could be a genuine answer for both of them.

The need to thank her in some way enveloped him. It took courage and kindness to offer advice to help someone you barely knew, much less held a grudge against.

A patch of wildflowers drew his attention and Bass asked if they might stop for a moment. Butterflies and hummingbirds fluttered here and there on the purplish-pink petals, vying for the succulent, fragrant nectar in their white centers.

"I'm sorry, have I been walking too fast?" Daisy halted, bending to let Ollie slide down from her perch upon her mother's shoulders. She'd insisted upon carrying the child so they could walk quicker. "Don't wander too far, Ollie. We'll rest just for a few minutes. And don't you and Butler play too close to that longhorn. She's enjoying the rest. She'll leave you alone if you do the same to her."

Ollie plopped down on her belly amid the wildflowers and cupped her chin in her hands, laughing as Butler bounced around the longhorn trying to act as if his little horns could challenge the six-foot spread of the bigger animal's. The longhorn didn't move, looking disdainfully at the brave interloper.

Bass took the checkered cloth off the picnic basket and spread it across the ground so they could sit and rest. He waited until she took a seat then joined her. After picking a stem full of the sweet verbena he faced Daisy. "I've wanted to do this since I caught sight of them this morning as I tumbled by and particularly now after we've spent some time together. Seems like we shouldn't waste the sweetest fragrance of spring. Thank you for allowing me to tag along."

He gently tucked a cluster of the wildflowers behind her ear. "There. The perfect place to showcase true beauty."

Let her wonder if he meant the blossoms or her. He didn't care if he sounded as if he were paying court but he actually admired the way she looked right now. Her image would etch itself in his mind for a long time to come.

"M-My hair's a mess." Her fingers reached to push back wayward strands that had come loose during the fall.

She couldn't have looked prettier, her cheeks staining with a blush.

"We're all a mess thanks to Butler. You just deserve something pretty for being so patient and such a good mother to Ollie."

Years of held-back emotion welled up to moisten his eyes. He'd never once allowed himself tears over his own upbringing. A man just didn't show that kind of vulnerability and he didn't want Pet to see him feeling weak. It would have frightened her since she relied on him so much. But he couldn't stop the tears from brimming now because he was truly taken with the beauty of Daisy's sincere care for her child. It touched him as few moments in his life ever had.

Best get hold of his emotions or Daisy would think he was some besotted fool with spring fever and run away as fast as she had from Maddox. Still, he couldn't let this go unsaid. "This morning has been a real pleasure for me."

"I enjoyed it very much, too," she whispered. "I look forward to next time."

"The sooner, the better." And he realized he meant those words, his mind already racing ahead to find a way to share her company this evening.

As they deposited everything in the kitchen, Daisy suggested he check on Petula while she found Myrtle and discussed their plans for the afternoon.

Bass found Pet in her room, apparently having just washed her hair and brushing it now. "Did you have a good morning?"

She was becoming a beautiful young woman. When she married, Bass would miss Pet immensely if she settled somewhere other than where he lived. As Daisy had reminded, his affection for his sister kept a measure of gentleness in his life.

"Yes, it was lovely. Cleaned my room and got a bath. Even learned a little bit about the stove from Myrtle," she replied, sitting on the chair in front of a mirrored vanity. "And you? You look quite messy."

"One of the best days I've had in a while. Got to get

my hands dirty and do a little work." He gave her a brief rundown of all they'd done.

"You miss working, don't you?" Petula stopped brushing her hair a moment and studied him. "Father never understood that about you, did he? You didn't like being his second-in-charge. You wanted to be out there among the coopers making the barrels."

Bass nodded. He made a point of never saying anything negative about their parents to Petula. It only reminded her of pain. "He didn't understand that I like to work with my hands."

He lifted his palms and was reminded of how many times his hands had served him in numerous ways, sometimes ways that didn't make him proud. But his emotions had always revealed themselves at his fingertips and that was the real Bass Parker. Not the spit-polished version that visited the Parker factories all over the North and South to make sure his father's industries maintained their quality. The only good that had ever come of being his father's puppet was meeting Knox at their barrel-making division in Florida. Bass shoved his hands into his pockets. "Got plans for the rest of the day?"

"I thought I'd go down and help Myrtle prepare lunch or supper, whichever she's working on now."

"What has brought on this sudden interest in cooking?" Bass knew but he was in too good of a mood to caution her.

She smiled. "Teague says he respects a good cook. You and I both know I need to learn. After all, I'm eighteen. So, what do you plan to do for the rest of the day?"

The stairs creaked and the fragrant scent of verbena announced the presence of who approached. Bass turned to find Daisy still wearing the flowers in her hair. If a heart could smile, his was grinning from chamber to chamber. He did his best to hide how pleased he was, but his mouth refused to comply.

Ollie tagged along beside her. The way the child stared at him, Bass thought it best not to let her start asking any questions. She'd be able to read his strange mood for sure. So he told his sister his intentions. "Depends on what our hostesses have planned for me. I hope I get to help make shoes."

"Later." Daisy pushed him toward his room. "Your brother had a fall this morning, Petula, and it's been a long walk both ways for him," she said, linking her arm through his. "He's going to take a nap and rest now." Her eyes met his. "Aren't you?"

"I don't need a nap," he replied, hearing Ollie relay with exuberance the details of their tumble down the slope. His argument went unheeded and Daisy gently tugged him inside his room.

"You rest and I'll wake you up in a couple of hours," she insisted. "You're looking a bit fragile and I won't have everyone thinking I'm not doing right by you. Now take your boots off and get some rest."

He didn't care for her babying him, but he finally agreed, shed his boots and socks, and lay back on the pillow. Maybe a nap would get his mind off Daisy's appeal.

After adjusting everywhere his body hurt and settling into the comfort of the bed, he realized Daisy wasn't coddling him, after all. She'd known what was best for him. Minutes later, sleep started to overtake him.

"Hey, Bass, ya asleep yet?"

The familiar voice made him blink himself awake.

He turned on his side to find Ollie's head poking around one corner of the door.

"How 'bout that trick with Butler?" she whispered and winked.

"What trick?" A strange feeling enveloped him that the wink boded something precocious.

"You know, my tri-i-ck." Her lips slanted to one side as she turned her head to look behind her then faced him again.

To make sure her mother was out of hearing distance, no doubt.

"Mama told me ya was gettin' a whole lot better, quicker than she thought. If she thinks ya hurt more she'll let ya stay longer. Didn't hurt ya too much, did I, Bass? I just bit his ol' ear, is all. How was I to know he could run so fast?"

A chuckle started deep in Bass's chest and barreled out his throat like a spewing geyser of water. He had to sit up to catch his breath.

"I've got a sneaking suspicion that you, Little Risk Taker," he said, wiping away tears caused from laughing so hard, "might just prove the death of me yet."

Chapter Nine

Daisy wondered what in the world had set Bass off to laughing so hard. His deep voice echoed throughout the house, filling the space with a sense of lighthearted joy. From the sound of his laughter, something or someone had delighted him.

She could think of only one person who would have bothered him as he rested. Ollie.

No telling what that child had said or done. Ollie clearly loved being with their houseguest and Bass seemed to enjoy her, as well.

Daisy appreciated that Bass took time with Ollie to show she mattered to him.

Reaching up to touch the sweet verbena in her hair, Daisy smiled. She had enjoyed his company, too. He'd been charming, kind and thoughtful. Helpful, when he should have been taking his recovery a little easier. Bass hadn't complained once this morning, though she knew within minutes of the fall that he'd hurt himself all over again.

She lifted the petals from her hair and looked for something she could save them in. Somewhere in the cupboard there should be a vase, but she hadn't set out any fresh flowers in her home since she couldn't re-member when. Any flowers she picked, Daisy always placed on Knox's grave.

A quick search allowed her to find the vase, but the flowers hadn't grown long-stemmed enough to rest well there. That would come in early summer provid-ing Myrtle didn't use too much in her verbena-and-mint tea or other medicinal concoctions.

Daisy took down a bowl and filled it with water, floating the cluster of flowers upon its surface. After setting the bowl in the middle of the kitchen table, she admired the gift and the reason he'd given for offer-ing it.

His words about taking care of Ollie seemed so sin-cere that they had touched her deeply. Sometimes she wondered if all she ever did was fail with raising her daughter, and people were quick to point it out. But most times she got it right and it pleased her that Bass had noticed this morning. She tried hard to make Ollie proud to call her Mama.

"That's a mighty smile on your face. What's put you in such a good mood?"

A masculine voice startled Daisy from her musings. She spun around to find Maddox towering in the door-way between the parlor and the kitchen. He held a sack in his hands and from the smell of its contents, the sack contained some kind of game animal. Good thing the verbena's reputation for being stronger-scented than prairie chips proved helpful at the moment.

"What are you doing here?" Daisy questioned rather than gave an answer to his. She couldn't recall any plans they'd made for the day and it was unusual for her brother-in-law to show up anytime other than on the weekend. In spring, he was just too busy at his own place to visit without reason.

"I knocked but nobody answered, so I just came on in. Figured ya wouldn't mind." He moved inside the kitchen and put the sack in the empty wash tin sitting on the cabinet filled with canned goods. "Brought you a message from Teague. Says he'll be back sometime before nightfall and don't wait supper on him. He'll just bed down in the barn and see y'all come mornin'. Didn't want y'all frettin' about who's staked out in the barn."

He nodded toward the sack. "But just in case you want to feed him, I brought ya somethin' for supper tonight so there'd be plenty for everybody. Hope you're hungry for turkey. Thought I'd have a sit-down with you and Ollie and have us a talk about how we're gonna make the three of us more family than we already are."

Maddox's forefinger shot to tug his buckskin shirt away from the edge of his Adam's apple as if it was choking him. "Little Britches said she had somethin' she needed me to do tonight and it would take a while, so I figured I might as well come on over and get started and done soon as I could. Wanted to see how good a cook ya turned out to be anyway."

"Myrtle does the bulk of the cooking, as you well know. You've been invited to supper many times." What was he implying?

"Can't say as I've ever eaten anything *you've* made."

"Myrtle's better in the kitchen than I am."

"Ya willing to keep paying her wages when ya move to my house?"

This was his idea of convincing a woman to marry him? "I haven't said yes, Maddox. There's something called love and, like I said, I just don't love you in that way. You are a great brother-in-law and I like you well enough as a friend, but we have a long way to go before I'd ever consider marrying you. And you owe me no obligation even if you are my husband's brother. I can take care of myself and Ollie."

He almost looked relieved, his face breaking into a grin. "Well, we see eye to eye on somethin' already. I ain't sure if I ever liked ya good enough and maybe won't ever love ya like Knox did."

Lines furrowed his broad forehead. "I guess it was all that preachin' at the service last night. I got a do-good feelin' stirred up in me and the first thing I could think of was gettin' Miz Jenkins off your back. The woman can be a pest, ya know. Don't know what got into me, but I ain't been able to shake it since I felt it. Once I said what I did, I figure I at least gotta court ya a little and keep my word or I'd be lying to Preacher Thistlewaite. Besides, who knows? I just might take more than a shine to ya."

He scratched his head as if he was stirring up a plan. "I promised ya a month to use your wiles on me and see what comes of it. I figure ya still got some since ya used 'em on my skirt-chasing brother, and it sure worked on him. We brothers never figured he'd settle down to one gal, but ya got him to. Guess it could happen to us all if we let it. I'm up to seeing if you can convince me."

No matter of his crude delivery, Maddox just stepped in last evening to give her a way out and it endeared him to her. Not enough to marry him, but to appreciate his kindheartedness. She owed Maddox a roasted turkey if it wouldn't upset Myrtle's plan for the evening meal. The cook and Petula should be headed in any moment now. They'd been in the salt shed long enough to make a choice of meats. "Are you staying while we cook or will you leave and come back later?"

He brushed dust from his knees, sending it cascading to the floor. "I figured since I'm already here, I'd wash up out in the barn and see what Ollie wants. Maybe I can get that done and eat then head back home. Told my brothers they can fend for themselves on the nights I come callin' on ya."

Myrtle and Petula entered through the back door, their arms loaded with a basket of vegetables and a ham. The cook frowned when she started to set the ham inside the wash tin now filled with the burlap sack.

"What's that?" She grabbed a towel hanging from a row of pegs near the sideboard. Myrtle spread the towel on the table and put the ham on top of it. Her helper deposited the vegetable basket next to the ham.

Daisy repeated the conversation she'd shared with Maddox and informed her that he would be joining them for supper.

The cook started laughing, setting her double chins to bobbing. "And this is what he calls courting? Making you cook and coming dressed no better than a road-sweaty mule skinner?"

If she shared the same opinion, Petula kept her silence and turned her face away. Not before Daisy noticed her guest's nose wrinkle delicately.

She couldn't fault the women for their reactions. She'd pretty much felt the same about his lack of looking his best, but she quickly defended Maddox as he had defended her against Mrs. Jenkins. "He came fresh from the hunt and said he'd wash up out in the barn. While I get the turkey and ham going, Myrtle, why don't you see if there's anything of Knox's that Maddox can wear? The old trunk's up in the hayloft. I didn't offer it to Bass that first night because...well, I just didn't."

Couldn't have was more like it, Daisy admitted silently.

No one had to ask why. She couldn't let the man whose actions had led her husband to his eventual death wear his clothes. Even now that she'd been in Bass's company and was beginning to discover him as a person instead of the hated stranger she'd considered no more than a coward, she still didn't know if she could have offered him anything that belonged to Knox. Giving him a place to recover was difficult enough.

Yet the care he'd shown at Knox's grave had been sincere. He'd straightened the cross, dug a trench to fill with water that would keep the flowers, which Ollie chose to leave there, fresh longer. He even bent in prayer with Ollie at her father's grave before they headed back.

Daisy now considered that the memorial he ached to leave on behalf of Knox could possibly be heartfelt respect and not simply guilt. Bass Parker seemed to want her husband's memory to live on and reap glory for his bravery and actions during the war. And, for that reason, she knew she might one day forgive Bass for all she'd blamed him for and possibly relent about the memorial.

It was just too soon to decide. Too soon to proceed without caution. Too soon to trust that Bass didn't have other motives to seem so sincere.

Still, she must admit that he hadn't taken Knox from Olivia. Knox took himself away. He allowed his sense of adventure to keep him from returning to his family. If not to her, then to their daughter. Bass had provided him money but, if it hadn't been him, Knox would have sought the funds from someone else.

Realizing her guests and cook were staring at her,

she wondered if they'd said something and she hadn't answered. "I'm sorry, I didn't hear what you said."

"I asked if you think they'll fit me." Maddox stood straighter to add to his height.

"The trousers will definitely be shorter, but I think his shirts will fit."

"I'll just give these a good scrub." His hands dusted here and there.

"They won't dry 'til morning," Myrtle argued before Daisy could intercede. "You ain't sitting wet buckskin on anything in this house, Maddox Trumbo."

The cook's eyes frosted like emerald icicles hanging from the roof and a few wisps of her salt-and-pepper hair stood on end. "If you plan on eating at my table or courting my boss you'll be wearing proper clothes. You got to do much better than this or you'll never make that child's list, either. Now bend down here."

Maddox complied.

The little rotund woman grabbed his ear and led him out the door, the giant of a man following like a sensible soul who knew what was best for him.

"She's a force to be reckoned with." Petula's voice echoed both compliment and respect. "I'm going to learn a lot from her. And from you, if you'll let me."

She lifted the tin that held the turkey and moved it over to where they usually washed dishes. "What do you want me to do first with this?"

Daisy motioned to the basket. "You wash off the potatoes and I'll take care of preparing the meat. I've cooked both before so I can handle this much myself. You might want to wait 'til Myrtle gets back to show you how she prepares everything else."

"Then I'll just watch what you do with the meat so I'll know for next time." Petula moved alongside her.

Daisy opened the sack and deposited the bird into the tin, setting the sack aside to use as a storage place for the feathers.

Then she prepared the stove so it would be warming while they plucked feathers. The task seemed relentless but, finally, the bird was bare and the oven ready for baking. Despite her obvious distaste of the process of plucking and cleaning the turkey, Petula proved diligent to the end and now both meats were roasting in their pans.

Daisy couldn't believe this was the same person reluctant to boil water before.

"How long will it take to cook them?" Petula faced Daisy, her cheeks flushed with heat from the stove. Blue eyes a shade darker than her brother's studied Daisy as if she had the answers to all things wise.

Daisy silently thanked her mother for teaching her the necessities of living life on her own. She knew how to cook, she just preferred not to. Having Myrtle cook was the single luxury she allowed herself. Maybe between her and Myrtle, they could help Petula learn whatever she had the desire to know about making a home.

Odd that few here in High Plains believed *her* of knowing how.

"About two hours for the ham, and about five or six for the turkey," Daisy informed. "It depends on the size of the bird." Petula looked tired and she was a guest, after all. "Why don't you let me and Myrtle finish up here? I don't know what's keeping her, but I'm sure she'll be back anytime now. Would you like to check on your brother or rest awhile?"

Petula seemed grateful to end the cooking lesson for the moment. "May I ask you something before I do, Mrs. Trumbo?"

"Certainly, but call me Daisy, please. I'd like to think we're becoming friends."

"That's just it. Bass and I never stay anywhere long enough to make friends. It means a lot to both of us."

Daisy washed her hands then motioned her guest into the parlor. "Let's sit and have a talk, shall we? The vegetables don't have to be dealt with until the last hour before we serve the meal."

Petula followed Daisy into the parlor and took a seat across from where Bass had sat last night. Daisy chose the settee so she could face her, wondering what might be revealed about the Parkers' pasts. She wanted to know more yet she felt as if she might be betraying Bass's trust in some way. Like how she'd asked him not to talk about Knox to Ollie.

"Where's my brother now?" Petula's gaze swept to the upstairs landing then back at Daisy. "In his room?"

She nodded. "I think so. At least he was earlier. You remember that I suggested he get some rest."

"You said he had a fall."

"I believe Ollie gave you the details."

"But you didn't say whether or not he hurt himself further."

"He didn't let me check his shoulder, but he said he probably bruised the other one, and it took him longer than expected to recover his breath. He was unsteady for ten minutes or so after the tumble and needed to rest once on the walk back."

"You won't make us leave until he's completely well, will you, even if a room opens up somewhere else?"

Daisy heard both concern and desperation in her voice, saw a plea in Pet's eyes. "Of course not. You might find a room soon if anyone gets tired of waiting on each race and leaves. They're being held twice a week all this month. But until Bass is capable of being on his own, with the return of his complete strength, I would be too worried that he'll suffer setbacks just as he's done today. I'll see him through his recovery. We owe him that."

"Even if Mrs. Jenkins or others like her tell you it's wrong to have him here?"

"He's done nothing wrong here. We're not doing anything we shouldn't be. Besides, having you and Myrtle in the house as suitable chaperones makes the arrangement proper enough." Daisy found courage in speaking her feelings and knowing that she had no reason to feel shame or worry about unfair judgments. "I'm not going to let others tell me not to make good on a promise I've given. I told you both you're welcome to stay here for as long as he needs to recover. I meant it and still do. He saved our lives, remember?"

Petula stood and reached over giving Daisy a hug. "Then you are a friend and I'm so glad to call you that, Daisy. You're the first in a very long time and it means the world to me. Thank you for standing up for us. I'm grateful, just as I know Bass is. He so much wants to feel at home somewhere and I…well, I haven't been much of a help making that easy for him. But now I know exactly where I want to belong and I'm going to see that he finds his place, too. I owe him, you see."

She ended the hug and paced a moment. "I need to tell you something I've never even told my brother." She finally stopped and stared Daisy in the eyes. "Because of me Bass hired someone else to take his place in the war. I didn't know until just before I arrived in High Plains that you are the man's widow. Bass didn't confide in me sooner for whatever reason. Probably because I was so young when he hired your husband.

Back then I didn't want to be left alone as somebody's ward after our folks died and we were left orphans. Like the other boys his age, he had wanted very much to go to battle and prove himself, but he chose not to for my sake. You see, I deliberately started acting wild and almost ruined my reputation so that he would have to stay home with me."

Tears welled up in her eyes. "I'm not proud of that and I don't know if I can ever tell him the truth about it. He deserves better than I treated him. Please don't think badly of him. It's my fault he did what he did."

Daisy felt guilty, her stubbornness to defend Bass's right to remain in her home not because it was the right thing to do but because she refused to be manipulated by anyone ever again. He'd been manipulated by his own sister.

Petula couldn't have been more than eleven or twelve years old at the time of Knox's conscription. A little girl afraid of being left in strangers' care. A brother needing to protect a sister from herself. Finally, Daisy understood and maybe, just maybe, there was room for a true friendship between her and Bass Parker.

She had thought Petula incapable of kindness, of being anything but selfish. Yet High Plains or someone here had changed her. And she could just about guess who that someone might be. The same someone who encouraged her to want to cook. To want to set things right.

Even though she wasn't sure Bass would approve, she decided to encourage Petula's pursuit of the particular man with whom she seemed so enamored. "By the way, before you head upstairs, I thought I'd let you know that Teague is due in late this evening. We'll save a plate of supper warming for him if he arrives later than the meal."

Petula's eyes lit up as she hurried to climb the stairs. "I've got a dozen things to do before he gets here. Make sure his bedroll's laid out and there's fresh straw under it. You know Butler messed all that up so I'll have to muck the stall again. And I need to get him a fresh blanket. Oh, and he likes a cup of coffee just before he turns in for the night."

She stopped midway on the stairs and looked at Daisy with uncertainty. "What am I forgetting? I'm forgetting something important. Why can't I remember?"

Daisy understood completely. She needed to offer sound suggestions. "Why not do the things you remember will please him, then fix your hair and put on something pretty. In fact, if you'd like me to help with your hair, I'd be glad to. Once you've done all that I think you'll remember whatever else you need to do to make him feel welcome."

That's certainly what she would do if she ever wanted to pursue another man's affections, but she no longer believed her life's journey would lead her down such a path.

Chapter Ten

Hunger rumbled in Bass's belly. The slices of cheese hadn't lasted long and he'd fallen asleep for the nap Daisy suggested before eating any lunch. The delicious aroma wafting through the house now made him hungry for something more substantial. He hurriedly dressed and headed downstairs to see how much longer it would be before the meal would be served.

He hoped the growling in his stomach didn't precede him and make him sound like a hungry old bear awakened from hibernation.

Living out of hotels and at the mercy of a café or diner for the past few months, he and Petula rarely enjoyed the benefit of good cooking. Fine restaurants didn't exactly dot this portion of the state of Texas, and staying in boardinghouses rarely awarded them anything but adequate meals.

Myrtle's food, on the other hand, measured up to the best he'd ever been served, and Bass hoped Petula enjoyed her lessons with the cook. Maybe once they made a genuine home for themselves again, she might want to practice some cooking of her own.

Experience had taught him that he suffered at the

craft, though he tried once in a while just to keep from having to eat out every single night. That habit got old, quickly. Petula rarely ate much when he attempted to master the use of a stove, but she'd been too polite to tell him how much he failed in the effort. She didn't ever have to say anything, though. He tasted it in every bite.

Maybe if he showed up in the kitchen and lent a hand this delicious-smelling meal could be hurried along.

A mingle of voices drew him to join Myrtle and who-ever else might already be helping her.

"Well, sleepyhead's up, I see," Maddox greeted him in a loud voice. His eyes blinked madly as he contin-ued peeling an onion, tears streaming down his cheeks. "Whew! Hope this didn't wake you up, Parker. You could probably smell these from here to Fort Worth. They taste good, but they sure got a stink about 'em."

He looked comical sitting in a chair with an apron tied high under each armpit, too short to fit where it should at his waist. Ruffles along each vertical side seam made him look as if he was wearing an ill-fitting pinafore over a shirt and trousers that rode high as knickers up his calves. His broken nose, massive hands and unshaven shadow of sandy whiskers couldn't have been more brutish in appearance against the frock he'd been made to wear as a helper.

Bass offered to add his hands to the mix, hoping he was assigned some task that didn't require an apron.

"I got it all under control." Myrtle refused his offer, stirring something in big boiling pots on the stove while Petula handed her items from a spice rack.

Daisy sat across from Maddox at the table sprinkling cinnamon and sugar on a pan full of sweet potatoes. She glanced at Bass. "Come join us. We all decided to make this a combined effort so we could get it done quicker. Ollie's asking her uncle some questions while we're at it. All we lack is about ten or fifteen minutes. These potatoes are already cooked, but I like to fancy them just before I serve the meal."

Bass took a seat between Ollie and Daisy. "I couldn't stay away from whatever's smelling so good." His eyes started blinking rapidly. He leaned a little closer to Daisy so the fragrance of the verbena would overpower the other scent. "Not that onion, by the way."

Maddox reached past his niece and waved it around Bass's nose. "God's way of makin' wimmen tougher than men, I'd say. Not a one of them spilt a tear yet. I'm squallin' like a piglet done lost its sow."

A quick dodge kept Bass from getting a nose full, but his eyes stung.

"Uncle Maddox, quit playin' with the onion," scolded Ollie. "Ya didn't answer my last question yet. I'm wai-ai-tin'."

Chastised, Maddox's hand shot back and finished chopping the onion. "All right, Speedy Britches, I'll just say that I'm sufferable at it."

Bass watched Ollie write down his answer. Instead of sufferable, she wrote *can*. "You know what that means?"

"Yeah." Ollie's gaze darted toward her mother. "Mama says it means ya can tolerate it. So I just put down can. Don't know why people don't just say things easy."

Bass noticed Daisy still wore the verbena. No, she'd brushed her hair and rebraided it first, then put it back in her hair. The thought pleased him yet made him uncomfortable, too. Had she changed her mind about letting Maddox court her? Had she spruced up for her brother-in-law? Was this her way of, how had she said it, looking for life's best again?

Ollie thumbed back several pages of her writing tablet. "How 'bout you, Bass? Can ya sing?"

Bass stared at the flowers thinking he didn't like her wearing them so much. Maybe she ought to be choosier when and where she wore them.

Daisy nodded toward her child. "Ollie asked you something."

"Oh, I'm sorry, I didn't hear." Bass swung around to face the seven-year-old. "What did you say?"

"You wasn't listenin'. I *asked* if you can sing. Uncle Mad can. Mama likes singin'."

"Hand me those potatoes and let me get them on," Myrtle interrupted. "Y'all move all that into the parlor, where you're supposed to play games, and me and Pet here will finish up with this. There's too many bodies in this kitchen. Now scoot."

She accepted the pan Daisy offered. "But you, Maddox Trumbo, you wash your hands so I don't smell 'em the whole meal. Then you can take your big ol' self out yonder with them."

"Would you let me carry something for you, Ollie?" Bass offered as he stood.

She shook her head, setting her braids to swaying. "Nope. I got it. Get Mama and let's go. But you sit on the big chair like ya did at prayer meetin' and leave some room for Uncle Maddox. He's gonna sit beside ya."

What was the little minx up to? Bass motioned for Daisy to precede him to the parlor and dutifully followed behind. He sat where the child indicated and watched her climb into a chair opposite the settee. Daisy took a seat in an adjacent chair.

"Okay now, you can answer me, Bass." Ollie had

her papers ready and was armed with a pencil. "Can ya sing?"

"We're not waiting on your uncle to join us?" Bass glanced toward the kitchen. "It shouldn't take but a minute or two."

"You can answer in a minute. I already know what he said about it."

"I'm eager to know, too. About you, I mean," Daisy admitted.

Sunset faded along the horizon beyond the window behind her to beckon fingers of twilight in its wake. When she lit the lamp on the table that sat between hers and Ollie's chairs, the color of Daisy's eyes softened to a warm honeyed hue in the lamplight.

"I'm not much of a singer." He was fair at playing a certain musical instrument, but that was saved for sadder times usually. Bass found it difficult to concentrate now, and the distraction came from the fact that he couldn't keep his attention from Daisy. The more times he enjoyed her company, the more he found something he liked about her. This was supposed to give him opportunity to put his plans into effect, not moon over what a beautiful woman she was.

"Let's hear ya," Ollie ordered. "You and Uncle Maddox."

"Oh, no. Please. I should have said that I can't sing at all." He silently pleaded with Daisy to intercede. She just smiled, leaving him to her daughter's insistence.

Maddox joined them just in time to hear Bass begging off.

"Sit by Bass, Uncle Mad. Y'all are gonna have a singin' battle."

He sat down and rubbed his hands vigorously as if he looked forward to the competition. "All right, what'cha want us to sing? 'Can't Plug The Hole'? 'My Pony's Gone Loco'? 'I Miss My Spittoo'—"

"None of those." Daisy frowned. "Something Ollie can appreciate."

"Oh, I know the words," Ollie informed her. "I heard Uncle Grissom and Uncle Jonas singin' them a couple of times before. 'Course when they remembered I was in the room, they kind of got stumbly-talkin' and changed the words real quick."

"Let's choose one Bass knows. It's only fair." Daisy looked askance at Bass.

Bass didn't want to sing any song.

"Well, spit it out, Bass," Ollie urged. "I got a lot more questions to go."

He might as well be done with it. They'd learn soon enough that Maddox held the upper hand in this particular round. "How about 'The Battle Hymn of the Republic'?"

"Do you know 'Dixie'?" Maddox countered. "Let's keep it Texan."

Bass knew Texans who had fought on both sides of the war. Knox had worn Union Blue for money, but he hadn't yet become Texan at that point. "Dixie" it would be to satisfy Maddox.

"Way down yonder in the land of—" Bass began, his voice resonant but ordinary. Having the talent to hold a long note might be something, but when the note pained someone's ear it was nothing to brag about. The eldest Trumbo piped in with a resounding rendition that would urge Rebel troops to stand proudly at attention.

Ollie scribbled something down and held her palm up to silence them. "You won that one, Uncle Mad, but Bass is a couple of points ahead of you right now."

"Let me see them pages, young'un." Maddox walked

over and peered down at Ollie's scribbles. "What's all that mean? A round circle and a smile? Or eyes and an O and a number?"

Exasperated, Ollie covered her writing with both palms. "It's for me to know. I'm only seven. I can write some words 'cause Mama taught me. I just make pictures of faces to show ya did it good or not so good. The numbers tell me how good or bad ya did. It's my own...what do ya call it, Mama?"

"Cypher or code. Symbols that substitute the word you mean."

Bass had read her notes last evening and was amazed at how well Ollie made her opinion clear. She would grow up to be quite an intelligent lady if her mother persisted in furthering Ollie's education.

Daisy had informed him the children in High Plains were out of school because it was planting season. They'd take another break from school during harvest, as well. Many helped their parents or their neighbors during these seasons.

If he stayed in High Plains, or if he decided to offer Daisy marriage, Bass decided to make sure he saw that Ollie could go to school any day she wanted.

"What about you and Daisy?" Bass hoped to swing the conversation to discovering more about his hostess and her daughter. "Do both of you sing well?"

Ollie shrugged. "When we hafta. Not now 'cause we want to find out about you and Uncle Mad. Supper's about ready and Mama said I can't do no more after we eat. I gotta wash up and go to bed after that."

Bass had read how extensive she'd made her list. It would take days for her to get through all the questions. "What if we just ask your mother to tell us what's most important to her? That seems like a quicker way of doing this for you. Are you willing, Daisy?"

Daisy's tall frame straightened as she sat closer to the edge of her chair. Her shoulders squared back and she seemed to be gathering her thoughts carefully. He sensed her discomfort immediately.

Daisy blew out the lamp, sending the room into shadows. Only the light from the kitchen remained.

"I did that for a reason. So you can see how hard it is to look in the dark. Can you see me well?"

"Your outline," Maddox answered.

"My eyes? The color of my hair? The size of my feet?"

"Not clearly," Bass admitted. Where was this leading?

"You sound mad, Mama," Ollie spoke up. "Like thunder when it's rumblin' and ready to flash."

"You're right, Ollie, but I'm not mad at you." Daisy sat back a little. "I'm angry at my past and the way I've dealt with it. I'm not looking for how a man appears, or what he does or how well he does it. Not how brave he's been or who he can impress. Those are all foolish, in my way of thinking, and I've come to that opinion in a hard way."

She took a deep breath. "I want to know the inner man, the sound of his heart and how he offers it to others. I want to hear his voice of reasoning and feel him use it to benefit not only himself but those he cares about. Most of all, I need to be certain that if I share my life with him, he'll be the light always there to see me through any darkness. That's what's important to me. Not a list of can-dos."

Her words enveloped Bass with a sense that she was talking from her heart as deeply as he'd shared his own with her this morning. He understood her even better now.

"If he can't find those things in himself and expect the same from me," she continued, "then he's not the right man for me. The only competition any man will have concerning my affection is with himself and what he's willing to reveal to me about how he feels, what he believes in and to what end that matters to him."

"Whew, that makes my head hurt, Mama. It must be hard being big," Ollie grumbled. "Can we turn the light back on now?"

A light had already lit in Bass's mind and he intended to follow its source.

"My head hurts, too," Maddox agreed, "and my do-goodin' is fadin' fast. I think I'm gonna have to sleep on it before I figure out what'cha mean for sure. Maybe some turkey and ham'll perk me up."

Bass remained quiet until she relit the lamp and could see his face. He wanted Daisy to know with every faculty she possessed that he meant to know the answer to the question that he couldn't let go of now, no matter what the cost.

"Supper's ready and the table's set." Myrtle stepped around the kitchen doorway. "Y'all come eat."

When everyone rose to heed the call, Bass reached out and touched Daisy. "Will you wait just a minute?"

Letting Maddox and Ollie move ahead, Daisy stopped. "Yes?"

Unconsciously he reached up to caress the flowers he'd given her and let his fingers slide slowly to press gently against her cheek. "Do you think you could ever forgive me for hiring Knox that day? For Ollie never getting to know him?"

Amber eyes met blue, studying him to the depths of

his soul. "We're supposed to forgive, aren't we? It's the forgetting that would be difficult for me to do."

Bass's fingers lowered and laced into her own, offering a gentle squeeze of her hand. "Okay, just as long as we both understand you didn't say impossible."

Chapter Eleven

Daisy sat back in her chair at the table and pushed her plate away only half-finished. She simply couldn't eat another bite and rested her hands in her lap. A sense of fullness so powerful consumed her that she just wanted to savor the moment.

All around her sat people she liked, loved or teetered on the edge of becoming good friends with. She studied every face, the enjoyment of the shared meal in the laughter that spiced the conversation and the sounds of satisfaction that made most of them reach for yet another bite.

She couldn't remember the last time she'd felt such a sense of family. She'd been hungering for simple moments of pure companionship and hadn't even realized it until now.

"You're smiling." Bass's hand reached out to pat hers beneath the table.

Daisy nodded and didn't try to quell her smile nor the fact that his touch genuinely pleased her. It was just a friendly gesture of companionship, wasn't it?

A thought escaped her into words that ached to have a voice. "Feels like we're a loud, rowdy family, doesn't it?"

"Sure does," he answered softly.

"What are you two whispering about down there?" Maddox craned his neck to see past Petula and Ollie. "I wanna hear any plans y'all are making."

Bass's fingers laced with hers, tracing figure eights along her skin.

She jerked her hand away immediately.

He'd gone too far.

She wasn't ready to offer more than forgiveness and a measure of friendship. Yet something about him drew Daisy like a hummingbird to nectar. Her heart still raced from his touch.

Bass laid down his fork and scooted his plate away and answered Maddox. "Matter of fact, I was just about to tell Daisy my plans."

He motioned to encompass the feast they'd shared. "I suggest we men wash the dishes while you fine cooks spend the rest of the evening however you wish. You've been at it all day, obviously."

Maddox looked as if he'd been asked to herd road-runners. "Oh, not me, partner. I got to get on home 'fore anybody sees me in these knee britches."

"We'll clean up everything." Daisy started stacking the empty plates, wishing she could regain the sense of companionship enjoyed during the meal. "You can go on if you like, Mad."

Myrtle immediately stood and grabbed the turkey platter, moving it past the giant, close to his nose. "If you expect to take any of this home for a midnight snack, I suggest you get your big old hide over there and start scrubbing right now. It'll do you some good cleaning up after yourself. You and I both know, ain't nobody in this territory brave enough to laugh at that long stretch of skinny chicken legs of yours. You'd boot 'em from here to Sunday if they tried."

"That's right, Uncle Mad," Ollie spoke up. "You don't let nobody laugh at ya 'cept me. I'll help ya with them dishes. I didn't do no cookin', neither."

Petula stood. "Thank you, Mr. Trumbo. It's sweet of you to help wash dishes. We'll clear the table and put away what's left of the food and, that way, cleaning won't take much time if we all work together."

Daisy noticed Bass's expression at his sister's offer. His eyes lit with what surely must be pride. He seemed pleased at Petula's change for the better in the time they'd spent here. Daisy found the whole situation a blessing since their stay had been a result of a disaster of her making. Of her not seeing to Ollie's care well enough. Maybe some real good would come of this after all.

Maddox grabbed a bite of one more piece of turkey before Myrtle could take it out of reach. "Okay," he muttered with his mouth full, "since you wimmen are gangin' up on me, I guess I'll let'cha win."

He grumbled as he put back on the frilly apron. "I can see how this is gonna go if we get hitched, Daisy. I ain't gonna win no more arguments in my house, that's for sure."

Ollie giggled. "That's right, Uncle Mad, or you'll be havin' some long droopy ears. Myrtie wins every time." The child reached up and rubbed one of her earlobes in sympathy. "You ought'a know."

Armed with two pans of water—one sudsy, one for rinsing—and a dry towel, the men worked shoulder to shoulder to clean the dishes. Daisy watched as Bass set a chair between him and Maddox so Ollie could rinse, but the plates were too heavy for her to handle.

Petula prepared the plate of food she must be setting back for Teague, and Myrtle wrapped up more than enough turkey and ham to send home with Maddox.

Ollie's little hands tried their best to do their part until she finally lost her temper and stomped a foot on the chair in frustration. Bass grabbed the forks and spoons from Maddox and handed them to her daughter while he took the heavier dishes.

"Swish those around good for me, will you?" He waited patiently until Ollie got over her irritation and rinsed the utensils as he'd asked.

She grinned at him.

He returned the pleasure. "Thanks a bunch, friend. That lets us work faster by using teamwork."

Bass held out his hand and she smacked her palm against his then shook it. The exuberant smack splattered droplets of water, making her giggle.

Ollie looked so proud of herself, she seemed to grow inches taller between her two daddy candidates.

Bass seemed to understand how important it was for her daughter to lend a helping hand, and Daisy appreciated his kindness. He would someday make some woman a wonderful husband if he allowed himself to marry. And, from what she'd seen so far, he would also prove a loving father. He was patient with his sister and Ollie, never criticizing them in front of anyone. Most likely out of his own desire to have been treated kindly as a child.

Her heart went out to him, and Daisy added another of his good traits to the list she mentally kept concerning him.

His actions all day had only increased her curiosity about Bass and the unexpected sympathy she felt toward him. While she was driven to see him completely recovered, she knew that once he left her home she would be less likely to share any time with him. The least she could do while he stayed here was show him how a good friend would treat him. That's what he seemed to need most, and she could offer that.

His nap today had clearly given him much-needed stamina, and it was holding up well the longer the evening progressed. Maybe tonight, as a sincere offer of friendship, she should apologize to him for thinking so badly of him and admit that she'd finally accepted Knox's role in his own death.

Once Maddox left, maybe she would ask Bass if he felt up to sharing another walk.

"You didn't get that spot," Ollie announced, slipping a fork back into her uncle's wash water.

"Looks good to me." Maddox scrubbed the fork fiercely and dipped it in Ollie's pan. "How's 'zat, Little Miss Spit Polish?"

"What do you think, Bass?" Ollie grabbed it and showed the fork to their patient.

Maddox glared at his inspector, frowning.

Daisy's breath caught as she wondered if Bass had the talent and wisdom to be tactful.

"*You're* in charge of rinsing, remember?" Bass tapped the dry towel on the tip of Ollie's nose. "That's your decision."

Ollie slipped the fork back into her uncle's pan. "It's still got food on it. Better do it again, Uncle Mad." She leaned over to Bass and looked up. "Remind me when my hands ain't wet that I gotta write somethin' down. Uncle Mad ain't no good at dishes and he might need to talk to Doc about orderin' him some spec-tickles."

Maddox stripped himself of the apron faster than a man picking a cocklebur from under his saddle. He tossed the apron over the back of Ollie's chair. "All right, that's it. I'm done, Fussy Britches. Somebody else can take over. A little leftover sweet taters on a fork ain't gonna hurt nobody."

"And remind me to put down that he sure gets cranky fast." Ollie grabbed the still-dirty fork, scrubbed it clean, rinsed it and thrust it at Bass.

"Myrtle, you got that plate you're gonna give me for eating later?" Maddox swung around and instantly accepted the basket the cook thrust at him.

"Sent some for your brothers, too," she said. "I appreciate you doing what dishes you did. Oh, and I wrapped the meat up in a bandanna. Didn't figure you'd want to have to wash up another platter and tote it back here. You can keep the bandanna."

"Thanks for the meal and the use of Knox's trousers." He pinched a wad of her cheek affectionately. "You're a fine cook, Myrtie Pearl. Hard-headed as an iron skillet, but a fine old gal."

"Daisy cooked the meat and lent you the clothes." Myrtle swatted away his hand but blushed all the same at his compliment. "Was none of my doing."

Bass glanced at Daisy at that moment and she wondered what must be going through his head as he laid down the towel. If Knox's clothes had been available when Bass first arrived, did he care that they'd slapped a pair of pantaloons on him quicker than she could shake a stick at a snapping crawdad?

Though he said nothing, his hands spoke volumes. Daisy watched his fingers flex as if trying to get a grip on something, then sink into the pockets of his trousers and remain there when he caught her studying them.

Bass definitely cared and was upset. But he'd been

born and bred a gentleman. She knew he'd never say anything to her now in front of the others.

Hopefully, he would agree to the walk and would wait until she bid Maddox good-night, got Ollie to bed and determined a way to explain without hurting him further.

Bass needed fresh air, but he didn't want to watch Daisy see Maddox off. Deciding it best to go the opposite direction, he headed out the back door toward some of the outer buildings by the salt shed.

He'd had enough of sharing the evening with Maddox and wondered why it had upset him so much that the oldest Trumbo had been given the privilege of wearing his brother's clothes. Or why they had not been offered to him.

Reason told Bass that it was a logical solution for whatever reason Maddox had needed the change. What seemed illogical was his reaction from being denied the loan.

Bass willed away the memory of Daisy pushing his hand away from hers beneath the table.

Was he jealous of Maddox? Or was it Daisy's rejection that stung the most? Either emotion was new to Bass. He'd hardened his heart so long ago that he'd never thought he would care if a woman rejected him. He understood her initial dislike of him for Knox's sake, but this rejection felt personal and directed at his offer of friendship.

Bass decided he was brooding too much and needed to get on with his purpose here. To determine how best to help Daisy, not question her reasoning.

Maddox was rough around the edges, but he had a good heart. He'd come to Daisy's rescue with Mrs.

Jenkins and let Ollie wrap him around her tiny finger anytime she wanted. He liked Maddox personally. If he thought Daisy's brother-in-law really was in love with her, he'd step away and not even consider the possibility of offering the widow marriage to settle his duty to her.

But their getting to know each other better at the cemetery and the fact that she'd worn his gift of flowers felt as if they had moved on to a friendlier connection. A reason to join forces and improve all their circumstances.

A squeaking door announced his solitude had ended. The house needed repair. Maybe tomorrow he could fix a few things if his shoulder could take the work.

"Could we talk, Bass?"

The scent of verbena wafted on the gentle breeze and he turned to discover Daisy walking toward him, her hair looking golden in the moonlight. He couldn't read her eyes as they remained in shadow, so he wondered if this would be a talk to look forward to or dread. His hands moved from his pockets to reach forward and help her catch up to him.

He wasn't sure she would accept his offer, but she did. Daisy laced her fingers through his this time. Though her skin felt soft at the top, her palms had calluses hardened by work. She seemed an enigma of opposites.

"I'd love a talk." A conversation might appease all that troubled him. "Would you like to walk a ways or do you want to stay closer to the house to listen for Ollie?"

"She went to her room when I was getting Maddox ready to leave. When I checked on her, she had dozed off writing notes. It took me a while to change her into nightclothes, but she's resting in her bed now. Myrtle said she'd check in on her just before she turns in. It's been quite a day for all of us."

Daisy motioned toward the stream that ran a few yards behind the shed, moonbeams dancing along its surface. "Let's walk over there. I like to listen to the water gurgle as it passes over the rocks and meanders down to the lake. I won't take too much of your time, I promise. I know you need your rest."

Bass headed for the bank, taking it slow at first then remembering she liked to walk much faster. "I'm feeling better. It's been a great day. There's no need to worry about me so much anymore. That nap did a lot of good earlier. Thank you for suggesting it."

Long, slender fingers tapered to fit perfectly into his. He couldn't help himself and traced her silken skin.

"Why do you do that?"

His caressing stopped. Would she move her hand away again? "Do what?"

"It's almost like you're drawing pictures."

He started to slide his hand apart from hers, but she squeezed gently to stop him.

"Please don't," she said. "I wasn't complaining. Just wondering. I've noticed that you're gentle with your touch even though your fists looked so fierce when you fought the bank robbers."

Bass hesitated. Should he tell her the truth? Reveal what no one really knew about him?

How did he expect Daisy to learn to trust him, if he didn't do the same to her?

"I was taught to never show my emotions. That doing so was a sign of weakness and wasn't considered good business. Where you're concerned, Daisy, my hands want to share my feelings with you and reflect how much I appreciate the kindness you've offered me and

Petula, even though you had no reason to. But I promise, you'll never have to be afraid of them, no matter how rough they look. I would never hurt you and I'll stop even this anytime you ask me to. I didn't mean to upset you earlier at the table."

She halted and stared into his eyes. "And the figure eight you draw on my thumb?"

"The eight is a never-ending path with no break to weaken it." His voice lowered, "I suppose it's my belief, and my hope, in no limitations between us."

"The other drawings?" she asked softly.

"Have you ever followed trail?"

Daisy nodded. "I've tracked Ollie many a time if that's what you mean."

A chuckle escaped him. "Sort of like that. When you trail someone, you learn their signs. You trace what you learn of their ways until they all become a familiar pattern that cloaks you like a second skin and resonates in your senses. I'm trying to learn your ways, Daisy. I enjoy what I'm learning about you and how it makes me feel. I hope you feel free to do the same and want to discover more about me, as well. I want to become your friend if you'll let me. The best of friends."

"I treated you so badly when I learned who you were. I couldn't offer you Knox's clothes," she began, letting go and spreading her palms wide. "I even used you to keep Maddox at bay, and I'm ashamed to admit it. That's why I wanted to talk to you and explain that I made assumptions about you I shouldn't have. You've proven yourself nothing but kind to us. It's going to take some time for me to forget what brought you into our lives, but I will try to set that all aside and be your friend."

Bass searched her eyes. "That's what I hoped to hear. That I have a chance to prove myself worthy of you."

"Just please, don't give me reason to ever regret this change of heart." Daisy's eyes met his directly. "I forgive the first time. From then on, I *walk from among them*, as the old saying goes."

Before he could say anything else, the sound of running steps captured Bass's attention. He noticed his sister rushing toward the barn. Petula kept looking back at the house as if she feared being spotted.

"Petula's carrying something to the barn," Bass grumbled. "I wonder why she's out here so late by herself. I've told her several times that good girls don't roam around in the dark and—"

"Teague must have returned from town," Daisy's voice suddenly held a sharp tone. "Your sister kept a plate of food warming for his supper and she's probably delivering it. There's not a thing wrong with that, Bass. I don't know if I like you assuming the worst of her."

Bass reached for Daisy's arm but she jerked away. "Why are you angry? What did I say? I thought we were getting along fine just now." He couldn't imagine what had changed her mood so quickly.

"Well, you thought wrong."

Daisy hurried ahead of him, long strides eating away the path leading to the house. He kept pace with her, not wanting her to go inside until whatever had just happened was settled between them. Clearly, he had a lot more to learn about what might set off her temper.

Just as she reached the porch, where someone had left a lit lantern, Daisy stopped and picked it up, spinning to shine it over his path. "Maybe if you'll remember that Petula can't be that good little *girl*. She's a grown, good *woman*, Bass, and you need to trust her and what she feels. You've seen her changing. I saw your expression at the table when you were proud of her offering to help. Give her a chance to prove herself. Quit being so tightly wound."

One fist shot to her hip. "And, by the way, maybe you also need to consider that I've been out here in the dark alone with you. How good does that make me?"

Of course, he should beg her pardon, but he hadn't meant to compare Daisy's behavior to Petula's. When Daisy stormed, her anger struck hard. His own flashed in defense of himself.

"I don't like being called judgmental when I only mean to protect my sister," he thundered, buffering it with, "I'm sorry you took it wrong."

"Oh, so it's my fault, is it?" One eye closed as she targeted the other at him like an arrow aimed and ready for release.

"I'm going to make mistakes and say thoughtless things," he admitted, "but I'm just now learning your ways and, by all that's fair, I want you to extend me the same patience as you learn mine."

"Well, I guess we'll just have to see, won't we?" Daisy's challenge met its mark. "Maybe neither of us will find each other worth spending more time with."

Chapter Twelve

Daisy realized she had reacted too quickly, knowing her anger cloaked the long-held fear that she might never be good enough for someone to give her importance in his life. When he'd said good girls don't roam around in the dark, she'd taken it as criticism of her as well as Pet and she'd let her own fears of inadequacy bother her yet again.

Bass was not Knox. He had done nothing but show her that she mattered in his eyes.

She'd never been enough for her husband. There was always one more woman Knox thought he had to win over. Daisy had married him only to discover that his real devotion focused on conquering the next woman who caught his fancy and maintaining his reputation among men who valued that particular skill.

"I've probably made you want to go in, but I hope you'll excuse my temper. I'm not used to allowing people close enough to tell me when I'm wrong. Will you walk with me instead and let me see if there's any way we can hurry Teague's delivery?" Bass held out his hand to Daisy. "I know I've got to trust her more, but I'll have to let go slowly."

Daisy appreciated that he apologized first. "Shall I take the lantern?"

"No. Leave it there. It was probably Pet's and meant to show her the path both ways."

Daisy returned the lantern to the porch and she reached out to accept his hand. "From what she's told me, she says she deserves you being such a watchdog over her."

"Really? She's spoken about our past?"

Daisy appreciated that he maintained his brotherly protection of Pet by referring to *our* past rather than just Petula's. "You may be glad to hear some of what she said if you don't know it already."

He frowned as they started walking. "I'm not sure I want to know anything more. What I've experienced is plenty."

His vulnerability overshadowed his eruption of anger moments ago. She shared all that Petula revealed about her manipulation of him to get her way.

Bass stopped and faced Daisy a moment, his expression solemn. "I'm glad to know her reputation was only almost ruined. I feared the worst but could never actually make her confess to the details. I knew what she was really afraid of. Few people liked us. We were Parkers, spoiled little rich kids who seemed to have everything others thought we wanted. No responsibilities but to be the socially elite product of our parents. Very few realized that we had nothing substantial in here."

He pressed a hand to his heart. "Our parents didn't love us. All we had was each other to keep kindness in our lives. We didn't care about all the wealthy trappings of being the children of a barrel-making baron."

He sighed heavily. "When Petula begged me to stay, I couldn't leave her alone. No matter that I wanted to prove on the battlefield that I was more than what people thought. I had more substance."

Daisy raised a palm to his cheek and whispered, "You chose to protect your sister. I'm so sorry that you both suffered so much and were loved so little. I at least have my parents, my sisters and my precious little Olivia."

"And Knox," he reminded.

Daisy wasn't ready to tell him that she'd never truly had Knox's love. She thought she did, at first. But the pain of discovery came soon after she told him they were going to have a child. His fear of forever being tied down to one way of life tainted their hope of ever experiencing real love. He'd sent her out of Florida to journey along with his brothers and instructed them to build her a home in Texas away from the war. She eventually discovered that Knox had demanded they stay out of service so they could ensure her safety. But the war followed her here.

Knox had never returned. And, frankly, she wasn't sure if he had really wanted to.

No, she wouldn't speak of her inability to love Knox after that point. Not now. Not while she still felt partially to blame that he hadn't loved her enough. That there must have been something wrong with the way she'd loved him. Therefore, she might have been equally to blame.

Thoughts about her husband settled slowly into a place in her heart where she might find some sort of peace that would eventually resolve them.

"And Knox," she finally added his name to the list of her mentioned loved ones.

The lie tasted bitter on her lips.

Bass gently took her hand from his cheek and pressed

a kiss atop her knuckles. "I will always be grateful that he allowed me to care for my sister and not leave her with people she feared would punish her simply because of who she was."

Daisy didn't move her hand away from his kiss. "Petula wouldn't talk of Knox to us. Just that you stayed with her and that she always said a prayer for the man who took your place in the war. Did you never tell her his name?"

"Not until I informed her that we were coming here. I felt I had to explain so she would understand why you kept refusing my money. She wasn't used to people not expecting money from us."

"It was good that you told her," Daisy said. "She needed to know how you might be greeted. I must say, though, she's becoming a friend to me and I'm deeply thankful that she prayed for Knox not even knowing him. Maybe that's why he lasted through all those battles. Someone caring enough to show what goodness really is prayed for him. Whatever you feel about her now in the barn with Teague, think the best of her, will you? She's got a good heart. Maybe all she needs is someone praying for her, too. I'll be glad to do that."

"Just hold my hand, will you?" He urged her forward. "I'm used to instantly reacting with my fists if she puts herself in a compromising position."

"I won't let go, Bass, I promise." Daisy fell in step with him. "You can count on me whenever you need me."

Bass closed the distance to the barn in quick steps and swung open the door. There in the third stall, they spotted Petula sitting on a pile of hay, crying as Teague stood over her.

Bass's fingers tensed and started to slip from Daisy's, but she held on tightly and refused to give his anger rein.

"What seems to be the problem?" Daisy gave Bass time to collect himself. "Why are you crying, Petula? Teague?"

Daisy noticed the lawman's coffee-colored eyes shift from Pet to Bass. He was a man who didn't back down from any sign of tension. If this ended in a fight, both men seemed capable of great damage to the other.

"Tell your brother or I will." Teague untied his bandanna from around his neck and offered it to Petula.

Pet wailed again, accepting his offer. "No, I can't say it."

"Say what?" Bass's stance widened.

This might escalate quicker than Daisy could stop it.

"He called me a…" Petula sniffed.

Oh no, Bass would have to defend her honor now if the slur was too harsh. What little Daisy knew of Teague, he didn't seem the type to set out to offend women. She squeezed Bass's fingers gently. "Don't do anything rash."

"What did you call her?" Bass demanded sharply.

"A half-grown petticoat, that's what. I told her she needed to get on back to the house if she was going to act like a moonfaced schoolgirl."

Bass stood there taking in what Teague had said, not balling up his fists as Daisy expected.

"Just because I told him that I'd waited up and kept that food warmed for him, and the least he could do was give me a proper good-night kiss for the effort." Petula blew her nose into the bandanna.

Daisy's eyes rounded, unsure how Bass would react to what he'd just heard. And to think, she'd just been trying to convince him minutes ago that he no longer needed to worry about Petula.

"A proper kiss? Have you kissed her once already, Teague?" Bass dropped Daisy's hand.

Teague didn't move an inch backward, standing there looking fierce in his worn duster and chaps.

Petula stood and grabbed her shawl from the stall post. "No, he has not and says he won't until he's had a long talk with you first. I told him I'm eighteen and I can decide for myself who is and isn't going to kiss me." She started to sob again. "I am fully grown and I intend to prove it." She thrust the bandanna back at Teague. "Thanks, I don't need it anymore."

Teague threw both palms up as if he was at gunpoint, refusing to touch it. "You keep it, but give it a wash."

Petula glared at him petulantly.

"Maybe we should leave the men alone to have their talk?" Daisy suggested though unsure that was such a good idea, either. Teague clearly wanted a conference of some sort. Depending on what he said, she couldn't be a buffer to Bass's reaction if she wasn't at his side. Maybe she could take Pet in and get back here quickly as possible. "How about us heading inside?"

Before Petula could give an answer, Teague shook his head. "Got some things to tell you first, Daisy, if you ladies will give me a minute before you go. Mr. Parker, are you willing to stick around 'til I'm done passing some messages to the widow?"

"I'm not moving."

"Good, I appreciate a reasonable man." Teague reached over and took a bite of turkey from the plate sitting on the cantle of his saddle lying near his bedroll. "Sorry, the sheriff's been catching me up on trouble and I haven't had time to grab anything to eat. Just need a bite."

They waited to let him finish swallowing.

"Seems he figures the bank gang might be circling back to pull another job. With all the extra pockets in town due to the races and some of the purses that will be awarded to the winners, he thinks we better keep an eye out for them. Being that you four and the banker are the only ones that got a good look at 'em, we think they might target you. I wanted to let you know, Parker, so you were aware of the possible threat."

"I'll keep my eyes open for them. Thanks for the warning."

Teague nodded at Daisy. "I plan to stick around here as much as I can, but I'm sending off for another man from Special Forces to help out when I have to be elsewhere. You'll know him on sight. Eyes squinted all the time. Scars that look like freckles unless you study him closer. I've seen him take down a dozen men by himself. You'll be safe with Gage Newcomb around."

Daisy thought of all the times she'd wondered about Teague and now she knew for sure. He belonged to a company of Texas Rangers. Everyone knew the governor called them his Special Forces.

"As for you, Widow. I know you're expecting your sisters soon. The next stage is due in tomorrow, a day earlier than expected. Seems they added an extra one because of the interest in the races. Don't know where you're going to put everyone, but thought I'd let you know so you'd have someone there waiting to pick 'em up, just in case."

"Thanks." Daisy appreciated the heads-up, although she wondered why it was taking her sisters so long to arrive for their visit. They should have been here a couple of weeks ago. What could be stalling them?

Maybe Petula would like to ride along with her to fetch them. Maybe her new friend would share the details of whatever else Bass and Teague talked about tonight if Bass confided in Petula.

And maybe, just maybe, Snow and Willow would not be on the stage yet. Once they arrived and came to know Bass, Daisy had no doubt the pair of them would admire the man and want to vie for his attention.

For the first time since inviting her sisters, Daisy wished they didn't hurry along and wondered if she would welcome them freely knowing that one of them might end up taking an interest in Bass.

The nightlong dream seemed so vivid Daisy could almost smell it. She and Bass had been walking for a long distance until suddenly he started running hand in hand with her downhill. She laughed and felt more alive than she'd ever been.

When he stopped to pick verbena and thread it gently through her hair, her gaze met his and filled Daisy with a happiness she'd never known before and couldn't define. Like thunder, voices called behind her, coming closer, faster, spoiling the moment she shared with Bass. Everything inside Daisy compelled her to run, to make sure that she and Bass reached their destination before something outraced them. Overtook them. When his hand grabbed hers again, she slipped and tumbled to the lake's edge. Wounds appeared everywhere on her.

Bass followed later, but in time to help her.

He took the verbena from her hair, crumbling the purplish-pink flowers into tiny, dry petals, which he rubbed on every wound. Each disappeared as if cured.

Bass carried her to the cemetery and let her rest while he lifted the cross from Knox's grave.

To her surprise, a stone marker lay to one side covered with words she understood more clearly than any she'd considered before. Bass's flower poultice had made her strong and it was she, not Bass, who moved the heavy stone into place.

The danger couldn't reach her anymore and she wondered why she'd felt so frightened that it might have separated her from Bass.

She thanked him for knowing how to use the verbena and saving her from the painful wounds that had seemed too many to survive.

He drew a figure eight upon her hand and was just about to say something she knew would forever change her life, but Daisy startled awake.

Her heart hammered, her breath racing to match its rhythm as she squeezed her eyes shut again. Desperately, she prayed for his words to return, knowing she must hear them. "Please," she begged, "don't leave them unsaid."

Try as she might to will them back into her awakened consciousness, she couldn't and tears welled in her lashes. She'd been so emotional since his arrival, and she'd never been the kind of woman given to crying.

Still, the tears came unbidden.

"What were you trying to say, Bass?" she wondered aloud as she sat up. "What does it all mean?"

She'd never been good at deciphering dreams. It had been too hard to allow herself to dream in real life, much less in her sleep. She simply accepted life as it came and ignored anything that made her hope too much. But she sensed that this dream, his words, had something to do with her future.

With part of it heartwarming, another portion frightening, maybe it meant she would ultimately survive the pain. All she could make of it was that every emotion felt real and erupted from some place deep within her.

Maybe she should confide in Myrtle and see what her cook thought of the dream.

Then again, maybe this was something to keep private and let life show her the meaning someday.

"Please, Lord, give me understanding." She reached for her pillow and started to fluff it before lying back to find sleep again.

It was then she remembered the verbena. She had taken the flowers from her hair and laid them beneath her pillow so she could enjoy their fragrance before they dried out and had to be put away. The press of her head had crushed the petals. Later this morning she would place them between the pages of her Bible as a reminder of Bass's gift to her.

She lifted a few in her hands and breathed in their sweet minty scent. *The Bible.* What was that old legend about sweet verbena? Daisy struggled to recall, then finally the ancient tale came to mind.

Many believed the flower was used to staunch the bleeding of Jesus's wounds as he was taken from the cross.

Maybe the dream meant that Bass's care for her could heal the wounds that kept her heart from happiness.

Did she want so much for a man like him to make her the most important person in his life, just as he had Petula, that her mind had created the hopeful images and a reason to let him in a little closer?

Chapter Thirteen

The talk with Teague gave Bass a lot to think about. He hadn't yet determined his answer, but he knew one thing after mulling the facts. He respected the Ranger immensely and would give him an answer as soon as possible.

Bass couldn't wait to discuss the matter with Daisy and see what she thought about it. After all, she wanted the best for Petula. She saw deep into his sister's heart at the woman Pet could become.

As he finished getting ready for the morning, Bass wondered what Daisy would say when he told her he planned to ride into town with everyone. She'd probably tell him it was too soon and that might prove true. But the thought of her and his sister leaving him here with Myrtle seemed less appealing. He liked the cook well enough, and she hadn't bitten his head off recently, but going to town sounded promising.

He'd just tell Daisy that he wanted to pay Doc Thomas a visit. If the medic saw him capable of a short fifteen- or twenty-minute ride then maybe he could determine how long the rest of the recovery might take.

Bass wanted to make sure he used every minute of what was left to build Daisy's trust in him.

Besides, he wanted to ride along and provide added protection for the wagonload of women. If the gang was in the vicinity, they might be less likely to attack if they saw two men among the mix.

After dressing, Bass headed downstairs. Petula and Ollie greeted him, each exiting the kitchen and both looking surprised that he had donned his best clothes.

"Where's Daisy?" Had she already eaten breakfast?

"Out helping Teague get the wagon ready," Petula informed him.

Bass decided not to eat. He could always get food in town.

"You taggin' along?" Ollie seemed pleased by the prospect.

"I thought the doctor wouldn't let you travel yet?" Worry and something else made Petula look less than enthusiastic to share the ride.

Since Teague would be riding alongside them as guard, she would probably have preferred that Bass stay home. But he'd thought she was angry with the Ranger and the pair wouldn't be talking this morning. Her infatuation with Teague clearly overrode any anger she bore him. Not that Bass could fault her. He'd done the same last night. He'd flared at Daisy then tried his best to ease the tension he'd caused between them.

Bass was grateful Teague opted to go with the women this morning. Myrtle hadn't seen the gang so she was no threat to the robbers; therefore she was safe from harm. For all the gang knew, Teague figured they couldn't be certain Bass had survived the shoot-out unless one of them stuck around town without anyone knowing it. Daisy, Ollie and Petula needed to stay together as a group, so there would be no leaving Ollie home with him and the cook.

"I'm going," Bass told his sister stubbornly, "to show Doc Thomas how well I'm doing and find out when he'll release me, and I could lend a hand if Teague needs me."

"Ya ain't gonna move out, are ya, Bass?" Ollie frowned. "I ain't ready for ya to skedaddle yet."

Touched by her display of affection, Bass reached out and gently tugged one of her braids. "Thanks, Ollie. I'm going to miss you, too, when that time comes, but I just decided I'd take the opportunity to check with the doctor since he hasn't had a chance to make it out here yet. I hope that doesn't mean Banker Cardwell is worse."

Ollie shook her head, freeing her braid from his hand. "Teague says Sam's a little better, but he ain't up and around much. I'm gonna stop at the store and buy him some licorice. It's his favorite candy and I figure I owe him." She dug in her pocket and held up two coins. "I got me some money saved and I'm gonna get him this much worth. I'm gonna promise him I ain't never takin' no more hostages ever. I been waitin' to tell him I'm real sorry."

The child sounded sincere.

"I'm sure he knows it." Maybe there was something Bass could do for the banker, too. After all, it was his fists that had ended up causing the man's place of business to be shot asunder. Another good reason to go into town.

"Ladies, what's keeping you?" Teague's shout heralded from the front yard. "We've got to get this wagon rolling if we're meeting the stage. It's due in before you know it."

Bass darted to the kitchen and told Myrtle he was

going into town so she wouldn't worry about him. She seemed glad to have some time alone.

Hurrying, he reached Petula and Ollie soon enough to help them into the wagon. Both took a place in the wagonbed, allowing Bass the seat on the driver's box next to Daisy. It took him a moment using only one hand and shoulder, but he managed fine.

"Just where do you think you're going?" Daisy set the brake again, studying him as she held the reins. "You are not to be traveling."

"Now, Daisy, I'm fed up with being treated like an invalid." Realizing how brusque that sounded, Bass softened his delivery. "You can see I'm feeling better."

Bass also mentioned all the other reasons he had planned to convince her he should go.

Not until Teague rode up alongside them and said, "The man knows his mind. Give him a chance to use it," did she relent and release the brake.

"All right, then." She flicked the leather straps and urged the team into a trot. "But you'll set yourself back a few days, mark my words."

"You can tell me I should have listened." He settled into the seat and resisted the impulse to grab the reins. Bass was usually in control, and it felt strange to rely on someone else to guide his journey. But Daisy seemed capable, quite skilled at commanding the horses. She was certainly self-sufficient. Too much so at times.

"Is something wrong?" Daisy's eyes turned from the trail to glance at him before resuming their original focus.

"No, in fact, everything's just great." Bass heard Petula and Ollie in the back laughing together. He hadn't been sure his sister liked being around a small child who tended to grab everyone's attention. Pet had always wanted his so desperately, he didn't know her capable of sharing with anyone but him. She was, indeed, becoming a lady. It seemed nobody really needed him.

"I want to talk something over with you, privately," he announced, "if you have the time."

Daisy laughed. "You've got fifteen minutes. You sure you don't mean if I can handle two things at once?"

"You said that. I wouldn't have dared." Bass liked her *usual* easygoing nature. He would learn to survive her storms, and her teasing, too.

"Funny thing is," she said, laughing again, "I have been a little distracted the past few days. I'm not on my best behavior."

The both of us, it seems. Bass studied her profile and saw nothing but ease in the set of her shoulders despite her criticism of herself. He couldn't help it; he had to know and the question escaped him before he could give it a second thought. "Distracted by what?"

Silence ensued for only a moment then she quirked an eyebrow at him. "You."

He liked her honesty and wondered what she might do if he threaded his arm through hers and pressed his bad shoulder against hers. "That's good to know, because you're doing the same to me. Strange way to become friends, isn't it?"

"Better that than enemies. Are you hurting, Bass?"

He decided to test her reaction and linked his arm as he imagined. She didn't try to make him move away, but her back straightened showing she was still guarded.

"Just getting a better hold." He wouldn't admit it, but he was in pain. The grab to lift himself to his position on the driver's box and the jarring from the rutted road took more effort than he'd prepared himself for.

"You aren't really upset that I came along for the ride, are you? I just wanted to tag along."

He didn't want her worrying, and he didn't want Petula and Ollie making presumptions about his and Daisy's closeness, either. Not yet anyway.

"Not really, but I told you so. If you need to lean against me to hang on, I don't mind. I know you must be hurting. So what exactly did you want to talk over?"

Though she sounded interested her eyes focused on the road now and he couldn't blame her. Sitting this close had his brain buzzing like bees feasting on honey. She smelled nice and the concern in her voice about his comfort pleased him. He had to remind himself about the talk between him and Teague and the decision that needed to be made.

Ollie's face suddenly appeared above their shoulders. "What you two doin'? Sure is quiet up here. Don't y'all got nothin' to say?"

"We're enjoying the quiet," Bass replied. The child had impeccable timing.

"That's what your sister said just now. Said she needed to practice somethin' on Teague and I ought'a come up here and keep y'all company."

Ollie had his full attention now. Bass turned just far enough around to find Petula talking to the Ranger riding closer than he'd done earlier. "Practice what?"

"Oh? Me and Petully thought up some ways to mess with him. She's mad at Teague for some reason, but I said that's okay. He told me once he liked feisty girls and that's why he hung around me so much. He said I needed savin' all the time and that was his job. I don't know 'zactly what that means, but I figured I'd learn Petully how to feist herself up some so he'd like her better."

"Why don't you turn around there, Little Miss Matchmaker," Daisy insisted, "and just enjoy resting your throat awhile. You wouldn't want to wear it out before your aunts get here. I'm certain you'll ask them endless questions."

Ollie looked from Daisy to Bass. "You sure ya don't need me up here, Bass? I got lots of stuff to talk about."

"Save your voice for later, like your mama said," Bass suggested. "I'm going to be curious about your aunts and which one you like the best."

Daisy's eyes met his a moment then returned to the task at hand. "Sit back down, Ollie. We'll be there in no time."

Ollie disappeared and did as she was told, but not without a loud grumble.

Daisy remained quiet and Bass wondered why she was waiting for him to pick up where they'd left off in their discussion.

"Uh, you know Teague and I talked quite a while after you and Petula went inside," he began again.

"I thought you two might have called me back to the barn to let me know what was discussed, but I got tired of waiting and fell asleep." She sighed heavily. "I wish I'd been able to rest more but I knew the stage arrives early and didn't want us to miss it."

"I'm sorry if waiting up for us caused you not to rest."

"No, just some silly dream I had. Do you want me to ask Petula to lean in so she can hear this?"

Bass shook his head then realized she couldn't see his answer. She'd have to take her attention off the road. "No, I'd like to get your opinion on the matter before I say anything to her."

"Will Teague want you sharing whatever this is with me?"

She was considerate about keeping someone's confidence, and Bass liked that. In fact, he'd found a great many things about Daisy Trumbo likable. "Yes, he said at one point to run it by you."

"Then go ahead."

"He's asked for Petula's hand in marriage."

Daisy nearly dropped the reins. "What?" She lowered her voice from a squeal of pleasure to disbelief. "He practically ran her out of the barn. You can't mean to say he really cares about her?"

Bass helped her regain the straps. "I think Teague spoke more words in that barn than he'd ever uttered in his whole life. A man like that doesn't give his affections lightly, but when he knows his mind and sets his heart to something, he's relentless until he gets what he's after."

Ever since he met Daisy, Bass felt relentless in seeing that he helped her and Ollie gain a better life. So he completely understood Teague. "He wants Petula for a bride, but he's not going to let her think she can lead him down the path just because she wants to. He wants to make her fight for him, to prove she wants him, too. Not just because he's the first man to tell her no. He's just as surprised as we are that he's fallen for…what did he call her? A half-grown petticoat."

"Love at first sight," Daisy whispered.

"At first fight is more like it," Bass countered.

"Still, whatever you call it, it's sweet. Both of them know it. Both feel it. How wonderful." Daisy hurried the team. "Maybe we'll have time to look for some cloth to make her a wedding dress."

"I'll buy her—" Bass changed his mind instantly. He

wouldn't buy her a ready-made dress though he could easily afford the price. He would let Daisy be involved any way she thought best. If she wanted to make the dress for Petula, it would be a kindness his sister would treasure. "Then you approve of the match?"

Daisy nodded. "I'm so happy for them both. It gives me faith that love can come at the least expected moment and with the most unimaginable person. As long as they both adore each other and put no other before them. When will he ask her?" A grin graced her lips. "Soon, I hope."

Bass started chuckling and it drew Petula's and Ollie's attention. Teague even asked what he was braying about.

"Oh sorry." Bass tried to quit smiling. He'd forgotten that robbers might be nearby and his laughter would only draw attention. "I'll be quieter."

"No need for that now. Anyone in the vicinity has a dead shot on our location." Teague fell back into position. "Big help you are."

Bass tried to look properly chastised but he leaned into Daisy and whispered, "He said he'd tell her when she straightened up and acted right. I figure they've got a long courtship ahead of them."

Daisy burst out laughing and Bass joined in, making them both the loudest targets on the trail.

They made it to town without mishap, much to Daisy's relief. The pure joy of learning the news of Petula's impending wedding and Bass's laughter concerning the subject had made the trip pleasant instead of just a necessary drudgery.

How wonderful that he took the news of Petula's future so well. Maybe with Pet here or wherever the

Ranger set up home, Bass wouldn't want to move on. She told herself that she wanted him to watch Petula build a love-filled life so that he might one day have a change of heart and build one for himself.

But the prospect of him staying held other promises if she allowed herself to admit the feelings that forgiving him had stirred within her.

Seeing no stagecoach yet, she decided to steer her team toward Doc Thomas's office.

"Where you headed?" Bass pointed toward the livery. "Aren't you afraid you'll miss your sisters?"

"Are they as pretty as you?" Petula had scooted close enough to hear. "Are they more Teague's age?"

Daisy understood Petula's concern. Her friend feared competition for the Ranger, just as she had wondered if Snow and Willow might vie for Bass's affections. It had surprised her to feel a twinge of jealousy. Bass was a handsome man with many fine qualities. He'd certainly be sought after if he allowed himself to court anyone.

Daisy decided right then and there to tell her sisters Teague would be hands-off. Not that she thought he would waver in his feelings for Petula. The Ranger was a man who made up his mind quick. Bass, on the other hand, was on his own with her sisters.

"I'm the least fair of the three of us, and the oldest," Daisy replied. "I don't know Teague's age, do you, Ollie?"

Ollie popped up again between Daisy's and Bass's shoulders. "Yep, said he was too young to fight in the Alamo and too old to wait on me to marry 'im." She sighed. "I had to scratch him off my list."

Bass tried to sound serious. "I thought your list was for possible fathers."

"It is, but I told him if he didn't marry Mama he

could wait on me. That's when he told me how old he was."

Daisy reined up at the doctor's office and set the brake, unlinking from Bass. "I'll go in and make sure Doc's here before I leave you. My sisters will wait if I'm late. Bear and his wife will give them a cup of tea until I get there, I'm sure. Ollie's going with me to meet her aunts officially. She was newborn the last time they got to see her. Though Mom and Dad encouraged them to just visit this time, I'm hoping to convince both to stay and make this their permanent home. I have plenty of room and Ollie needs to get to know them better."

Refusing Bass's help down, Daisy managed quite nicely and gave her houseguest an option. "Petula, you have a choice. Either go with Ollie and me or stay with Bass."

Teague spoke up. "Why don't you women keep together? Security would be easier that way."

All of a sudden Petula yelped. "Oww! Why'd you elbow me?"

Ollie whispered, "Feisty, 'member?"

"Oh. I'll stick with Teague," Petula announced. "I mean, with you and Ollie, Daisy."

"And when I'm done, do I meet you ladies at the livery or the mercantile?" Bass seemed satisfied with Petula's decision. "Thought you might want to spend some time in town with your sisters before we head home."

Daisy shook her head. "This won't be the first stage they've missed and they might not have known an extra one was scheduled, so I'm not even sure they'll be here. Why don't you meet us at the mercantile when you're done? You know I plan to buy a few things and Ollie wants to get some licorice. We'll be there at some point.

Just take your time with Doc. Don't leave without him examining you thoroughly."

With a brief plan set for everyone's needs, Daisy went inside. The waiting room was empty. "Doc, are you here?"

"In the back with Sam. Don't come back. I'm changing his bandages then we'll be right out."

Daisy needed to stretch her legs so she paced in the parlor. "You better, Sam?"

"Fit as a warped fiddle."

"Glad to hear you talking. Ollie has something to tell you in a little while."

"Tell her to give Doc a bit and I'll be glad to listen."

"Oh, she'll come back later. She has to go with me now, but she'll catch you before we leave." That was settled. Ollie was afraid he'd never speak to her again. Glad Sam was such an understanding friend.

"Doc, do you have time to give us an update on Bass, I mean, Mr. Parker? He thought he'd ride in so you wouldn't have to come out there."

"He's feeling that much better?"

Daisy shook her head then remembered the physician was at least a room away. "Not really, but he'll try to convince you he is. In fact, I'm sure you'll find bruises on the other side of him. He thinks he's tough as Wild Bill and indestructible."

"Sure, I'll take a look at him as soon as I'm finished here. Myrtle smack him upside the head a few times? Or was it your brothers-in-law?"

She gave him a brief description of the tumble.

"That billy goat did it? He got me the last time I was out there. You need to throw him in a pit and mesquite-smoke him if he doesn't settle down."

"Believe me, Myrtle will do just that if he ever gets

loose in her kitchen again. She's still scrubbing up flour." Daisy shared Bass's first run-in with the goat.

"Sounds like your patient's had a time of it and not getting much rest."

She needed to hurry things along. "You be the judge for yourself. I don't mind letting him stay awhile longer with us, just to be fair." *Among other reasons.*

Daisy said a quick prayer that Doc would agree with her that Bass wasn't ready to leave town.

"That's good to hear. There's still no rooms anywhere and I hear tell they're sending extra stages. Folks are going to have to rent out their barns or set up tents. Who'd have thought footraces could draw such interest."

Daisy hadn't had time to think about the races, making shoes or even remember to bring some with her today to consign to the mercantile for display. She needed to get done, get home and settle in her sisters.

"Well, I'll go and tell him you can see him," she called out. "I've got people to pick up. Maybe we'll have a chance to talk after the races tomorrow and you can give me a progress report on him. Take care, Sam. I'm glad you're feeling better."

This bright wonderful morning had started out fun but now threatened to become a whirlwind of must-get-dones. And that was no fun at all.

As she'd confessed to Bass, she was certainly allowing him to distract her.

And experience had taught her long ago when she became distracted that's when trouble rode hardest in her direction.

Chapter Fourteen

Fifteen minutes later Daisy waited at the livery with Petula and Ollie, wondering how much longer the stage would be and why. Sitting on this driver's box was making her hips hurt and she was ready to get off the wagon and enjoy a softer chair at the café when her sisters arrived.

Worry was just about to set in that the stage might have met with some sort of disaster when Ollie stood in the wagonbed and started jumping up and down, shouting and waving.

"Here it comes, Mama! Look at them horses go!"

The stagecoach rushed into view, the driver pulling up reins. The team dug in their hooves as the coach springs halted with the scraping of brakes and a billowing cloud of dust, setting everyone to coughing.

While Daisy tried to recover, she waved the dust away from her face and dabbed at her eyes with her sleeve. "Good gracious, I'll never get used to that."

"It's even worse if you're riding inside." Petula coughed and flicked her fan rapidly. "I've ridden so many I've decided to put some of my money into railroad stock in the future. There's got to be a cleaner way to travel than this."

The door swung wide and the leather straps cradling the coach creaked as a man stepped down and his nostrils immediately flared. The reek of the steaming, blowing team had him reaching for his handkerchief before turning to help the next passenger.

A redheaded, full-figured woman accepted his hand and stepped down, her legs nearly buckling beneath her. Daisy gasped, afraid the lady would crumple to the ground before anyone could prevent the fall.

Ollie jumped off the wagon and raced up to help, but the man swept the lady up into his arms just in time.

"You ain't my aunt, are ya?" Ollie kept craning her neck to get a good look at the redhead. She turned and frowned at Daisy. "She don't look nothin' like ya, Mama."

"She's not my sister, sweetheart."

"Whew! Good." Gratitude swept over Ollie's face as she backed up a ways. "I don't think I could'a caught her. She would'a squashed me for sure."

"I'm fine," the newcomer told her rescuer, her green eyes opening and shutting against the battering dust. "Just let me catch my breath and get my feet under me again."

The back of her right hand pressed against her forehead, trembling. "Everything swayed a moment and my stomach turned. I…I think some water might help."

When her hand returned to her side, Daisy noticed a flash of amber in the ring the stranger wore. Leaves made of gold formed a circle around a pair of honey-colored ovals. Surprise filled Daisy making her study the ring on her own finger.

Knox had married her with it, telling Daisy the ring

was one of a kind and made to match her eyes. Apparently not.

"My wife has some tea made." Bear stepped in to offer help. "I'll just be a moment."

"I'm gonna help Bear, Mama." Ollie maneuvered through the crowd to reach him.

"Stay with your mom, Tadpole," Bear told her as he headed off to his home attached to the livery.

Ollie grumbled and rejoined Daisy. "Don't worry about that lady," she told Bass's sister. "Teague didn't even come runnin'. She's probably one of them funeral-faintin' ladies that wants ever'body to see how sad she is. He probably don't figure she's for real sick."

Petula patted Ollie's shoulder. "Or feisty."

"That's sure as shootin'."

"You're welcome to rest on our wagonbed, ma'am," Daisy called down from the driver's box.

The woman's rescuer lowered the redhead to her feet and allowed her to test her strength, but decided to take Daisy up on her offer. He lifted her again and placed her in the wagon next to where Ollie and Petula sat. Both scooted over.

The overwhelmed redhead offered a smile to both the man and Daisy. "I'll only need a moment."

"Take what time you need." Daisy knew no matter how powerful one's constitution was, journeying in an overland coach could wear down even the strongest.

Already men were unhitching the horses and harnessing new ones to keep the driver on schedule. The passengers going to the next destination would have an hour's reprieve to get something to eat and a few moments' rest from the coach's rock and sway.

Since Bear normally gave the passengers instructions, Daisy stepped in and pointed out where the café and mercantile were located to allow them as much time as possible to enjoy themselves and grab what they needed. To the fragile lady, she asked, "Would you like for me to send someone over to get you something to eat?"

"If you do, bring back something for two," said a familiar voice, stepping out of the coach with a boy barely taller than Ollie in hand. "This young man is her son."

"You're finally here!" Daisy's heart warmed to the sight of her beloved sister's solid white tresses and hazel eyes, not really concentrating on the boy at all. Snow McMurtry had been born with a headful of the unusual-colored hair, which pleased their father immensely. He'd dubbed her his little snow bunny from that day forth and the name had stuck.

Daisy couldn't believe how much she had missed Snow. She hurriedly jumped from the wagon and hugged her sister, looking past Snow's shorter shoulders, anticipating her first sight of Willow in a very long time.

"Ma'am?" Ollie's voice echoed from behind Daisy.

"I'm here alone. Wait just a minute, will you?" Snow pointed to one man unloading baggage. "Handle that with care, sir. I'd appreciate it."

"Excuse me, ma'am." Impatience filled Ollie's tone.

"Alone?" Daisy tried to hide her disappointment as the fragrance of oranges fought for prominence over her sister's travel-weary perspiration. Daisy recalled Snow's favorite scent and her love of playing in the orange groves of their youth.

"I said maaa-yummm." Ollie's bid for attention took on a cadence.

"She took a position recently," Snow informed Daisy, "and she wanted to finish the job. Said she would come as soon as she could or it's done, whichever comes first. You know Will, how she's always wanting to surprise us. Let's just get this little fella to his mother and I would very much like to answer that persistent little girl behind you." She finally let go of the boy and he ran to his parent. "Could this be darling Ollie?"

"That would be me." Ollie grabbed a hunk of calico from each hip and curtsied. "Are ya really my aunt Snow? I don't usually dress up like this. So if you ain't, I wanna change."

As Snow's gaze swept over Olivia, Daisy wondered how the two would measure up to each other. Ollie reminded her of Snow in so many ways.

Snow bent down and held out a palm. "Proud to finally meet you, Olivia, and yes I am your aunt. Actually, I was here at your birth, but you were more concerned with your mother at the time. You just call me Snow from now on. The less names, the better, don't you think? And frankly—" she chuckled "—I can't wait to change into some overalls myself."

Ollie let go of the calico and shook her aunt's hand, nearly melting with pure happiness on the spot. "Mama, she's just like me. She likes to wear pants."

Daisy laughed. "She's older so you're just like her, my sweet. I can see this is going to be a mutual meeting of the minds where you two are concerned. I think I'm in double trouble now."

Teague drifted by on his horse as if he had no interest in the gathering.

"Daisy?" Petula jumped down from the wagon and shook the wrinkles from her skirt. "Would you mind if I head over to the mercantile in case Bass might be done? I'd like to do some shopping before we leave."

More likely wanting to chase down the Ranger than rejoin Bass. Daisy wasn't fooled.

"Before you go," Daisy said, "let me introduce you to my sister." Petula waited and once Daisy finished telling Snow about her guests, she ended with, "I'll explain everything on the way home. I'm sure you'll want to make a stop at the mercantile. Maybe gather a few items before we leave?"

Snow nodded to Petula then smiled. "A *few*."

Daisy's middle sister was not one to collect much. Snow liked things uncluttered and necessary. No stockpiles for her.

"Well, then," Snow said as she grabbed her bag and lifted it onto Daisy's wagon, "it seems we need to see how much longer that tea will be for Abigail. She and Thad should get some food so they won't miss the stage."

As Petula bid her leave, Ollie raised her hand to get their attention. "I'll hurry Bear up."

The child grabbed something from out of the wagon and took off in a rush before Daisy could remind her that Teague didn't want them all separated. The Ranger would skin her hide if the gang was nearby.

"The tea will do, Miss McMurtry," the redhead assured them. "I'd like to get a room first. We'll eat later."

Abigail and Thad? Snow must have shared the stagecoach journey for a great stretch for her sister to feel free to use their names. Such close quarters often jostled the passengers about so it was hard to keep personal space. Being friendly seemed a better way to excuse yourself from pitch and parries.

Bear and Ollie, now dressed in overalls and a white blouse rolled up at the sleeves, the dress she'd worn bundled beneath one armpit, approached with the tea.

Ollie looked as haphazard as the amount of time she'd used to change clothes.

Daisy felt a moment's responsibility to warn Abigail of the lack of rooms. As Abigail accepted the cup and took a drink, the sight of her ring rattled Daisy.

She shouldn't have been surprised by Knox's lie concerning the ring's uniqueness, but it hurt that he'd thought he needed to. There before her sat a woman with an identical ring to the one Knox had given her.

You're just working yourself up for no reason, Daisy told herself. *It wasn't the first time he lied to you about something.* "Because of the races and so many people in town, ma'am, there's probably not a room available anywhere."

"Races?" Abigail's expression revealed she had no clue what Daisy meant. She handed the blacksmith the cup and thanked him.

Daisy quickly told her about the series of upcoming competitions.

Snow sighed. "You're actually involved in them out here? I'd thought you were done with all that back home."

"Definitely involved and in the running, so to speak." Daisy and Snow never saw eye to eye on her love of chasing the wind. Of letting it help gather her thoughts and spur her decision making. "I placed second just last Sunday."

Had that only been days ago? A lifetime, it seemed.

"And the next one happens tomorrow." Daisy glanced apologetically at Abigail and she wasn't sure why she felt guilty for any reason. It wasn't her fault every place in town was filled to capacity. "I'd be very surprised if you can find a room for the night. You might have to ask around and see if someone will rent you a room in their home. Or maybe you have family here?"

"I don't, but my son does. Do you know the Trumbos?"

Dread engulfed Daisy as she looked more closely at the boy and his mother. The boy's features sent ripples of gooseflesh up Daisy's arms as if something cold scurried to the top of her head and danced on spider legs.

Snow appeared stunned. "You didn't mention them on the journey, Abigail."

Ollie stuffed her dress into the wagon and spoke up. "We're Trumbos. I don't know that boy."

The unsettling feeling began to chill Daisy to the bone. The woman could be anybody. Her son some relation Maddox and his brothers never mentioned. But surely she would have heard of him by now. She'd known the Trumbos years before she married into the family.

Bile rose to burn Daisy's throat and replace the chill of misgivings that consumed her.

She tried to regain her composure, not wanting to give way to the hurt stirring from the past. But the similarity of rings now took on an even more dreadful possibility. The boy's features couldn't deny his ancestry.

"Which particular Trumbo are you looking for, may I ask?" Her heart hammered hard in her ears, the beat rushing from her throat to tighten her cheeks as if they were being gripped in a vise. *Please don't say it*, Daisy prayed. *Please let the matching ring just be coincidence.*

Abigail's hand dipped into the lace that formed a wealth of ruffles above her bosom, pulled out a folded piece of parchment and handed it to Daisy. "Daisy Trumbo. Do you know her?"

"I'm Daisy. His widow." Daisy's announcement escaped her as the rush of reality hit her full force. Her hands trembled when she dared open the paper and saw her husband's handwriting. She could hardly focus.

Dearest Daisy,
If you're reading this letter it means I need your help. I know you have plenty of reason not to do this for me. Will probably even hate me for asking you. Still, we've been friends for a long time. More than that, not long enough. Do you think you could find it in your heart to give my…

Daisy's eyes blurred with emotion. Unable to believe what she'd read, all she could do was repeat, "I'm Knox's widow."

Ollie tugged on Daisy's skirt. "What's wrong, Mama? Why do ya look so sad?"

"And you are?" Snow asked Abigail what Daisy could not, linking an arm through her sister's to steady her.

Abigail must surely know Snow wasn't simply asking her name. Daisy wasn't sure she wanted to know the answer. Could she bear to hear it?

"I'm the mother of his son."

It took everything inside Daisy to keep from swaying, not to sink where she stood. Her sister's strength beside her buoyed Daisy up and she would be forever grateful.

Daisy opened the note again, her eyes desperately needing to see confirmation of Abigail's announcement.

…son a place to stay if he ever needs one?
Ever Loving You,
Knox

Her eyes focused on Thad, and Daisy saw what Knox would have looked like at that age. The boy had to be about Ollie's age or maybe slightly older. She'd met Knox at eleven years old, but she could see that this boy would be her husband's spitting image in a few years. The color of Thad's sandy hair would never be anything but the blond of his Nordic heritage, his eyes as gray as his father's and uncles'. His nose sloped sharp and lean. Long legs hinted he would enjoy the Trumbo height. She immediately glanced at his fingers. The smallest of them crooked like Ollie's, the family trait.

Suddenly, Daisy wished Bass was here and all she could think of was to get to him. To talk to him about this woman and her son. Knox's son. Thad. Shortened obviously from Thaddeus.

Daisy put the note away in her skirt pocket, trying to forget what the words implied. There was only one thing she could do. As distasteful as it would be, she must honor her husband's request.

"Let me collect the rest of my family and guests and we'll head back to the house. All of us. You and…" She struggled to say the boy's name because it hurt too much, so she elected not to. She and Knox had wanted to name their firstborn son Thaddeus after a family relative, and he'd given the pleasure to another woman. "…your son will stay at my place for tonight at least until we decide what to do."

Daisy let go of Snow's arm. "I have an extra room since my other sister didn't come."

"No, Mama. Don't let 'em stay." Ollie nearly tore Daisy's skirt yanking so hard.

"Hush, baby. We must. It's the right thing to do. It's our duty."

Snow held a hand out to Ollie. Surprisingly Ollie left Daisy's side and accepted it.

"Thank you, we're grateful." Abigail held her child tightly. "I'm finally glad to put a face to your name."

"Wish I could say the same," Daisy admitted. "This is the first I've heard of you, I'm afraid."

The redhead straightened. "Abigail Rutcliffe, and this is my son, Thaddeus Rutcliffe."

At least they did not carry Knox's name, no matter that Abigail wore his ring. Knox had spared Daisy the disgrace of bigamy. "How old are you, Thaddeus?"

"Eight."

"He just had a birthday."

Daisy had always known Knox had broken his marriage vows. She'd always feared there would be a child elsewhere. Always thought Knox would be honest enough to tell her.

Eight. Slightly older than Ollie. Daisy's stomach knotted as if she'd been punched there. She and Abigail must have been carrying Knox's children close to the same time. He had been consorting with Abigail in Florida months before she'd told him of Ollie's forthcoming birth. His reasoning to send them all to Texas to protect them from war apparently meant to also keep any of them from finding out about his indiscretion with Thad's mother. No wonder he'd never come home to High Plains. His heart remained in Florida with his son and he didn't want her to discover the truth.

"Ollie, will you get Teague and tell him I'm headed to the mercantile then home if he wants to follow us back. And don't be too long, honey. You've got to go home with me. You can't stay in town and have someone bring you back. I need you home, understood? I expect you to be at the mercantile in no less than ten minutes or I'm coming looking for you."

"Okay, Mama." Ollie glanced in the direction of the boy and frowned, letting go of Snow's hand. She wiggled a finger at her mama to bend down closer.

The sight of Ollie's smallest finger almost proved Daisy's undoing and she had to stifle a whimper.

Ollie hugged her fiercely and whispered into her ear. "Don't worry, Mama. I'll hurry. Me and you'll fix things up good."

As Daisy watched her daughter take off at a run, she doubted anyone could repair this particular hurt in her life. Even Bass.

Bass wondered what had happened during his separation from the others.

From the looks of the widow, she must have surely seen one or more of the gang. She walked into the mercantile, linked arm in arm with a white-haired woman who surely must be her sister. They had similar features though Daisy was taller, but the sister didn't lack that much in height. Where was the other one?

Pale-faced, Daisy's amber eyes rounded with some emotion Bass couldn't fathom. She let go of her sister and rushed to him, making quick introductions and asking that he load whatever purchases he'd made into the wagon so that they could be on their way.

"No one but me shopping?" That meant something was clearly amiss. He knew Pet, Ollie and Daisy had all wanted to do that before they left town.

He pulled Daisy to one side. "What's wrong?"

"No time to tell you now. Let's just get home as soon as we can."

"Are you ill?"

She shook her head and gave a half-baked smile. "Asks the man who didn't want to be treated as an invalid."

Whatever disturbed her, Bass sensed she was fighting to keep control of her emotions.

Teague, Petula and Ollie instantly showed up and Bass could tell something was not right just by the look in each one's eyes. The Ranger stared out the door and Ollie glared angrily out the front window. Even Petula remained close to the door, not perusing the inventory as she normally would have.

"Will somebody please let me in on what's happened?" Bass asked, wondering what was outside awaiting them.

Had the gang been spotted? Worse, were the women threatened? Bass made note of each one's location in case trouble started.

The sister introduced to him as Snow McMurtry answered him.

"Daisy's received some upsetting news. I know you don't know me well, but believe me we need to get her home, where she can deal with it privately."

"Nothing to do with your other sister, is it?" He feared the worst.

"No, she's fine."

"I'll finish this up tomorrow, then, when we come for the races," Bass told the merchant. "Sam can verify that I'm good for all this. Put everything on my account, and send some licorice to the banker. Say it's from Olivia Trumbo and that she'll drop by tomorrow. We couldn't visit with him now."

Bass grabbed the packages and headed out of the store, wondering what upsetting news Daisy had received and why everyone seemed so tense.

No hail of bullets riddled him with lead.

Another woman sat in the wagon with a small boy, her back turned away from Bass. He had forgotten the other sister. What was her name?

What had Daisy told him at the cemetery? Their parents named them after parts of nature: a flower/ Daisy, the weather/Snow, and what was the other one? A tree/Willow!

Was this Willow? Her hair was definitely a different shade than Daisy's or Snow's. She seemed plumper in frame than her sisters. And there was no way to determine how tall she might be, given that he couldn't see much of anything below the sideboards.

It looked as if Daisy had added a third seat to accommodate the added passengers. She hadn't mentioned another child would be tagging along. Had she known the boy was coming? He'd just assumed both sisters were unmarried since she mentioned that they still lived at home.

"It's safe out here," he hollered at the others, deciding he should introduce himself properly to the new passengers while everyone took their seats. He needed to make himself known as part of their travel party. Bass walked around the wagon and said, "Hello, I'm Bass Parker and you must be Wil—"

His mouth gaped and he forgot to finish his greeting, nearly dropping his purchases.

The redheaded woman pulled the child closer as if Bass was threatening to steal him.

Daisy came around to the back of the wagon and quickly made introductions. "This is Abigail Rutcliffe and her son, Thaddeus. Miss Rutcliffe, another of my boarders, Bass Parker."

Another boarder? Was Daisy taking on visitors other

than her sisters? Where was her younger sister? Did Daisy have any idea who this woman was? His pulse raced so hard he thought his heart might beat out of his chest. Surely not.

Bass waited for some spark of recognition to register on the woman's face, but she apparently didn't remember him.

Maybe, just maybe, he wouldn't have to admit he already knew her. "Pleased to meet you, ma'am. You, too, young man."

"It's Miss," Daisy corrected, her face salt-white with whatever tension gripped her, "not ma'am. On the way home, I'd appreciate you telling them our schedule and how we run things at the house. I'll count on you to help make them feel welcome. Think you can do that?"

She finally asked him to help her, and talking to Abigail Rutcliffe was the last thing on earth he wanted to agree to.

"Sure," he said, crawling into the wagonbed and taking a seat beside the woman who could destroy every positive move he'd made in gaining Daisy's trust. "Count on me."

Chapter Fifteen

Bass barely survived the ride back to Daisy's, though no ambushes occurred and no delays kept them from the trail. When they left this morning, Bass had expected the return journey to be full of women's chatter. Daisy catching up with all that was new with her sisters, Ollie with licorice tales about Sam and Petula badgering him for details about what he and Teague had discussed.

Instead, the wagonload of people remained three rows of brooding silence except for his brief discussion about the Trumbos' meal times and house rules.

His hands fidgeted, not knowing quite what to do with themselves. So he laced his fingers with one of Ollie's hands and waited to see if she would accept his gesture. The tyke squeezed his palm, reassuring Bass as if she knew she was giving him comfort of some kind.

She kept peeking at the boy when he turned his head away to spot something along the roadway. The observant little girl clearly knew that Thaddeus's and his mother's presence had upset Daisy, but Bass wasn't sure if she understood exactly why. And he hoped she didn't. Ollie needed to stay innocent-minded as long as life would let her. If only he could shield her.

He knew her well enough now that there was no doubt her silent glances meant she was plotting some kind of retaliation on the boy. She could be a little schemer and that worried Bass about the position in which that might place Daisy.

Petula seemed ready to talk and ask questions, but he wanted to put her off until they were alone and could discuss all the decisions needed to be made. She kept quirking an eyebrow at him as if asking why no one was speaking to each other. He shook his head, hoping she'd get the message that now was not the time. After the third eyebrow raising, she sighed in frustration.

Later, he mouthed silently.

"Hey, mister."

The boy's voice startled Bass from his thoughts. He glanced in the child's direction. "Yes?"

"Did you know my daddy? Do I look like him?"

Thaddeus had not only inherited his father's features but definitely the resonant voice of the male Trumbos. Bass hoped Daisy had not heard the child's question.

Bass's heart went out to Knox's children. He knew how it felt to want to really know a parent you understood so little about. Maybe one day, Daisy would revoke her demand and he could tell Ollie and the boy anything they wanted to hear about their father. But for now, he would assume it best to wait on Daisy's approval before he shared any such knowledge with Knox's son. She'd expect him to treat both children the same.

"That depends on who your daddy is, son." Bass was not proud of himself for giving an offhanded reply. He felt as though he was trying to tiptoe across quicksand.

Would this disaster of a ride ever end?

Despite the fact that Doc Thomas refused to release

him yet and Daisy saying he and Pet could stay, Bass saw only trouble brewing ahead if he and Abigail spent time in the same house. Maybe the best thing to do was make plans to set up a trust for Daisy and Ollie, then just leave and hope she would eventually relent in accepting money from him. If Daisy ever found out the secret he hid from her, she'd kick him out anyway. She'd certainly never agree to an offer of marriage.

Teague and Bass were kind enough to volunteer to put away the wagon and team, allowing Daisy and the women to take their purchases and baggage inside. To her surprise, the men even asked the children if they would like to help and both chomped at the bit to stretch their legs.

Ollie was madder than bees in an empty honeycomb and the best thing to do was let her work off the sting.

Myrtle wasn't in the best of moods, either, not expecting the additional houseguests. Daisy's temper proved too quick and she'd reminded the cook that the only difference in number was one small boy since Abigail would be substituting for Willow.

How much trouble could one more child be? Daisy didn't miss the irony of her own thought. Trouble rode in hard today.

But after calming down, she felt ashamed of herself for baring her teeth at her dear cook when it was really Abigail's presence that galled her. What were the woman's motives? Daisy needed time to think. Time to regain her balance. Time to run and run hard.

Maybe the races tomorrow would pound in a plan of action to get her through all this.

"Ready for me to show you to your rooms?" Daisy motioned upstairs as Snow and Abigail followed behind her. "Lunch will be ready in about thirty minutes. I'm sure you both would like to freshen up."

Snow moved past Daisy. "I'll find it on my own. You're sort of predictable, sis. You know perfectly well how to make me comfortable, the colors I like, the sparseness of the room, biggest windows I can open and climb out onto the trees if I take a notion."

Daisy appreciated her sister trying to lighten the moment. "You guessed it. Nevertheless, after I get the Rutcliffes settled in, I'll be up to check and make sure you didn't choose Ollie's. You two like the same sort of room, but I've set up my sewing machine in hers. Ollie and I are sharing a room at the moment."

Snow turned, her hazel eyes searching Daisy's. "I'll find it, but if you need me for anything, I mean anything, I'm just a shout away."

Daisy understood what she was and wasn't saying. "I'm fine now, sis. I've got it all under control."

She plastered a smile of welcome on her face and asked her unexpected houseguest, "May I carry those bags for you? You're still a little pale."

Abigail's skin looked ashen. The jarring wagon ride after almost fainting when she exited the coach would be hard on anyone. Daisy tried her best to remember her manners and offer sincere hospitality.

"I would appreciate it, Mrs. Trumbo." She set one bag down and held on to the stair railing. "I haven't quite been able to regain my balance."

Daisy grabbed the bag and reached out to take the one from her hand, leaving her guest with nothing to carry. She led Abigail upstairs, stopping once to make sure the woman was able to follow. Abigail did but not easily. Was she ill from something other than the rides?

Daisy hoped she hadn't brought further caregiving

needs into her home. She certainly didn't want anything to prolong Abigail's stay.

Once Abigail caught up to her on the landing, Daisy gave her a moment to catch her breath. "Normally I would have several rooms for you to choose from, miss. But as you've noticed, I've got lots of visitors. I hope the room I've assigned you and Thaddeus will be sufficient." It was getting easier to speak his name.

"We're grateful. Anything will do, really."

"To your right, then. You'll be next to Petula Parker." Daisy didn't know if Bass had introduced his sister to the woman during the ride home.

Daisy opened the door to the room and walked in long enough to set the baggage down near the armoire that provided storage drawers and a small closet for hanging clothes. Every bedroom in the house offered the minimal necessities. Nothing fancy, just serviceable. The color of curtains, quilts, braided rugs and window views provided the only variance to each room.

She motioned to the bed and its feathered ticking. "Please rest for a while. If you sleep through lunch I'll keep a plate warm for you and make sure the boy eats. Oh, and I'll set a bedroll outside your door in case he would prefer not to share. I'm afraid that's all I have left, but there's hay out in the barn. I can make it comfortable for him." Daisy didn't know why she was prattling on so.

The sound of the woman taking a seat on the bed echoed in the room. "Mrs. Trumbo," she began. "*Daisy*. Now that we're alone together, may we talk?"

Daisy stiffened, feeling awkward with the instant anger that flared within her. She wasn't ready yet for a talk alone with Knox's consort. "I thought that's what we were doing."

"I mean, will you close the door and take a seat in that chair? I need to say something to you. Something that wasn't on Knox's note."

"With the door closed?"

"It's your business only."

The woman had understood Snow's meaning on the stairs, *"I'm just a shout away."*

Not wanting Abigail to think she feared her for any reason, Daisy shut the door and sat. She wouldn't encourage her guest to speak, but she waited.

"You've surprised me, ma'am. I didn't expect you to be so decent to me. To take me into your home." Green eyes studied Daisy.

What did she expect her to do? Pull out every hair on her head? Claw her fingers down her face? Stuff the note down her throat? What purpose would that serve?

"Oh, make no mistake, Miss Rutcliffe...*Abigail*. The decency is not purposely extended to you. I owe you nothing. It's for your son, because he's clearly Knox's boy. Knox's note asked me to give him a place to stay if he ever needed it. That's what I'm doing, giving Thaddeus a room while you're here. You just happen to be along for the ride."

Daisy unleashed her anger. "Thaddeus is the innocent one in this matter. I can't say the same about the rest of us. You for chasing another woman's husband. Knox for—" Daisy couldn't hold back the resentment and hurt "—adding another notch to his holster. Me for not caring anymore to demand he kept his vows."

"He loved me." Green fire sparked in Abigail's gaze.

"I know." Daisy admitted the truth. "He loved each one of us and I suspected there were many others but, as far as I know, he only married me."

Abigail looked chastised before defending herself.

"Thad and I may have never carried his name, but you never carried his heart." Her thumb rubbed the ring Knox had given her. "We truly loved each other and I gave him the son he wanted. He told me how proud he was of that fact when he took leave to see Thad when he was born."

The words pierced Daisy's heart, twisting open the old wound that had festered between her and Knox. Daisy had written and asked Knox to come after Ollie's birth. He'd supposedly never requested a leave before and should have been allowed the time. He'd written that he'd been denied leave and that he must lead his men into an important impending battle. Though Daisy had suspected there was more to the decision than what she was told, she knew now Knox had chosen to visit his son rather than Ollie.

She wanted nothing more than to hurt Abigail as she'd been hurt, to resent the boy, but Daisy didn't want to live this way, with so much hate and remembered pain. She wanted love, kindness, a new beginning and a better rest-of-her-life's journey.

Why had life brought this to her door now to endure? Hadn't she suffered enough?

She prayed that Ollie never found out her daddy had chosen another child over her.

Daisy stood, ready to end the discussion. "We could batter this back and forth between us forever wallowing in the past. I'm not willing to do that to myself nor will I allow that grief to reach my daughter. We need to put this behind us and do what's best for his children."

As Daisy scooted the chair back under the reading table so she could leave, Abigail reached out a gloved hand to cover Daisy's. "Wait. That's why I came. I'm trying to do what's best for Thaddeus and, in the long run, I hope that includes your Ollie."

Daisy jerked her hand away.

"I'm dying, Mrs. Trumbo. *Daisy.*"

Daisy studied Abigail. She'd certainly seen moments of ill health within the stranger this morning, but dying? Was this some kind of ruse? "Why?"

"The long death. I have a growth. They say they can't operate. I take medicine that makes me not of my own mind at times. I need to find Thad a *permanent*, safe home. He's too little to leave alone."

Starting to pace, Daisy fired off questions. "Don't you have family who already knows him? Who loves him? Who he'll want to stay with?" And then came the most important one of all. "Why us?"

"Because he deserves his true name. He has a true sister." The plea in Abigail's eyes seemed sincere. "Someone who will grow to love him one day, if he's blessed. Then he would not be shunned as a by-product of my wayward choices." Abigail laughed bitterly. "No, Daisy. Thad has no family who loves him other than me. I have to count on you and your Ollie to be the answer to his future."

She began to sob. "May I leave him with you? Will you honor Knox's request? Will you give him a place in his father's home? His sister's life? Can you forgive Knox and me enough to give our son a chance?"

The storm of emotions thundering inside Daisy threatened to flood her with tears. She had to get out of here now, away from her wretched past and the decision she must make for her and Ollie's happiness. To preserve Knox's memory for his children.

"I need time," she muttered, trying to keep her lips from trembling and the tears at bay. "Time to think."

Daisy jerked open the door unable to quell the need to escape.

"Please don't take too long," a warning came urgently from behind her. "I must know what to do with his son."

The echo of a slamming door reverberated in the house just as Bass trudged up the last step to the landing. All of a sudden, Daisy rushed toward the room she and Ollie shared.

"Daisy?" He noticed her hands covering her eyes. Her wretched sobbing flooded him with the need to soothe her. "Daisy, please let me help."

At the sound of his voice, she turned and threw herself into his arms, burying her face into his chest. She wouldn't answer Bass and just kept weeping, clinging.

His hand reached up to pet her back, to stroke her braid, but the touch seemed to offer no comfort. So he simply stood there, cooing words of comfort. "There, there. Everything will be all right. Whatever's wrong, we'll work it out. There's nothing we can't fix together."

The creak of a bedroom door made Daisy stiffen in his arms. She finally spoke. "Can we go somewhere? Alone? I need to talk."

He was weary from the morning and probably should have agreed to another time later when he was rested and could offer better advice. But Daisy needed him now, and he wasn't about to deny her.

She wouldn't want to use either of their bedrooms for the talk since that wouldn't seem appropriate. The parlor was too close to where Myrtle worked. The children and Teague were still out in the barn. "How about down by the stream? Do you feel up to it?"

"The question is, do you?" She stepped out of his

embrace and searched his eyes. "I know you didn't convince Doc Thomas of anything this morning. You couldn't have. You're not ready to move out yet even if I wanted you to."

"Let's take a blanket so we can sit by the stream while we talk." He wouldn't remind her that she was treating him like an invalid yet again, so he chose to tread cautiously while she was in such a fragile state of mind.

She grabbed an extra blanket from Ollie's bed then rejoined him. Daisy reached out. "Will you take my hand?"

"Of course." He couldn't help but wonder what more had upset her. He laced his fingers through Daisy's and took the blanket from her in the other.

As they started to head downstairs, Daisy called back over her shoulder, "Sis, tell Myrtle not to hold lunch for me and Bass. Go ahead and eat. Okay?"

"Sure." The creaky door sounded again, footsteps pattered across the floor and the sound of a window opening sent them on their way.

Bass wondered how Daisy had known her sister was listening, but he didn't ask.

The farther he walked with Daisy, the more control she regained of her emotions. By the time they reached the stream and he had spread the blanket to keep the grass from soiling their clothes, they sat down side by side staring off into the distance.

Silence held Daisy now, and he decided she had changed her mind about telling him what led her into his arms a few minutes ago. He didn't push her to talk, wanting her to initiate the answer. Instead, he looked around to see if any verbena grew nearby. If ever a woman needed flowers, she might appreciate them now.

"As you've probably already guessed, Thaddeus is Knox's son. Now Abigail has asked me to raise him." Daisy's voice quivered with the abrupt announcement. "And there's more."

He didn't say anything, but Bass was surprised that Miss Rutcliffe wanted to give up her son. He'd half expected she came to seek money or part of Knox's holdings for the boy. That seemed the most logical reason for her to travel this far. Maybe it was best to hear the rest before he offered any advice.

His impulse proved wise. Words started to flow from Daisy as she told him all that had been said between her and Knox's consort.

Abigail was dying. Thaddeus would have no real home. Not even Knox's last name.

Bass let those facts sink in as he realized Daisy was mired in a dilemma not of her own making. Was there anything he could do to help her? Would she even let him? Yet she had come to him on her own.

Surely there was a practical way to resolve this and he told her so. "Thaddeus is Ollie's brother. His mother won't live much longer apparently. The boy has no one else willing to raise him but you or possibly his uncles. I don't believe she would leave him in anyone's hands but yours. You do have plenty of room here for him."

Bass listed the last, most important, consideration. "You're too good-hearted to send him to an orphanage, and I think that leaves you only one choice."

The possibility he'd been mulling stirred in his thoughts again, although he took his personal reasons out of the equation before offering it to her. "If you'll allow me to help, I can buffer the added burden of his education and expenses. That way, you don't carry the brunt of adding him to your family. If we look at this with open hearts, we'll be of real help to the boy."

Daisy frowned at him. "You've been around Ollie too much and sound like he's some list you've checked off to fill. Thaddeus needs someone who's going to be able to love him like a true son. Not just take him in. You, of all people, know the kind of need he'll really have. I've just met him. I don't know if I'm capable of giving him that kind of affection. Especially now, when she leaves him and he needs it most."

Daisy had hit on Bass's personal reason for offering this solution. He *could* give the boy the very thing he and Petula had needed. The very thing he wanted his parents to have offered them. Even if it took all the rest of his life. God was giving him a chance to give another soul what he'd wanted and that gave Bass purpose. He would set aside his own plans and would do this for Thaddeus or die trying.

"I believe you can, Daisy. I believe we both can and I want to give the boy his due. None of this was his doing." The dilemma was not only Daisy's now but his own. How could he make her see that the answer would come from daring to love enough?

"Marry me," he challenged, "and both he and Ollie will have a home with two parents who'll love them."

Chapter Sixteen

"I want the best for you, no matter how you feel I've wronged you." Bass ran his hand along her arm, needing to reassure her. "I've been trying my best to show you that I'm an answer for you and whatever trouble comes your way. Give me a chance to learn to be kind and caring enough. I need that as much as you need to rely on me."

Daisy's mind shouted with joy at the logic of his proposal, but her heart resisted knowing that she would be settling yet again for a marriage without love. Could she be happy doing what was best for everyone else but herself?

His thumb lifted to her cheek and wiped away the stain of teardrops that lingered there. "Moments ago, you trusted me with your deepest feelings. Trusted me to give you good advice. I'll spend the rest of my life becoming your best friend, Daisy, and make it enough for me. I'm willing to give you forever to forgive and forget my wrongs. Let me take care of you and the children. I promise I'll never make you sorry you counted on me. Say you'll marry me. Under whatever terms you want. For whatever reason you choose. I won't disappoint you, ever."

She started backing away, shaking her head. "I need time to think. To decide what's best for all of us."

Bass's hand slowly dropped to his side. "How will you do that?"

"Run. Run like the wind." She began to pace back and forth.

"Run?" What kind of plan was that? Frustration and, if he gave it rein, disappointment boiled up inside *him*. He'd offered nothing but the best of himself, hadn't he? He pushed away the twinge of hurt that enveloped him and realized he'd allowed her in closer than he'd meant to. "At least give my offer some thought, will you?"

"That's what I plan to do," she said. "Think about the right way to go from here. I do a lot of that when I run, and I make my best decisions that way. My mind goes into a special place while I'm racing. Clear answers come and help me leave behind the troubles that chase me. I'll know better what to do after tomorrow."

"Will Miss Rutcliffe wait for an answer?" He would have to leave if Daisy rejected his proposal and he had no chance of giving her and the two children what they deserved. He would be too hurt to stay and watch them all struggle. If he did leave there were needs to be taken care of before going. Repairing the squeaking doors here and paying for the reconstruction of Sam Cardwell's bank. Informing his sister of Teague's intentions and then making arrangements for their impending marriage.

"I know the urgency, but she'll just have to wait," Daisy said.

Her answer stirred Bass from his thoughts. Her insistence echoed like a death knell being pounded into his plans to do right by them.

"As will you," she said, "but I promise I'll at least

consider what you've offered and do my best to give you an answer after the race."

"I've got some things to do in town tomorrow," he announced abruptly, starting to go inside. "Save me a seat in the morning. I'll be catching a ride with you."

"Did Doc Thomas release you? Do you have to go in?" she called after him.

Bass halted and faced her. "I intend to be there directly after your race and possibly no longer."

He saw the hurt in her eyes and took an ounce of hope with him. Daisy cared. But did she care enough to accept his proposal?

Daisy barely slept through the night. The ride to town had been difficult with everyone except Bass so full of gaiety and anticipation concerning the races. Teague and Petula seemed companionable today, and she wondered if Bass had told his sister of Teague's plans for them. Ollie was at least talking to Thaddeus, which seemed a good sign. Maybe the two would get to know each other quickly.

Fortunately, Abigail stayed behind with Myrtle and begged off from attending the activities.

Bass just sat there saying nothing and she noticed he had brought his baggage, but not Petula's, with him. Was he seriously considering leaving if she refused his proposal? Was she ready for him to go?

Though Daisy had done her best to make light of all the worries on her mind, she'd been unable to convince Snow that nothing was wrong that she wasn't already aware of. Snow offered her opinion and that only blurred the solution even further.

Yawning, Daisy pulled up to the mercantile, where the races were to begin, and set the brake. She turned around on the seat. "Okay, everybody out. Ollie, you and Thaddeus stick with me. Petula, will you mind helping Snow with the children during the race? They can't run with me, of course. And I'd like her to be able to enjoy her first day in town."

"You'll do that for her, won't you, Pet?" Teague answered for her. "It'll make it easier for me to watch you four. I figure if they try to make a play it will come during the race when everyone's distracted."

"I don't mind helping." Petula offered Teague a smile.

The Ranger pushed back his hat. "You sure it's wise to do this run, Daisy? Could be plenty of places for ambush along the trail."

As she watched Bass climb out of the wagon and help Snow down, Daisy nodded. "I know, but I've got to, Teague. Haven't had much time for sewing these past few days. So I'll not make much on shoe sales and I need the money. Plus, if I don't make the top five, I might not earn enough points for the finals. I can't let those bank scavengers ruin my chances. I won't let them."

"Parker? How about you? Where you headed?"

Bass motioned in another direction after he settled Snow on her feet. "To see if the banker's still at Doc's. I've got some business to talk over with him."

He helped Petula down, as well.

"Let's set a meet-back-here time for everybody." The Ranger's gaze looked as if it was already sweeping the gathering crowd along the sidewalks.

"The race starts at twelve-thirty." Daisy pointed to the town clock that formed part of the height of a water tower behind the livery. "So how about no later than fifteen after? If nothing happens during the race we'll have something to eat before we head home. I told Myrtle not to make anything for us until supper."

"Then I'm off. Y'all keep watch for trouble." Teague tipped his hat to Petula then commanded his dun down the street.

When Daisy started to get down from the wagon, Bass was waiting to help her. She accepted his hand but, due to his injuries, wouldn't let him grab her waist to set her down.

His blue eyes studied hers. "I hope you win, Daisy. You deserve some victories."

He grabbed his baggage from the wagonbed and walked away.

Daisy watched him go, feeling as if it might be the last time she'd ever see him. Her heart sank. If he left, could she survive losing their blossoming friendship? No matter what her decision would be today, not having him around was the last thing she really wanted.

She wished she hadn't confided in him yesterday, but one look at Bass had compelled her to throw herself into his arms, take comfort and seek his advice. That need for him had surprised her more than any of the revelations Abigail made.

Daisy had to get her mind off Bass or she'd never be able to concentrate during the race or make the decision that must be made without taking his proposal into account. She had to know whatever she chose to do about Thaddeus would be the same even if Bass hadn't offered marriage as a solution.

"All right, everybody, what would you like to do first?" She checked the time once more. "I've got about thirty minutes before I must start warming up. Do we shop awhile or would you prefer if we get something to drink at the café or—"

"Ice cream. Let's get some ice cream!" Ollie jumped down and raced ahead of them. "Come on, Thaddie-Wumpus. I can beat ya there!"

Knox's lookalike jumped down and raced after her. "No fair, I don't know where I'm goin'."

"I think I'll do some quick shopping. Breakfast will last me 'til later." Snow gently nudged Daisy. "You best hightail it after those kids. Petula, it's your choice, but I say we take advantage of some time getting to know one another. I'm sure we'll be too busy with the children later to get much else done. You with me?"

Petula agreed to stay and shop.

"We'll meet you out front here when you're ready for us to watch the kids." Snow nudged Daisy again.

"Thanks," Daisy said, taking off after her daughter and possible new son.

She hurried to the café, fighting off a yawn. Between not sleeping and now chasing the children, she would not be at her best when the race started. But she needed to stay with Ollie and make sure she remained safe.

Stepping inside the small dining establishment connected to the only hotel in town, Daisy spotted the children already taking a seat despite the crowded room. To her dismay, Ollie had joined her uncles at their table.

"Come on in, Daisy." Maddox waved her over, looking as if he'd been in some kind of scuffle. Strands of hair escaped from the leather rawhide he'd tied it back with. Red marks darkened his cheeks and a dirty footprint stained the middle of his buckskinned chest, making her wonder if he'd been kicked there. If he looked this bad how must the man on the opposite end of his fists have fared?

A glance at his younger brothers' disheveled states

hinted that Maddox hadn't fought alone. Hopefully, the fight had not been among the brothers.

She joined them at the table.

"We all came to see how you'll do this morning, but we figured we'd grab some breakfast first. Had a little difference of opinion with a redheaded fella and his partners. Don't have to worry none about 'em now, do we, brothers?" Maddox shared a grin with Grissom and Jonas. "Won't be winking and calling us names no more, I guarantee it."

Redheaded? Winking? A shudder ran down Daisy's spine. Had the Trumbos met up with the men who'd robbed Sam's bank? Daisy needed to ask where Maddox had left them. "Did you turn them in to the sheriff?"

"Naw, we handle our own skirmishes. If he put someone in jail every time I got aggravated he'd have to build a couple of stockades. We just sent the fellas runnin' for high cotton. Figure you won't see 'em around here for a few days. They're hurtin' some now. Won't you go ahead and sit down and rest awhile before your race."

The proprietor of the diner always gave the Trumbo men the largest of the red checkered tables because of their commanding size, so all she had to do was see if another chair was available. The waitress set a bench down for Ollie and Thaddeus to share opposite Grissom and Jonas.

Grissom stood and offered his seat. "I was just finishing, Daisy. You can have my chair." He elbowed Jonas. "You 'bout done, brother?"

Jonas looked up from his meal, then stuffed his mouth with three more bites of eggs before he stood. "I guess. Oh, I mean sure. Good to see ya, Daisy." He leaned across and yanked one of Ollie's braids, not taking the time to wipe off the grease from his hands. "You, too, Little Britches."

She smacked his hand. "Wipe your hands first, Uncle Jonas. Butler'll try to eat my hair when I get home."

"You don't need to rush off. I won't be here long." Daisy waved for the waitress to come back. "The children just wanted some ice cream."

"Yeah, two scoops," Ollie demanded. "Two for me and two for him."

Daisy shook her head. "One for each of you. You just had breakfast."

Maddox rubbed his buckskinned belly. "Aww, she's a growin' gal, Daisy darlin'. I'll pay for her and her little pal there, too. Let 'em both have what they want."

Thaddeus scooted away from Ollie on the bench. "I'm not her pal. I'm her brother. Mama says so."

It seemed the whole room suddenly got quiet and everybody leaned in as if buffeted by a fierce wind.

"Her brother?" Maddox roared, pounding his fist on the table, setting the dishes to jangling. "How is that so?"

"Open your eyes and take a good look." Grissom walked over and stood behind Thaddeus, putting his hands on the boy's shoulders. "Spittin' image of Knox, if you ask me."

Daisy sank into the chair Grissom left behind.

"I don't think so." Jonas bent down to stare the boy in the face. "But then I don't remember much about Knox when he was that little."

"He's got Grandpa's crooked finger," Grissom noted, "and I'm sure if we stripped off his shoes, his little toe is crooked, too."

"Is that a fact, boy?" Maddox demanded.

"Yeah." Thaddeus lifted his chin and shirked his shoulders away from Grissom. "What of it?"

Maddox's gray eyes lit with something Daisy feared might be pride.

"Did'ja hear that?" Maddox roared. "He's a Trumbo, all right. What's your name, boy, and where have you been?"

Maddox and Knox had discussed the name Knox planned to give his first son. Thaddeus was their grandfather's given name.

"Please, let's not discuss this here, shall we?" All the staring eyes made Daisy want to melt into a puddle of nothingness in her chair. "I'll tell you where he's been after the races if you'll come to the house, where we can speak alone as a family."

Please, Lord. Let the running work. Help me make a quick decision.

If she chose to give Thaddeus and Ollie the security of both a mother and a father then may Heaven help her choose the right man.

Maddox, his true uncle.

Or Bass, the man she knew could give a little boy what he himself had never known in his own life.

Chapter Seventeen

"Well, I guess that just about does it." Sam Cardwell extended his hand to Bass. "I can have papers ready for your signature by Friday so you're not having to deal with this at the last minute before you leave town. You sure you want to do this? She's been pretty stubborn about taking money for the memorial. I don't imagine she's going to be too happy about a trust fund in Ollie's name."

Bass shook the banker's hand and eyed him one more time to make certain he looked stable enough to contend with the crowd outside Doc's office. "Ollie can decide for herself when she turns eighteen, if her mother elects not to use any of it for her before then. Make sure you let Daisy know she's also in charge of the other trust I set up for Thaddeus Rutcliffe."

"Fortunate young man," Sam said. "Whoever he is."

"Thanks for letting me store my bag here." Bass would let Daisy disclose Thad's relationship to her. "I'll pick it up after the race."

He hadn't planned on having to stay longer if Daisy rejected his proposal. Now he'd have to buy and pitch a tent somewhere until Friday if she declined.

"Doc won't mind. He's used to always having somebody's belongings in his parlor." Sam wore a patch over the eye he'd almost lost, and he'd completely shaven to make himself look better from his bullet-creased whiskers. A sling protected his injured arm and shoulder.

Holding open the door that led out to the street, Bass squinted, adjusting to the bright glare of the Texas sun. "Looks like a good day to race. Plenty of sunshine."

"Don't lock the door. Doc wants it so he doesn't have to mess with keys if he has to come back for any reason. He took his medicine bag and plans to roam the crowd since a lot of young'uns will test their oats while their parents are preoccupied with the festivities."

"Smart man." Bass closed the door and took up a gait that matched the banker's. "Ollie will most likely be one of them for sure. Especially with Daisy busy running."

"You're right about that. Pickens delivered the licorice to me yesterday. I need to catch up with the little scamp and thank her."

"She seems genuinely sorry about causing the ruckus, and I regret you got hurt, too. I want you to take what you need from my funds to pay for the repairs and whatever you owe Doc Thomas."

"I can't accept them, but I'll see that Doc's paid."

"I insist." Bass's hands rubbed together as the two men started weaving through the meandering crowd. "I allowed my fists to start the fight. They caused your business to have to shut down this week and ended up getting both of us hurt. I can't leave knowing that I haven't compensated you in some way."

"You saved our lives. It could have been a lot worse, Parker. Let's just call everything even and come out of it friends."

Bass would see that the reconstruction of the bank

was immediate and of no cost to Sam. From the construction Maddox and his brothers had done on Knox's home they seemed the likely choice to rebuild the bank. He would make the price plenty beneficial to them to take on the job.

As he and Sam turned the corner, the crowd suddenly halted and pooled in the area directly out front of the mercantile. A banner had been strung from the top of the storefront to the other side of the street to the second story of the Twisted Spur Saloon.

Sporting two lines, it read Welcome High Plains Footracers. Catch the Wind and Don't Stub Your Toes.

Red, white and blue half-moon-shaped garlands hung under eaves jutting out from the businesses that formed the runners' raceway leading out of town. Must be those saved from the Fourth of July celebrations.

He searched for sight of Daisy and Ollie in the crowd, thankful Snow's unusual hair color would make it easier to locate them. But it was Maddox's towering height that helped him draw a bead on them.

Maddox had set up position near the saloon. Ollie balanced on his right shoulder and, surprisingly, Thaddeus rode piggyback on Grissom's shoulders. Looked as though the boy had made fast friends. Jonas stood next to Snow and Petula beside him. At the corner of the Twisted Spur, Teague kept watch over all, reining his dun in the alleyway between the saloon and another building.

"I'm headed this way." Bass motioned Sam toward his fellow passengers. "You want to join us?"

"I'll head back to the mercantile in case someone needs to see me about banking." He chuckled. "Standing by the saloon can get dangerous. So for the sake of self-preservation, I'll watch the race from a safer viewpoint."

Bass encouraged him to change his mind. "It looks like Daisy's lined up closer to her in-laws. You'll see her better there."

Daisy looked more beautiful than Bass had ever seen her. All focused and determined. So alive doing what she loved. He was glad he'd been given an opportunity to watch her race and get to see her doing something she enjoyed. What a difference she'd make in his life if she would grace him with a yes today. She would allow him to do something he knew he would find worthwhile— helping her and the children.

"Guess I could watch her start," Sam said, "but I prefer to wait for her to cross under the banner on her way back. Folks stand out of the roadway so the runners can get by. It's a better view."

"Why don't you go ahead then and get the spot you planned. Think I'll take your advice and grab the others. Besides, Ollie wants to give you that apology I told you about." Bass parted ways and hurried toward the saloon.

He didn't get far before a loud voice hollered.

"Runners! On your marks."

As he moved, Bass focused on Daisy's tall form amid the competitors, not surprised that male participants far outnumbered the female.

"Get set!"

Daisy's head and shoulders dipped. A glimpse revealed her knees and elbows now locked into position.

The sound of the starting gun rent the air. The crowd shouted the race into action with a mighty Texas yell, "Yee-haw!"

Bass wove and sliced through the excited watchers to reach Maddox and the others. Ollie bounced on her uncle's shoulder, shouting encouragement. "Go, Mama, go! You can beat 'em. I know ya can!"

"Trip 'em up, Daiz," Maddox's booming voice echoed over those nearby. "Give 'em what for. Hitch up that hem and run like wildfire!"

Snow swatted him with her parasol, obviously upset with Maddox's word choices. Bass admired her gumption.

Grissom and Jonas laughed. She swung around to swat them, but both took the better side of valor and dodged.

"Let me take Ollie a minute." Bass hurried to grab her from her perch, wanting to get the child as far away from the saloon's batwing doors as possible. Already men were rushing in, shifting the crowd's position on the sidewalk. Maddox stepped aside a few times then elected to elbow a couple he clearly didn't appreciate trying to adjust his space.

His face flushed with temper the more he got jostled.

Trouble loomed a few more elbows away.

Bass knew Teague had his eyes set on keeping Petula safe so he left her in the Ranger's good care. Snow looked as if she could handle even the roughest of them. If they got too close, she kept poking the offenders with the tip end of her parasol.

Once Bass could get Ollie to Sam, he'd come back for Thad.

Bass stripped Ollie from Maddox's shoulders and carefully set her on his own so she wouldn't miss out on watching her mother run. It took a little effort, but as long as she didn't bounce, he thought he could hold her weight long enough to make it across the roadway.

"I'm taking her out of this stampede," he told Maddox. "Sam wants to talk to her."

Maddox allowed the transfer only to grab Thaddeus from Grissom and give the boy Ollie's former perch.

Relief washed over Bass. The giant would kill a man before letting his niece or nephew get hurt.

Trying to reach the banker was like swimming upstream. "When did your uncles meet Thaddeus?" Bass shouted, dodging and weaving to keep Ollie seated.

She leaned down to explain and he could barely hear her from all the noise the crowd made.

"Does he know anything about who the boy is?"

"Thaddie-Wumpus told him he was my brother." Ollie almost lost her balance and grabbed Bass by the throat to hang on.

Bass's hands jerked from her ankles to capture her fingers, so her grip would ease and he could breathe. He coughed several times then finally assured her, "That's b-better. You safe, honey?"

"Mama's out in front!" Ollie screamed, bouncing with excitement.

He barely kept from shouting in pain.

"Oh, sorry." In an instant, she stopped bouncing. "Mama's gettin' so little I ain't gonna see her in a minute. She's faster'n anybody, ain't she, Bass? The best runner in the whole wide world of Texas!"

"She sure is. Not only in Texas, but anywhere else I've been."

"Ahh, that's just 'cause you like her a whole bunch."

"Do I?" Maybe he did and it showed. Would he have offered marriage to anyone else under the circumstances? Was there more than the need to fulfill his duty driving his actions? Mulling the disappointment and the twinge of hurt he'd felt at having to wait for an answer, he wasn't quite sure anymore of all the reasons he offered marriage.

They finally reached Sam.

Ollie asked to be set down then wiggled one forefinger and told the banker to bend down. "Oooh." She touched his eye patch. "'Zat hurt?"

Not anymore, Bass thought even though he knew her question was for Sam.

"A bit, but the patch makes me look handsome, don't you think?"

Ollie shook her head. "Not 'zactly, but ya look better than ya did."

"How about you tell him the *nice* thing you wanted to say to him?" Bass suggested, motioning them farther away from the stream of movement and closer to the store's door.

"Oh, yeah. I'm sorry ya got hurt 'cause of me. I didn't mean them hostages to steal all your money and shoot ya up so bad. Maybe ya ought'a get Uncle Mad to learn you how to shoot some better 'fore I mess up again."

Ollie looked past him and pointed to the counter filled with candy jars. "I had Mr. Pickens send ya two whole pieces of licorice. Sure hope he didn't lick 'em 'fore ya got 'em."

"He didn't, Little Pistol, and I just wanted to say thank you for sending the candy my way. They were mighty good. My favorite, matter of fact."

"Okay, I'm done now." She dismissed him, but her eyes suddenly rolled upward into her lashes. "Oh, yeah, I forgot." Ollie gave a reluctant curtsy and then looked at Bass. "Be sure you tell Mama I did this."

Bass shared a grin with the banker. "I will. Sam, can I leave her with you a minute while I go grab the ladies and the little boy that's with them?"

"Thaddie-Wumpus," Ollie's voice echoed with disapproval.

Sam offered Ollie his hand. "I can't carry you like Bass did. My shoulder's still pretty sore, but if you'll grab my hand, I think we'll manage just fine. We'll see if there's any licorice left while he's gone. Is that boy Daisy's nephew? I thought only her sisters were due in."

"I don't need no help." Ollie wouldn't take his hand. "Only Aunt Snow came. Thaddie-Wumpus is my brother."

Sam stared at Bass for verification. "Her brother?"

Once again Bass didn't say anything, assuming that was Daisy's tale to tell. "Long story. I'm sure Daisy will catch you up on it when she has some time. Speaking of which, how long will it be before we need to watch for the dash to the finish line?"

"The whole race takes about fifteen or so minutes. Three miles." Sam took another glance at those waiting across the way. "Don't let the Trumbos lure you inside the Twisted Spur."

"I'll be right back with the others. Just save me a place."

As he headed back, Bass hoped there would be a spot for him alongside Daisy here. With Ollie, as well. Even with all the other colorful characters who'd made his life feel so full since arriving in town. All seemed pieces that completed the whole sense of crossing over some line he'd drawn for himself.

Unable to maintain the lead, Daisy had fallen back to third place. Two men raced ahead of her. Another woman she didn't know followed close behind. A proud moment she decided for the Pedestriennes, the association of women runners who had formed a running league making a name for itself across the country. At least two, or if they were blessed three, might rank high in this particular race.

Winded, she decided to set a medium pace until the leaders approached the halfway turning point. Once the runners hit the homestretch, she would resume her best speed and push to finish well.

The woman passed her.

Daisy kept her pace steady, resisting the urge to catch up and challenge her competitor's will. Not yet. Timing was the key in a three-mile race. *I'm in the top four*, Daisy told herself. *No lower than five, five, five, five*, her steps echoed the warning in case her strategy failed.

No heavy breathing. No rapid footfalls behind her. Now was the time to take advantage of maintaining the pace she'd set for resting.

The sound of her footsteps kept a steady rhythm. Abigail. Bass. Maddox. Yes. Yes. No. Abigail. Bass.

Decisions she'd struggled with that had kept her from sleeping soon crept in to take on a rhythm of reasoning at her temples.

Daisy pondered Abigail's arrival, all that she revealed, the ring she wore and the claim she made that Knox truly loved her. Thaddeus's presence was more than enough evidence that the relationship Abigail and Knox shared was as strong as the one he'd shared with *her*.

The fact that he'd written the note to protect his son meant he wanted her to learn the importance Abigail served in his life since he'd left the note in the woman's possession.

All that kept running through Daisy's mind was that he had cared deeply for Thaddeus's mother, maybe even more than he ever had her. As much as a man like Knox could for anyone and know his own heart.

Had he been searching for true love when he found Abigail? Could Daisy accept that possibility and forgive Knox his trespasses?

She wanted to. She didn't want to live her life consumed with hurt and anger. She wanted to find a way to go on and turn the other cheek. Bury the past and its betrayal.

Had his solemn marriage vow *'til death do us part* kept Knox married to her when all he wanted was to pledge his true heart to another?

Daisy tried to find the good in herself. To know when she was wrong about something. To make sure she could still recognize it and work with it to make her life better. Did she still have that within her?

Thad's image rose in her mind.

The boy was like the wind rushing past her face while she ran. Things happened over time usually and a person could study and make a well-thought-out decision. But the really big experiences in life often happened in an instant and pointed to the moment when it changed forever because you trusted your heart, not your logic, to make the right choice.

Trust was the issue. It could also be the answer. Did she trust her own heart to be wise?

Could she grow to love Thaddeus as her son with or without the help of Maddox or Bass or any man for that matter? Did she want to give Knox's son—Ollie's brother—a better chance in life?

Yes. For all the practical reasons first. She had plenty of room. They always prepared too much food. God never failed to provide her needs and a way to get them. Life got hard sometimes, but she'd faced every storm. Even found strength in surviving them.

This would give Ollie a sibling. She would get to know her father in a way Daisy had never considered. Thaddeus seemed to be similar to his daddy at that age and, hopefully, with Ollie and her help, he would grow up to follow a better path than his father had taken. How could that ever prove a mistake? It would only add to Ollie's experiences. That way, each child would have one another when the time came that they lost her someday.

Daisy decided to talk to Abigail and find out if Thad even knew his mother's plans to leave him in her care. What objections might he have to the possibility? Only then could she know for sure how to answer Abigail. Even though Daisy's heart had pretty much made its decision already.

The halfway mark loomed a few yards ahead. A long-dead trunk of a lightning-struck tree, scarred and petrified, stood sentinel to the ravaging storms of the Texas sky. Beneath it, a patch of spring green grappled among its tangled roots.

Daisy sped up, her footfalls keeping time with her heartbeat. She passed her female competitor.

Third.

Her mind filled with the image of Knox again. The shared knowledge of youth and friendship sometimes could not bring true love. They'd been young, ready to start the adventure of life, eager to learn how they could find their purpose in the world. They'd made plenty of mistakes, but they'd grown from them.

Forgiveness rushed through her, filling Daisy with a sense of joy and understanding. Forgiveness that neither she nor Knox should blame the other for what they were or were not to each other. Their path had taken them in different directions and she had to trust whatever caused that parting would prove God's good purpose.

Freedom from the past lifted from her a burden that had weighed down her body and soul for far too long. The strategy to save her stamina now proved its worth. Daisy's feet took wing.

She passed the sentinel and noted that, though

scarred and almost stone, it had dared to replenish its life by dropping seeds.

Daisy passed the man who'd won last Sunday. She was in second and the leader only a stretch ahead of her.

On she raced, one decision blooming perfectly clear. She could never agree to be Maddox's wife. The promise of a new life, the seeds of courage strong enough to challenge the gnarled roots of her past, had been planted with Bass. He'd not promised love, but he had promised his best. Something Knox had never done.

Daisy knew the moment she'd told him to wait for her answer that she was seriously considering accepting his proposal. She thought of him as more than a friend now. Someone she could trust. Someone who would not betray that trust.

Bass had become the light to point the way out of her darkness, the courage to withstand any hurt that might touch her life now.

Was what she had begun to feel for him enough to believe they could provide a happy family for each other and the children? Could friendship and respect for each other ever overcome the need to know true love? Or would she end up twice burned?

She must let Bass know that she was willing to wait for them to learn more of one another's ways. That, with time, she thought she could actually accept his hand in marriage. For now, she would concentrate on getting to know Thaddeus and prove to the boy she sincerely had enough love within her to take him in as her son and be glad of it.

Someone fired a gun, signaling the leader was in sight of town. Shedding the past behind her and racing toward what she prayed would be a bright future, Daisy focused on the path to winning.

Chapter Eighteen

Bass wished Maddox had gone into the saloon as the banker predicted he would. Instead, Maddox followed Bass and the ladies to the other side of the street, determined to hang on to Knox's lookalike.

He wasn't certain how much the giant-sized Trumbo knew about the boy, but Maddox clearly staked an early claim. Was he waiting until Daisy finished her race to learn more?

Just as he was, but for different reasons.

"Let that boy go play." Snow poked Maddox with her parasol. "Let him have a little fun. We're all out here watching him and Ollie like hawks. You act as if he's going to disappear." She continued to fuss until Maddox finally set Thaddeus down.

Thaddeus took off as if he had red ants in his shoes, joining a group of boys closer to the corner. Bass thought Ollie might follow her brother, but she elected to stay with him.

"Quit pokin' me with that shade stick, woman, or it's gonna end up in the trough." Maddox batted away the parasol.

Snow looked about as afraid of him as a longhorn

nose to nose with a horned toad. Bass tried to keep one eye trained on Thad, another on Petula in the mercantile, Ollie at her aunt's side and his curiosity listening to the quarrel. How did Daisy keep up with everybody?

Their argument continued, making Bass aware that these two people had some sort of long-standing feud between them. They obviously didn't like one another.

"I take it you two have met," he interrupted, wondering if he should referee the feud.

"Our families were neighbors back in Florida until they moved out here to...what did you call it?" Snow's cupid bow of a lip curled in derision. "'Texify' themselves. Maddox thought himself in love with me way back when and wanted me to wag after him like a lovestruck puppy."

"You wish," Maddox snarled. "We wanted our neighbors safe from the war, that's what. It's why Knox up and married Daisy. Thought himself one of them white knight fellas, rescuing his damsel—you know those wimmen what needs savin'. Might get Snow out of the sun awhile, Parker. She's hallu... You know, her gun sight's off a few yards."

The parasol darted toward Maddox again and this time he grabbed it, snapped the offending weapon over one thigh and tossed it over everybody's head to land in the horse trough. "There. Don't say I didn't warn you. Could have been your neck if I was in the mind to be mean."

"She ain't scared, Uncle Mad." Ollie tugged on his buckskinned leg, studying her uncle and aunt closely. "Not one bit."

Snow glanced at the children, then her hazel eyes swept to Bass in apology. "Sorry. How about I go inside for a while and cool off like Mr. Trumbo...*suggested.*

I'll join you and the kids as soon as I pick up a few birthday presents."

Birthday? Bass hadn't told anybody his birthday was tomorrow. Had Petula confided the fact to Snow and Daisy? Birthdays were such a sore spot with him; he preferred to forget them. "Please don't go to any trouble."

"Buy lots and lots, Aunt Snow." Ollie jumped high and drew an imaginary line across Maddox's belly. "A pile this big."

"Of course I will. It isn't every day somebody turns a whole eight years old."

Snow meant to celebrate Ollie's birthday, not his. Bass realized how his reaction must have sounded to Ollie. "Would you choose a couple of gifts for me to give her? Just tell Mr. Jenkins to put them on my account."

"Can I go with her and watch?"

"No." Bass denied Ollie her request for reasons too deep he might never share them with her. "Birthday presents should be surprises. That way, you get to have that happy anticipation wondering what they could possibly be."

"Aunt-tizzie-patient? Does that mean waitin'?" Ollie frowned.

Bass laughed, grateful she lightened the darkness where his thoughts had headed. "Yes, you have to wait sometimes to be happy."

"I'm sure glad my birthday's only one more day, then."

He and Ollie shared the date. An exciting prospect for future reference. He'd never forget one of her birthdays and, for that, Bass was grateful. He could always make sure her presents arrived in time even if he didn't stay in High Plains.

Bass asked Snow to wait a second longer. "Please tell the merchant that Daisy will pick up my gifts in case I'm unable to."

Snow's brows knitted in puzzlement, but she nodded. "Will do." She glared at Maddox one last time. "By the way, Trumbo, should I tell them why I'm not scared of your big, bad self?"

"Just get your sassy petticoat in there and go shop." Maddox pointed the way. "Leave me alone."

Her snort of laughter echoed as she bid them all farewell, causing curious onlookers to turn their way.

"Hey, look who's ahead!" somebody shouted, causing everyone to refocus on the race.

"It's Daisy Trumbo," another person relayed the leader's identity.

"Daisy, Daisy, Daisy," the crowd chanted.

Ollie started to move through the horde, but Bass managed to grab her and pull her back. "Stay here, Little Britches. She'll cross the finish line under that banner. Watch her win here, not up the road."

Thaddeus left the crowd of boys and ran toward Ollie.

"It's your mama," he shouted. "She's gonna win!"

"Run, Mama, run!" Ollie's shout got lost among the other cheers.

"Go, love, go," Bass couldn't help himself, hollering encouragement. It dawned on him what he'd called her right about the time Maddox's fist landed on his lip, bursting it open.

"Don't be calling my intended 'love,'" Maddox bellowed. "'Least not until after she turns me down for sure. It ain't respectful."

Ollie kicked her uncle's shin and punched Maddox's stomach. "Don'tcha be hittin' my future daddy's face."

"Fight!" a man in the crowd yelled.

Men poured out of the Twisted Spur and headed for the fray. Two of them Grissom and Jonas.

"Why are you so upset?" Bass asked. "You said you didn't really want to marry her."

"Yeah, but nobody else knows that yet," Maddox complained. "They'll expect me to slug ya. Let's work off some steam."

This is going to hurt, Bass realized before he could completely duck Maddox's next swing.

The massive fist grazed Bass's head and he felt the impact clear to his toes.

A shot rang out. Two. The crowd instantly froze in place.

Bass dived, grabbing Ollie and Thaddeus at the same time, covering them with his body.

When he turned to see Snow and Petula heading to check on what had happened, he shouted a warning. "Stay inside! Don't come out here."

Where was Teague? He'd disappeared from the alley.

Bass needed to know if the shots were meant merely to stop the fight.

"Oh no." Disbelief echoed in Maddox's voice as he tapped Bass on the shoulder and offered a hand to help him stand, the fight long forgotten. "Daisy's down. Get up."

"Mama!" Ollie wiggled beneath Bass. "Is Mama hurt?"

"Stay right here. I'll go see." Bass accepted Maddox's help and rose, letting the children up. His head whirled but he did his best to focus.

Anger and fear battled within him. Who would dare hurt Daisy, the woman he…? The woman he what? Bass couldn't calm his thoughts enough to find an answer to the question. Was it the robbers trying to rid themselves of a witness? She'd made herself a clear target.

Lord help me. If I get my hands on them...

The children. Get the children safe first. Bass pushed each inside the mercantile. People all around them suddenly bolted, men searching for weapons, women grabbing loved ones and scurrying to safety indoors. Curiosity seekers rushed toward the runners. "Go in with Snow and Petula and don't leave there, whatever you do," Bass ordered. "Grissom, Jonas, stay with them so you'll all be in one place and I know they're safe. Maddox, staying or going?"

"Going."

"Let's move." Though Bass ordered him into action, he couldn't keep up with Maddox's longer stretch of legs. His head was finally clearing from the punch and he managed to be only a minute behind Trumbo. Other people who'd chosen to spot the race leaders already surrounded Daisy, checking her condition.

Bass's heart beat so fast from running, he was sure everybody around him could hear it thumping. He bent beside her and gripped her hand, rubbing furious figure eights with his thumb. "Daisy, Daisy honey, open your eyes."

"I warned you about that 'love, honey' business a minute ago." Maddox fanned her face, giving her some air. He elbowed those closest to her and ordered, "Y'all back off a ways."

"Is she shot?" someone speculated.

Bass didn't see any place she was bleeding, but that didn't mean she wasn't.

Her lashes fluttered as if she was trying to regain consciousness. "That's it, Daisy," Bass encouraged.

"Open those pretty eyes for me. You can do it. Come back to me."

Amber eyes blinked open, staring at him but Bass noted not with full comprehension.

"What happened?" she muttered.

Doc Thomas's thin body fought its way through the curious crowd. He pushed up his spectacles on the bridge of his nose as he bent to examine her. "Anybody check to see where she's hurt?"

"Tell us where you're shot," Bass demanded.

"Shot?" Daisy attempted to sit up, allowing Maddox to help her. Her eyelashes blinked rapidly until she focused on the fingers laced through hers.

Bass squeezed her hand gently. Let Maddox do what he would, he refused to let go of her.

"I remember hearing two shots, but I'm not hit anywhere that I can feel."

The boiling anger in Bass's veins lowered to a simmer.

A combined sigh of relief echoed over the gathering. Word passed down the roadway to others waiting to hear how she fared.

"Do you remember anything?" Relieved that there was no immediate danger, Bass hoped to understand what had knocked her out.

Daisy's eyes swept the crowd. "I was racing to town thinking that I might actually win. All of a sudden I saw two men on horseback ride from behind the church. I just assumed they wanted to escort me in. Then each of them raised a rifle and took aim. I saw only one of the guns flash, but I heard two reports. The next thing I knew, dirt and rocks splattered the road and made me dodge. I lost my momentum, stumbled and down I went. I…I don't remember much more until I came to."

She was almost too calm. Bass could sense she wasn't telling all she'd seen. Daisy didn't want to frighten anyone, making light of her own fear. She wanted her storm to end and move away as quickly as possible.

As she attempted to stand, Bass helped her, refusing to let go of her hand in case she wasn't steady.

"Looks like I'm fine except for not winning the race." Daisy shrugged. "I'll have to work harder to earn those points next time."

Maddox grabbed her arm and linked it through his. Bass kept his hand laced in hers. They provided Daisy a two-sided escort forming a barrier to any other shooter. She insisted on crossing the finish line, though running was definitely out of the question.

The official race committee met them at the banner and told Daisy that the runners who'd passed her had conferred and decided they didn't feel justified in taking advantage of her accident. That she had been the clear winner and lost through no fault of her own. Since all the runners agreed, the committee determined that each competitor would receive equal points and the race would be called a draw. A cheer from the crowd went up.

Good-hearted people had won the day.

"Are we done now?" Bass wanted nothing more than to pick up their passengers, grab his baggage from Doc's and head to Daisy's place. His head hurt as though he'd been hit by a boulder. No way could he leave Daisy now. Not with her unsteady. "Let's go home."

The last word echoed with reverence from his lips.

Daisy studied him as they headed inside the store. "I'm ready when you are."

Bass wouldn't step aside even as Maddox tried to

make it impossible for the three of them to fit in the doorway together.

"I have a lot to tell everybody." Daisy dropped her hold on each man, stepping ahead of them to relieve Maddox's stubbornness.

"Well, I'm gonna ride out to the ranch with y'all," Maddox insisted, finally moving aside when Snow approached and hugged Daisy. "I got plenty of questions I want answered."

"Mama!" Ollie threw her arms around Daisy's skirt. "You ain't hurt!"

"You're tough." Thaddeus's compliment echoed in his voice though he stood next to Grissom and refrained from showing any sense of relief.

Petula joined them and hugged Daisy. "The minute Teague saw what happened, he told the Trumbos to make sure we all stayed and don't leave town until he could ride guard for us when we go home. Then he took off at a high gallop."

Bass heard reverence from his sister for the sanctuary Daisy had provided them. Petula had found the place she wanted to belong and the man she hoped to marry. Bass couldn't be happier for her since Teague equally returned her feelings.

"I hope he doesn't take long. I have something to tell him." Daisy's voice lowered. "Something that affects us all."

Their extended family moved in to form a tight-knit circle.

"You know who shot at you, don't you." Bass wasn't asking a question. He'd known all along she held something back.

Daisy nodded. "I didn't want word to spread through the crowd so I saved it until I could tell all of you."

She stared at each face, ending at his. "The shooters are two of the robbers, the redheaded winker and one of the three cowboys who had been working out at the Rafford place before the robbery."

Bass had known he was right to suspect them.

"I think they only meant to scare me, or else they would have just killed me. They had a clear enough shot. It was a warning of some kind, I think. Maybe to see if I'd go running to the sheriff. Which I didn't and I won't. I'll tell Teague if he doesn't already know when he returns, but I want us all on sharp lookout."

Bass found no joy in her confession. He could forgive her reasoning, just as he hoped she would someday forgive him the knowledge of Abigail in Knox's life if she ever learned his omission.

Daisy continued to whisper, "I may ask Bear to let us all stay in the livery rather than head back tonight. I think the robbers will expect us to go home now so it would be safer to wait until morning and give Teague a chance to capture them."

Bass agreed that it was too dangerous to leave and Daisy wanted as few people as possible hearing her plans.

She motioned to him. "If Bear does, you and the children could bed down in the wagon and we women could sleep in the hayloft."

Her gaze went to Maddox. "I don't see any problem with all of you brothers heading back to your place." Her voice lowered. "Nobody's after you three. You weren't witnesses to the robbery."

Maddox shook his head. "We'll muck out a stall if we have to. Won't be the first time we threw down a saddle for a pillow." He tried his best to whisper, but his voice was so resonant, it did little good. "I ain't leavin' ya, Daisy, 'til you're home and safe. You, and Ollie, and the boy."

"Thank you." Daisy exhaled a deep breath.

He glared at Snow. "Her, too, I guess."

He nodded politely at Petula. "No offense, miss, but you got your brother to guard you."

"No offense taken." Petula fanned herself.

Snow glared back. "Thanks a bunch. I know where I stack up in the to-save list."

"If we gotta stay here, 'zat mean I ain't gettin' no birthday cake in the mornin'?" Ollie grumbled.

She didn't seem to care who did and did not hear her as long as she got her point across.

"You know I like to eat it for breakfast, and Myrtie probably already made it and it'll just sit there and get all dried up like a cow patty and—" She had to stop to catch her breath so she could complain more.

"If it does," Petula reassured the child, "then you can have the one I'm cooking for Bass. It's his birthday, too, and I'll make sure it's fresh. I'm sure he won't mind swapping with you."

"I didn't know," Daisy admitted, her face crestfallen. "You should have told me, Bass."

He had no reason to tell her, so he shrugged it off. "Wasn't sure I'd still be here. Don't concern yourself. None of you." His statement targeted his sister and his caretaker.

Then it dawned on him how Daisy might have taken the news. "I just didn't mention it because—" *Give her the truth, so she'll understand.* "I don't celebrate my birthdays."

Hopefully, she would remember what he'd told her at the cemetery and she would forgive him for not wanting to explain his thirteenth birthday. Rather, the lack thereof. His parents had totally forgotten the day and it had shown Bass how deeply he hadn't mattered in the scheme of their priorities.

Yes, he had become a man of twenty-seven, but the boy of thirteen still craved to understand why he hadn't known their love.

"You mean, you never had a birthday cake?" Ollie's voice sounded full of disbelief. "No presents?"

"Oh, I've had lots of them." And he had. Gifts bought and chosen by someone hired by his father. Bass suddenly realized he'd done the very same thing today via Snow. No, he didn't hire her, but she'd substituted for him. He'd never make that mistake again concerning Ollie.

Bass didn't want pity, and he couldn't bear to have Ollie fretting about him. "Grown-ups have got to wait sometimes, honey, like I told you before. My special happy birthday will come along someday."

Thaddeus looked with such longing at all the aisles, Bass knew the boy was envious of Ollie's good fortune.

Ollie's forefinger wagged at Bass silently asking him to move closer. "Can you bend down?"

He did.

Ollie threw her arms around him and squeezed him tightly. "I'm gonna give you my happy birthday tomorrow, Bass. And you can have both of the cakes, too. 'Cept for one bitty, tiny piece, okay?"

Bass returned her squeeze gently and held on for a long time to the sincerest act of love he'd ever received, making him unable to speak.

Chapter Nineteen

The soft amber glow from the lantern hanging on the livery wall blended with the gentle hum of a mouth harp as one of the men lulled everyone to sleep. Daisy would have succumbed to the lullaby, but the sound of his music drew her to discover whose hands and breath conveyed such soulful majesty.

After climbing down from the hayloft, she grabbed the lantern and found Bass steps away from her wagon pulled inside the livery to keep their presence in town undisclosed. For a while she stood there just watching him, not knowing whether to disturb him or let him know she was there.

He sat on a bale of straw, a wagon wheel propping the livery door open slightly to relieve the smell of animals and offer fresh air. Moonbeams danced in the night shining through to silhouette his profile as his hands played the beauty of his heart.

She wondered why he'd never shown or spoken of this talent before.

One of the stabled horses nickered as she finally moved to lean over the wagonbed and check on the children. Back to back, their heads nestled over one arm raised high above them and one leg bent at the knee as if in a dance of opposites. Another similarity of their kinship. Knox used to sleep in the same manner.

The music stopped.

Assured the children were asleep, she moved toward Bass and shone the lantern light upon him.

He scooted over on the bale and patted the edge of it, welcoming her to join him. "Couldn't sleep?"

Daisy accepted his silent offer. "I wanted to see who was making such beautiful music. I didn't know you could play. You should have told us the night Ollie tried to make you sing."

Bass chuckled low. "I didn't want to interfere with Maddox's bragging rights that evening. When we picked up my baggage at the sawbones's office this afternoon, I just happened to remember the harp was among my belongings. Ollie asked me to sing her to sleep with a birthday song close to midnight, so I decided to whip this out instead."

He tapped it against his palm. "There are adventures to play or be imagined spending the night in a livery, and both kids were reluctant to go to sleep. But the harp seems to have done the trick."

"You certainly earned some points on her list with this. May I see it?"

As he handed it to Daisy, their fingers touched. Warmth traveled up her wrists and made her wish that he would take her hand in his.

"It doesn't look like much," Bass apologized, "but it was my most prized possession for most of my life."

"Why?" Daisy turned the mouth harp over in her hand, studying the instrument. No elaborate inlay of design encrusted the silver casing. Nothing set it apart from a dozen others she'd ever noticed for sale. She rubbed her thumb across the silver and noted that the metal had not yet cooled from being played so expertly. She traced the heat, ending in the circle of eights he'd introduced so sweetly into her sense of awareness.

One of the Trumbos snored loudly from the stall they'd mucked out. Daisy and Bass smiled at each other.

"Seems it worked on more than just the children." Daisy handed the mouth harp back to Bass. "What does this mean to you?"

Bass returned it to his inside vest pocket and stared out the door. "I bought it with the first money I ever earned that had nothing to do with my father's companies. Hard-won money and independence. It became like a friend to me. When life disappointed me, I played it. The few times happiness visited me, I played it. And, this sounds childish, I played it when my birthdays were forgotten or a belated afterthought."

He stared out at the moon. "I played tonight, not only for Ollie's sake, but to give thanks to the Lord for the bounty of friends He's offered me here. For this new journey with Teague for my sister. For keeping you safe from harm. Life is looking up, literally."

Daisy's heart gladdened. *Thank You, Lord*, she added her praise, feeling the loneliness that must have been Bass's for so long easing into the Heavens beyond the shadowed night.

Bass reached out and took her hand. "I want to know the choice you made today."

He raised her hand to his lips and pressed the gentlest of kisses against her skin. The soft glow of the moon and lantern light allowed Daisy to see anticipation in his eyes as well as sincerity in his tone.

"I waited this evening while you told Maddox and his brothers about Thad's circumstances," Bass informed

her. "I heard Maddox make his argument about whether
or not you decide to marry him, he should be the one
to raise Knox's son. I was so proud of you when you
stood up for yourself and told him that Abigail wanted
you and no other to take in the boy. And I must admit,
I felt relieved when I saw that Maddox's true disappointment concerned Thaddeus, not your rejection of
his proposal."

Bass's gaze slanted to the wagon. "I watched you
interact with Thad all evening and talk to him about
him and Abigail staying on for a while. That's when
I knew that you'd decided to raise him as your own. I
appreciated you sending Jonas to the mercantile to add
presents so Thad could be celebrated, too. Daisy, I can't
tell you how much I admire your kindness and ability
to love. But you forgot one very important issue before
you suggested we call it a day."

His eyes returned to search hers so intensely that
Daisy felt herself swimming in their fathoms.

"You didn't tell me if you'd decided if I can be part
of offering him the same. Of giving all three of you the
best I can offer." Bass gently squeezed her hand. "When
I saw you collapse on the road, I thought your life was
over. Please live a long one and let me help make this
a happy family."

*Give me the words. The right way to reassure him.
The right way to make him willing to wait.* "I thought
about it the whole race," Daisy began, "how you said
that we could do this by learning each other's ways and
doing what's best for one another. And that would, in
turn, help us become the loving parents Ollie and Thad
need. I believe that could be good for us. All of us."

"You're saying *us*. Does that mean—"

Could she be enough for him? Would his willing-

ness to do his best for her and the children help her
overcome never knowing true love if it never came to
her and Bass?

Dare she trust her heart and muster the courage and
strength to accept God's plan for them...whatever that
might be?

She needed to be completely honest with Bass about
the rest of her decision before she braced herself for the
challenge ahead.

Daisy stepped away. "I'll need a measure of time for
the engagement. You asked for us to learn more about
each other. I'll need to make wedding preparations as
you do for Petula. Snow has just arrived, and I don't
want to shortchange her visit. I don't know how long
Abigail intends to stay, but I want her to remain as long
as she can for Thad's sake. Then there's—"

His palm raised, his voice solemn, Bass said, "I
understand. You agree to marry me but only when
everyone else's life is made right first." Bass backed
away. "It may sound selfish, but that's not quite the
priority I hoped to be in your life, Daisy. You better
go on up and get some rest. Sounds like you've got a
lot of things planned and I need to consider how long
an engagement I'm willing to consider."

"I do care about you, Bass," she whispered, "a great
deal."

Bass headed outside, stopping short at the livery door
to face her. "Just let me know when you care enough
to set the date."

Daisy stood there for a long time waiting for him to
come back in. When he didn't return, she checked on
the children again and headed up the ladder to the hayloft. As she got halfway, Maddox's voice stopped her.

"Why didn't you tell the poor moondog you love him and put him out of his misery?"

Moondog? What did Maddox mean?

"How long have you been listening?" she whispered, glad Maddox couldn't see the tears welling in her eyes.

"Long enough. Don't avoid me. Why ain't you tellin' him you love him? Can't you see he loves you and just don't know it yet? Looks like he's going out to howl at the moon."

"Even though I pretty much said yes to his proposal, I know I disappointed him. I really don't know if I can offer Bass anything less than he deserves and yet he's offering the best that's in him. Can that ever become love?"

"How would I know? I just know I ain't gonna sleep right no more 'til you're took care of, and I promised Knox I'd see ya happy. Sitchy-ations like this keeps a fella awake. The man has a deep hankering for ya. And you're sounding mighty concerned about a fella you're trying to convince yourself you don't care enough about. Quit hemming and hawing and put the two of you out of y'all's misery. Marry him and let him be the hero he wants to be for ya."

His common sense eased her tears, and her affection for Maddox as a watchful "brother" needed to be spoken. "Did I ever tell you how much I like you, Maddox?"

"Get on up that ladder, gal. Ya know ya done damaged my pride a couple'a hours ago when ya turned me down flat. I would'a made them two kids a real good daddy, but ya didn't like me enough for that."

She laughed. "I did exactly what you really wanted me to, and we both know it. You can still be a fine uncle to them."

"I guess you're right on both accounts. But that don't

mean you should leave that Parker fella in the dark about what you really feel for him. I'll get over it. He might not. He's one of those forever kind of fellas. Better tie your bonnet on him."

Daisy finished her climb. "I promise, I'll tell him if you give me your word to let me do it at my own timing."

"Life's short, Daiz. Get it lived. Quit thinkin' and feel. Knox wouldn't blame ya one bit."

By the time Daisy nestled into the corner and sleep readied to overtake her, the mouth harp resumed playing, echoing a sad sense that she had hurt Bass and he might yet choose to walk away from her.

Just before dawn, the Texas Ranger walked into the barn and insisted it would be best to leave immediately for the ranch. Ambush, if it came, would be easier to spot at first light. Bass wondered when the man ever slept, but Teague didn't look any worse for the wear in tracking the shooters.

The sleepy town hadn't yet awakened for the day and no one seemed to be on the streets except an old mutt chasing a rooster strutting to announce the sunrise. The aroma of baking bread hinted that the diner cook had started preparing her morning menu and that would surely wake up others.

Snow and Petula remained quiet alongside Bass in the back of the wagon, letting the rock and sway of the wheels keep the children resting. Grissom and Jonas scouted ahead for ambush while the Ranger made sure no one followed. Maddox had hitched his horse to the wagon gate to trail behind and took command of the team instead.

The Trumbo brothers and Teague were alert and

armed to the hilt. Maddox had a rifle behind his boot heels. Even Bass stored a pistol under his baggage. It would take an army to stop them if fighting started.

Bass tried to keep focused and ready for action, but the sleepless night and his aching shoulder threatened to dull his senses. His jaw hurt and he felt like a giant bruise. The rutted road only added to his misery.

Moving closer to the driver's box, Bass tugged on Daisy's sleeve. "Did Teague say he found any sign of the shooters?"

She leaned over, worry carving her expression. "Just blood out near the church, where they'd been waiting to spot me. I think that must have been Winker. Mad had a run-in with him yesterday morning, but he had no clue Winker was one of the gang or he never would have let him up."

"I'd of done more than broke his nose and put the boot to him." Maddox explained what had taken place.

"Teague also said that one of the men's horses has need of a new shoe from the looks of his trail," Daisy informed them. "The animal's favoring the right foreleg. Teague warned Bear to let him know if a rider came in needing his horse shod for that reason."

"Has he seen sign near hom…your place?" Bass caught himself before paying the respect. He had to distance himself until he knew for sure it would ever be his true sanctuary. Daisy had said a lot of things last night. She'd marry him eventually. She cared for him, which would make their marriage easier if she liked him as much as he liked her. But when he realized she chose to put her obligations first, he'd been hurt to be considered less of a priority.

He hadn't known he wanted her to say yes for any other reason than to fulfill his own obligations and his desire to care for the children. When he'd walked out into the night to think, Bass soon decided he had no reason to feel hurt about the way she'd answered him. He'd been just as guilty of putting his duties first. Trouble was, he also acknowledged that he truly felt something more than just friendship for Daisy.

"Teague said he saw no signs whatsoever as of last night," Daisy interrupted his thoughts. "I told him that the gang might not consider Myrtle or Abigail a threat since they weren't witnesses to the robbery."

She straightened her back a moment to relieve the awkward riding position, then leaned down again to keep their conversation close to Bass's ear. "I could tell he was being patient with me by not saying anything else about my theory."

"Smarter move when a woman's figurin' out things," Maddox interjected, "but Teague's got a head on him. He's thought it through. If I was them, I'd set a bear trap for ya. Take a hostage. Myrtle, probably, 'cause she means the most to ya."

That's the way, Maddox, Bass warned silently. *Keep her stirred up.*

"He saw no sign," Daisy countered, the worry on her face now echoing her tone.

Bass hoped Daisy's reassurance proved reality, but Maddox's logic made sense. "Let's pray Teague's right. I don't want anything to spoil the children's party. We need to make it the most exciting they've ever had."

He glanced at the children. Presents wrapped in calico cloth and tied with a variety of colored string were stacked in piles all around Ollie. Those in brown butcher paper, tied with blue string, lay near Thaddeus.

Calico or butcher paper made no difference to a child who wanted to be remembered. Such wrappings would be quickly dismissed. What awaited inside would linger in the children's minds.

"If everything's as it should be," Bass suggested as the children began to stir, "once we get the team put away, I'll help Petula bake two fresh cakes. One for Ollie. The other for Thad. Myrtle may need some help with breakfast, too, since she's not expecting this many of us."

"Rough up them boots a little, Parker." Maddox flicked the reins. "These wimmen got ya too willin' to sport an apron."

"Speaking of us, Bass, would you wake up Snow and Petula? They'll want to be ready to unload their packages." Daisy corrected her position on the driver's seat, elbowing Maddox as the team's trot sped up. "The turn toward home's coming up."

Had it only been fifteen minutes since they'd left town? It seemed longer than that, but Bass had been so focused on watching for trouble that the time had flown.

Maybe Maddox's mention of possible danger to Myrtle and Abigail had gotten too close to what had happened a few days ago. Bass would have never believed the mess he found himself in at the bank.

By the time he woke the women, the children were wide awake and full of excitement about gathering their packages.

Grissom and Jonas hailed the house to announce their arrival.

A shout rent the air as the door flung open. Bass grabbed his gun. Aimed. Praying he didn't have to shoot. The swish of Maddox's rifle leaving its scabbard echoed over the yard.

Myrtle ran down the porch steps to reach them. "Oh, I'm so glad you're back."

"Liked to have got yourself shot, woman," Maddox grumbled, putting his rifle away.

She eyed each of them, ran past the brothers, searching every face exiting the wagon.

Bass lowered his gun and helped the ladies down.

Teague rode up within seconds. "What's wrong?"

Myrtle's hand pressed against the chignon at the top of her head, trembling. "The boy's mama. She's gone. I thought maybe she decided to walk to town and see what was keeping you all yesterday. She took her bag and asked if she could borrow a lantern from the barn in case it got dark before she reached town. I tried to talk her out of it, but she insisted. I figured she knew her own mind and she was determined to go."

Daisy pressed a finger to her lips as if to silence Myrtle, her eyes slanting toward Thaddeus.

Bass quickly gave the children instructions. "Take in your gifts. We'll have the party in a little while. We've got to take care of a few things first."

Thad stood rooted to the spot. "Where's my mama?"

"In town." Bass did his best to keep his voice even to relieve the boy's sense of fear. "Remember, she didn't know where we were and we left town before anybody was awake."

He felt guilty that he'd never told Daisy that he knew the woman from before and he suspected her of not being trustworthy, but here he was defending her.

Distrust darkened Thad's eyes to slate. "Miz Daisy said there wasn't no place for us to sleep in town. Where did Mama sleep?"

Bass answered him truthfully. "I don't know. I'm hoping I'll find that out soon, but I can't do that until I saddle up and bring her home, can I?"

"Come on, Thaddie-Wumpus." Ollie yanked on his

suspenders. "Teague and my uncles are the best finders in the whole wide world of Texas. And I'm sure Bass is, too, for a city slicker. Don't worry, if she ain't dead, they'll find her for sure."

Daisy's hand covered her eyes at Ollie's lack of sensitivity.

The cook grabbed Ollie's ear. "You, Little Miss Wide Mouth, come with me. Now!" She pulled Ollie into the house, spouting words about knowing when to say what to someone.

Daisy offered to help Thad with his packages, but he wouldn't let go of them. "Your mama will want to watch you unwrap all those," she encouraged. "Why don't you come with me and set them in your room? You can wash up and look real nice when she gets back. I know she'd appreciate that, and Bass said he'd find her for you."

Thad's eyes searched Bass's. "You promise?"

"I'll do my best," Bass offered the truth. He would do everything possible. He had no clue if he would find her dead from illness or, worse, from possibly being taken hostage as Maddox speculated before.

Bass could only pray that the woman had not used this opportunity to leave her son without having to say goodbye forever.

Whether Abigail's request of Daisy to raise Thaddeus stemmed from true need or ended as a scam to take the boy off her hands, leaving without telling him goodbye was unforgivable.

Thaddeus deserved to tell her goodbye, no matter if she cared to do the same to him.

"Grissom and Jonas, stay here and protect the house. Nobody outside until we ride back in," Bass instructed. "Maddox, I'll take one of their horses for now and ride with you and Teague. Is that good with you, Ranger?"

"Good enough."

"Daisy, in the meantime, find what you did with Knox's note." Bass walked over and pressed his hand against her cheek. "Check that handwriting again and match it against something else he's written. Make sure it's genuinely his. I don't trust the woman."

Chapter Twenty

Thad wanted to wait until his mother returned before eating the cake or opening his presents and said so as the children helped Daisy put up the team.

Ollie was not at all pleased by the prospect and didn't mind letting her brother know it. She kicked him in the shin. "Stupid Head, what if they don't find her? Then I'll never get to eat my cake."

"He'll find her. Mr. Parker promised." He pushed her back. "Besides, Mama likes him. Said he gave her some money a long time ago."

"When was that?" Daisy asked.

"Before I was borned, Mama said."

Daisy frowned, wondering why Bass had never mentioned he'd known Abigail before. She'd have to ask him about it when he returned. Why would he hold back that fact? "You two work on different sides and keep your hands and feet to yourselves."

The children argued back and forth until tempers ruled and they tried to wrestle each other to the ground. Thad prevailed and Ollie went down. She grabbed a handful of sand and straw, throwing it at him. Thad clutched something darker staining the stall floor and retaliated.

"Stop this right now!" Daisy rushed between them to hold up a palm and ward off another throw from either direction. "Now you're both going to have to take a bath before anybody gets cake."

Ollie let go of the next wad and stood, staring at Thad like Butler intent on charging an unsuspecting victim. Thad raised his fist, warning that he had no qualms in fighting a girl.

A bad habit Daisy planned to change as soon as possible with both her children. "Jonas! Can you come in here?" she shouted, then realized what she'd thought. Both her children. Had her heart already accepted the boy? "I need you."

In seconds the barn door opened and Jonas rushed inside, his eyes scanning for the source of trouble.

"Oohwee, who raised the stink in here?" His broken nose wiggled in reaction to the odor as he halted where he stood.

"That would be your nephew and his target." Daisy explained what Thad had thrown that now covered Ollie's face and clothes. "He was provoked, though."

Studying the animosity between the younger Trumbo generation, Jonas shrugged. "What do you expect me to do about it? It's a family tradition…fightin', I mean. Looks like a draw to me, all things square."

"I want you to give Thad a bath. Tell Grissom he'll have to stand guard by himself until you're done. I'll get Myrtle heating up some water for you." Daisy glared at the boy. "And you better wash up good. I expect the bar of soap to be smaller when you're finished with it and I always check behind ears."

"Toes. Knees. Elbows, too," jeered Ollie.

Daisy spun to glare at her daughter, whose stuck-out tongue didn't get back into her mouth in time.

"Olivia Jane Trumbo." Daisy used Ollie's getting-in-trouble name, warning that the storm brewing inside her was well underway. "*I'll* be scrubbing you."

Ollie's eyes aimed amber daggers at her brother. "I'm gonna get you for this. Making me take a bath on my birthday."

"Not another word from either of you until you're clean and ready to apologize to each other." Daisy would have taken each child in hand, but the prospect of touching either of their dirty little selves made her nose wrinkle. Instead she ordered, "Now march," and dared either of them to disobey.

In little time, Snow and Petula had helped Myrtle warm the bathwater for both scrubbings, and Daisy convinced Ollie that it wouldn't be fair to make Bass, Maddox or Teague miss the party.

The cakes were baked and resting on the pie safe to cool, waiting to be frosted once the searchers returned and the party could get underway.

As hungry as they all were, no one but Grissom and Jonas wanted breakfast, which allowed Myrtle to concentrate on cooking the noon meal for the planned party.

After their baths, Daisy took both children into the parlor to finish grooming their hair and making sure each looked his or her best in the fresh clothes they'd donned. Knowing they were nervous about giving an apology, she made them take a seat and began with her own.

"I'm sorry I yelled at you. I've been tense from worrying about getting us home safe since the race was over." She also had a thing or two to say to Bass about his previous knowledge of Abigail. "I'm feeling out of sorts, I'd guess you'd say, and that made me quick to spill anger. I shouldn't have taken my worry out on you."

Ollie scooted to the edge of her chair. "Couldn't you told us sorry before the bath?"

Daisy shook her head, but grinned inwardly. Her precocious daughter could always relieve a tense moment. "No, Little Miss, I couldn't. You took a bath because you smelled awful. I'm still very disappointed in the way you both acted. You're brother and sister. You're supposed to love each other, protect each other and not try to hurt the other for any reason."

She targeted this portion to Thad so he'd know how she operated. Ollie knew her ways already. "No more fighting from now on, so you won't disappoint me. I tend to give long talks when people let me down."

"Sore bottoms, too." Ollie used scare tactics.

Daisy had spanked Ollie once in her entire eight years. She'd endangered another child's life when one of her pranks went awry. Hopefully, Thad would never give cause to use such punishment again. "Do you think you could learn to be friends as well as relatives?"

Thaddeus stood and spit into his freshly scrubbed hand, extending it to Ollie. "Guess I was out of those same things your mama was. I just wanted to hit somethin', so I got mad and hit you. I been worried about Mama and them shooters. Reckon they got her?"

Ollie spit as well and pumped his hand vigorously.

Daisy just shook her head, wondering if she'd saddled up on more than she could ride with raising two feisty children.

She knew Thad was waiting for her answer and Daisy concentrated on the best way to reassure him.

If Bass didn't get back soon and the wait bled on much longer, there was a strong possibility his mother had left. Fifteen minutes there and back, scouting the trail, trying to find Abigail in town with so many new people in the crowd, would require a couple of hours at least. Stopping at Bear's to see if Abigail had bought a way out of town would certainly take up part of their time since no stage was due today.

"You remember how many folks are there right now, don't you?" Daisy tried to keep Thad calm.

He let go of Ollie's hand and nodded. "Lots."

"Then keep in mind your mama's trying to find all of us the same as we're trying to find her. No telling where she's searched. The mercantile, the diner, maybe even the livery. She, Mr. Parker, your uncle and Teague may have bypassed each other. We've got to wait until they all look in the same place at the same time. I'm sure that's why this is taking so long. No need to worry."

"Okay." Relief washed over his face as he sat back down.

"Yeah, if the robbers shot her on the trail, we'd already know it by now, wouldn't we, Mama? They would'a slung her over the saddle and hauled her home and—"

"Olivia, that's enough. Why don't you go to your room and find something to do that'll keep you clean until we start the party."

Her child's idea of helping had only served to make Thad's face turn ashen.

Ollie escaped upstairs at lightning speed more than willing to follow the instructions.

Daisy stood and moved past the settee to bend down in front of Thad. She looked him straight in the eyes, wanting him to trust what she said. "You don't need to worry about those men harming your mama. She will not die by their hands."

He blinked and closed his eyes a moment. When he

opened them again, tears filled the rims. "I know," he sobbed, "but maybe Mama ought'a."

A cold chill ran down Daisy's spine and hot tears swelled from her heart into her throat, threatening to rise farther and make her cry. *Thaddeus knew.*

She'd wondered if Abigail had told him she would be leaving him here and, more important, why. But no matter how hard it would tear her heart apart to hear it, Daisy knew he must say the words. Must share the fear or die from the pure torture of his own heartbreak.

"Why would you think or say that?" she asked softly.

"Because she's gonna die anyway and maybe she'd hurt only a little bit this way. She hurts so much alla time. She doesn't know I hear her, but Mama cries when she thinks I'm sleepin'." His tears became a torrent. "Why do people have to die?"

Daisy pulled him close and hugged him. His little arms accepted her embrace so fiercely she thought he would melt into her like a candle burning the last edge of its wick.

"I don't know, baby," Daisy whispered, thinking of Knox and all she'd felt when he'd passed. "We all end our journeys on this earth one day, and only God knows the hour and the reason that must happen. What I do know is that your mama loves you very much."

No matter what she felt about Abigail, she couldn't let Thaddeus feel any uncertainty about his mother.

The next words that would have once choked Daisy exited in gales of forgiveness as she recalled Knox's note. *This* had been hers and Knox's purpose all along. To help this little boy find a better path than the one dealt him.

"Your father loved you, too. Let them do for you what they can before they join each other in Heaven.

They only want to make sure you'll have a family to love who'll love you in return. That's us, Thad. Me and Ollie, your uncles and maybe even Mr. Parker if I marry him. He's already told me how much he likes you and would love to be a good father to you."

She looked beyond the window behind him, praying for sight of Abigail returning with Bass. "I know you're scared, but you don't have to be afraid of being alone when your mama's time comes. When it happens, I promise to love you as she would if she could stay. Would you allow me to do that? Do you think we could make her happy if she knew you didn't mind being my son?"

He nodded then finally chose to meet Daisy's gaze. "I promise I won't be no trouble."

Daisy gently rustled his hair and felt his little soul trust hers. "I'm used to a little trouble now and then, Thad. It makes me stronger when I come out on the other side of it. How about we shake hands on the deal? We'll promise to do our best for each other." Bass's words echoed in her thoughts. "If we mess up, then we promise to come out of it stronger people, okay?"

"I'm strong already."

"The bravest little boy I've ever met." And he was. No child should have to be this kind of strong. "We've got to do one really easy thing now and that's to wish your mama every moment left to her. After that, you belong to me and I'll start loving you for her and you can start loving me back. Until you're ready, we'll just like each other very much. Shake on it?"

Daisy offered him her hand.

Thad shook it vigorously. "Do I gotta love Ollie, too?"

"Is that a deal breaker?"

Thaddeus didn't answer quickly, and Daisy wondered if she needed to say it differently.

Finally a grin spread from ear to ear, easing the outpouring of grief that glistened in his eyes. "I think I know what that means. I get to choose, right?"

"Yes."

"She's my sister, huh?"

Daisy nodded.

"I don't ever have to marry-her-kind-of-love-her, do I?"

She shook her head.

"Then yeah," he said with a sigh, "I might can love Ollie-Golly someday. If she'll keep her feet off me."

"Which reminds me—" Daisy decided the two children must have liked each other at some point if they had nicknames for each other "—let's figure out what size shoe you wear. I've got to do something real quick, then I'll look for you in your room."

Maybe she could get some of the orders done while waiting for Bass's return.

"'Zat gonna be my stick-around room?"

Daisy shooed him upstairs. "Until you grow up and get married."

"I ain't gettin' married. No way ever."

"That's what we all think, sweetie. Until we change our minds."

Daisy enjoyed watching Thad run to his room in anticipation of claiming it as his own forever sanctuary.

Her feet felt lighter while she headed to where she had stored Knox's note, ready to finally claim her own peace of mind.

Chapter Twenty-One

The sun dipped low in the horizon when Bass and his fellow searchers rode wearily toward Daisy's barn. Grissom and Jonas waved their rifles, signaling that they'd spotted them and were headed in.

"I hope Myrtle's got plenty of grub cooked." Maddox dismounted. "I could eat the rump end of a buffalo by myself right now."

"I might wrestle you for a leg or two," Bass admitted, then decided if Maddox was in a fighting mood he'd just settle for a piece of cake. "I'm exhausted."

"I'm gonna brush down my horse and stay the night here," Teague informed. "If they followed us, they know we're on the edge of tired. They'll strike at our weakest."

The door of the house flapped open and Daisy came running out with Ollie and Thaddeus following like goslings behind her. Her gaze swept over the men and the horses. "You didn't find her, did you?"

Bass noticed Thad move up to stand beside Daisy and slip his hand into hers. Something had happened between Daisy and the boy while he'd been gone. His body language showed new trust in her, and Bass was glad. Thad would need it when he heard what had to be said.

Shaking his head, Bass brushed back the dark strands of disheveled hair hanging across his forehead. Somewhere along the way, he'd lost his hat trying to hang on to the reins. His shoulder hurt like fire, trying to keep up with the Ranger's expert horsemanship and the pace he set.

"Go in and get some coffee or tea. Myrtle's got supper waiting on us all." Daisy took the reins from Bass before he could make his way into the barn. "The children and I will put the horses away then we'll be in to join you."

To Bass's surprise, even Thad complied. He'd half expected the boy to spout rapid-fire questions about all they'd done to find his mother.

Maddox gladly handed over his horse and headed inside, his brothers following after him.

After Bass told Daisy what Teague had said, she nodded. "I'll ask him to join us for supper."

"I doubt he'll let you take care of his horse."

Ollie spoke up. "He don't let nobody touch Lupe but me."

"Lupe?" Bass was surprised that Teague had shared the dun's name with the child.

"Yeah, said he calls him Lupe for short, even though Lupe's named after a big old river. God-a-lupe, or something like that."

"Guadalupe," Daisy corrected gently. "Well, let's get done so we all can eat and share some cake, shall we? We still got presents to open."

Bass assumed they hadn't waited, the children had been so eager to unwrap them. "Can Ollie and Thad lead the horses in and you stay here a second? Teague will make sure they won't get hurt. The beasts are spent and just want something to eat and drink."

"I can spare a moment. I'm sure Teague is tired, too."

Once the children led the horses inside the barn, Daisy turned from her careful watch of them and faced him.

He kissed her forehead.

"What's that for?"

Her cheeks blushed, making her look even more beautiful than the last time he'd seen her. "A hundred things, but the most important…for being here for Thaddeus. Taking him in. Making him matter to you."

"She's not coming back, is she?" Daisy took a step back.

Bass shook his head, wondering why she seemed to have some sort of guard up. "We checked everywhere. Asked Bear if she rented a buggy or horse, talked to Maggie at the Twisted Spur to see if Abigail took off with, pardon my frankness, a new consort. Got a lead at Junior Pickens. He bought this from her."

He held up a ring made of gold leaves and two amber stones, much like the one Daisy wore on her left hand. Bass's gaze went immediately to her hand; only a pale circle of white remained where her ring once rested. Had she been wearing it this morning? He hadn't ever recalled it off her finger before.

"I'll tell you about it later, after supper. We do need to talk." She put her hands in her skirt pockets. "I really need to get in there or the children will wear Teague out with questions rather than feeding the horses."

"Pickens handed me this to give you." Bass reached into his inside vest pocket and gave her a wad of cash and a note. "I read it to make sure I didn't need to do something about it before I headed back. She says she sold the ring for that amount of money and she wants the money to be given to Thaddeus. It's a small stake for whatever he wants to do with it when he reaches sixteen or graduates from school, whichever comes first."

Bass gave Daisy the ring, too. "I figured since it was his mother's, the boy ought to have it to remember her by. Maybe give it to his bride when he finds her. I hope you don't mind me buying it for him."

Daisy accepted the ring, shook her head and said quietly, "I don't, and his mother and father would have been thankful that you've done this for him. It was the ring Knox pledged his love to Abigail with."

"Then Knox's note was truly written in his hand?"

"I checked it, in fact, only moments ago after I had a long talk with Thad. I was glad to discover Knox really had written the request. It gives my heart peace."

Puzzled, Bass didn't quite understand.

"I can let it all go now. Let Knox go. I'm free. My hurt served a purpose bigger than myself. And while I hope I never have to go through that again, I understand why it's led me here to this point in my life."

Led me here to you, Bass willed her to add the words.

But she didn't and until he heard them, he wouldn't place the other ring he'd bought today on her finger.

She scanned Abigail's note and read all that Bass had already told her, tucking it into her pocket. "So I'm assuming she found a way out of town?"

"With the glass supplier from Fort Worth. He'd been making a delivery at the diner, restocking the glassware and china that had been purchased. Sam even met with the man before he left, giving him an order for new windows at the bank. Evidently, Abigail hitched a ride with him to parts unknown."

Bass's eyes met Daisy's, keeping nothing else back.

"The man hadn't mentioned which way he was headed next, but Teague said we couldn't take a chance on following her because that would leave you and the children without much protection. I didn't want to leave you vulnerable to the robbers, especially when it was clear Abigail wanted to leave Thad without having to say goodbye. I did do my best to find her, Daisy, but I'm not bringing her back to him just to prolong his hurt."

Bass searched her face. "I wanted to tell you so I could give you time to prepare your words for the boy. He's going to be heartbroken. Would you prefer I tell him?"

Daisy shook her head. "No, thank you. I know just what to say."

She only hoped that Abigail had not left for any other reason than to truly spare her son from watching her pass away.

While she and the children fed the horses, Daisy wondered when the best time would be to have the talk with Bass and Thad. She didn't want to ruin the party, but she feared Thaddeus wouldn't enjoy the celebration until he knew exactly what Bass had learned about Abigail. The talk with the boy needed to come first so she would have her emotions in check. She couldn't guarantee that would be the case after she spoke to Bass.

Thad placed a feed bucket in the stall of the last horse curried. He dusted the oats from his hand and announced, "I'm done with this one. Can I talk to you by myself, Miz Daisy? Just you and me? Before the party?"

His eyes slanted toward Ollie, his meaning clear. *Get rid of her.*

"Ollie, are you done?" Daisy checked to make sure she'd completed her chore.

"Sure am."

"Then why don't you go wash your hands. Tell Myrtle the rest of us will be quick to follow."

Ollie didn't have to be told twice. She rushed out of the barn.

"Think I'll mosey out and relieve Jonas for a while so he can enjoy some cake." Teague took his leave, giving the requested privacy.

Now that the time had come, Daisy wasn't so certain her words would be enough to help Thad accept his mother's disappearance.

Daisy grabbed a blanket hanging on a peg near one of the stalls. "Want me to spread this and we'll sit or would you prefer to take a walk instead?"

"I'll stand. You can sit if you want."

Daisy elected to sit, realizing he needed to stand tall to brace himself for whatever he was about to say. He'd been dwelling in his thoughts as he'd worked, not saying a word the whole time.

She dared to broach the difficult subject she knew was on his mind. "Is this about your mama?"

"Yeah. I been thinkin' real hard. Thinkin' that she ain't comin' back. She didn't let Mr. Parker or nobody find her, did she?"

His brave little face nearly tore Daisy's heart apart. She wanted to reach out to him and pull him into her arms, but he wanted answers not soothing.

"Why do you think she didn't want to be found?"

"She had to go to Heaven and didn't want me to see. She figured I'd just follow her and I sure would'a."

"You're not old enough, Thad. She wants you to stay here and grow up and become the best man you can be. She wants you to have a long, happy life and maybe, one day, raise a little boy or girl of your own."

Surprise filled his face. "How'd you know? Mama told me that about a hunnerd times."

"Because that's what all mamas want for their children."

"Well, I told her I ain't ever gonna have no kids, 'specially not no girl kid. And mostly, I ain't never gonna die and make nobody cry or miss me. It hurts way too hard."

The soft rap on Bass's bedroom door almost didn't wake him, he was so exhausted. "Yes?"

"Can we talk?" Ollie's voice came from the other side of the door.

"Give me a minute." He sat up, fiddled with the lamp until a soft glow pushed the night shadows away. It had to be well past midnight. What was she doing up this late? Daisy said they had a full schedule come morning. He was ready for a little less activity if possible.

Bass quickly dressed.

Impatience echoed from his visitor. "What's taking ya so long?"

"Sorry." He yawned again and finally opened the door. "What's so important that it can't wait?"

"I'm worried, Bass." Ollie padded over and flopped down in the chair next to his bed. She had pencil and papers in hand.

"Does your mother know you're still up?"

"Uh-uh. She was usin' her sewin' machine and fell asleep on it. She said she was supposed to have a talk with you, so I figured I'd sneak out and get my talk to you done 'fore she wakes up again."

"What's got you so worried?" He sat on the edge of the bed.

"I'm trying to come up with a plan on how I can get rid of Thaddie-Wumpus and nothin's workin'."

"Why do you want to get rid of him?"

Ollie stuck her pencil behind her left ear and threw out both hands in exasperation. "You seen him at the party. Actin' like he likes it here so good. And Mama talkin' to him like…well, like she likes him better than me. He got almost as many presents as me and everybody ate some of his cake. Only me and my uncles and you ate mine."

Bass didn't know how much Daisy had explained to Ollie about what Thad suffered today. "Ladies always tend to fret over fellas that get bad news. So the women wanted to make sure they made him feel better. I think that's why all of them paid so much attention to him, don't you?"

She shook her head, nearly upsetting the pencil's position. "Nope. I think they're tired of me. Well, I don't care. I'm tired of him and I say we get rid of him. You with me?"

The papers slipped from her lap and Bass bent down to gather them. He happened to see a few of her possible plans for Thad. This resentment Ollie felt could develop into dangerous repercussions. He needed to tread cautiously with her. "What did you have in mind?"

As she started naming ways to make life hard for the boy, Bass wondered how much of this she'd learned from her uncles. Surely no eight-year-old child could come up with such deviousness. Had she consulted them on the issue?

This was Ollie, hostage-taker.

Goat-biter.

Inheritor of the Trumbo knack for fighting.

He best not put anything past her. "I can't help you with this, Little Britches."

She jumped up and glared at him. "You like him better than me."

"I've known you longer, so I love you, not just like you. But I expect someday to love him just as much."

"That does it, then." Ollie turned some of her pages and scribbled. "See ya."

"What did you just do?"

"Scratched you off my daddy list, that's what. You ain't gonna help me, I ain't gonna help you no more. Mama won't marry you if I don't like you. So there."

She stuck her tongue out at Bass and stomped away.

Chapter Twenty-Two

A couple of days later, Daisy still had not broached the subject of Abigail with Bass. Thunderheads rolled in over the plains, the west wind relentlessly seeking out Daisy and smothering her with its hot breath. Her mouth felt parched and her tongue licked her lips to moisten them. She glanced at Bass beside her on the driver's seat, and he didn't seem to suffer from the heat. She sensed the approach of a heated discussion, and she didn't look forward to it at all.

Shaking the reins gently, she urged the team into a quicker trot toward town. Maybe a swifter pace would add time to grab something to drink at the diner before the race started.

Though rain would put a damper over the competition, she would certainly welcome the wet spell. Maybe the long-standing drought would be less fierce this summer if moisture came this early in the season.

She'd deliberately ignored breakfast, not wanting to run on a full belly. But she'd been in such a hurry to get everyone underway that she'd forgotten to drink something. With town only minutes away, she hadn't thought it necessary to pack a canteen and didn't want to call a halt just to ask one of the men to lend her his.

"You're nervous about the race, aren't you?" asked Bass, a rifle lying in his lap for quick access in case the robbers attacked. "Looks like you might get rained out."

"A little nervous, I admit, but we can always use the rain." She answered him to quiet the thoughts that had plagued her about his previous knowledge of Abigail. How did she approach the subject? No opportunity had presented itself so far. Or maybe she just didn't want to hear his answer.

"I want to do well, but I don't want it to bring harm to any of us. I keep going back and forth in my mind whether visiting town will ease some of the strange mood at the house."

Lifting one rein so she could wipe the perspiration from her forehead with the back of her hand, she added, "Maybe I'm just stirring up even more trouble by running today. Just look how it's been for all you men at the ranch. Maddox and his brothers won't go home until the robbers are no more threat."

Bass glanced at the riders trailing the wagon on either side. "Part of that's because they like Myrtle's tasty cooking."

She appreciated him trying to lighten her concern. "True, but their presence may have helped stave off any attack. It certainly has been quiet at the house. *Outside*, at least."

"Thad seems to be settling in pretty well."

"You think so?" Daisy wondered if this could be her opening to question him.

"He made quick pals with Butler, and the goat seems to appreciate wrestling with him. Both have rowdy bones in their bodies. They'll enjoy growing up together. And the boy's taken a real liking to his uncles. He followed them everywhere until Teague ruled against it. They weren't being mindful of how far from the house they let him wander."

"And do you like him, Bass? Now that you've been around him a couple of days?"

"How could I not? He's as lovable as Ollie when she wants to be."

Something remained unspoken about Ollie, and Daisy intended to find out what he was reluctant to tell her. But first she wanted to ask his opinion concerning Thad before moving on to another subject.

"Have you noticed Thad's staying as far away from us women and Ollie as he can? Until mealtime, that is."

"Steering clear of Ollie is predictable, don't you think?" One of Bass's eyebrows rose. "Considering it's clear she's trying to get rid of him. I don't blame him. But I couldn't say why he's chosen not to be near you women. I guess I've been so busy, I hadn't really noticed. It's been an eye-opener being around small children."

How would he do with being a forever parent? she wondered. Could she rid herself enough of the anger she felt about him already knowing Abigail to make him a father to Ollie and Thad?

"Thad's vowed to never marry so he'll never have children. He doesn't want to make them hurt or cry if they lose him. So I think he's taken on a 'keep away from girls' policy." Daisy sought Bass's opinion. "Do you think he'll ever feel comfortable staying since the house is primarily female?"

"Since I've been out with Teague and the men most of the time, what have you ladies been doing? That might explain some of his reluctance to be near you."

Daisy thought about it. She and Snow had finally managed some time to visit with each other, reviewing old memories, reveling in their shared company and hatching ways to keep Snow in High Plains. They'd sewn a fair amount of shoes. Even Ollie had volunteered to help. Daisy related that to Bass.

"I didn't make enough to call the month a profit yet, but at least the orders that are due today are filled. I have some extras to take with me. I'll ask Junior Pickens to display them." What she didn't say was that she hoped to bring in some new orders, as well.

"I'm sure that's most of the reason Thad's avoiding you. He wants to do boy kind of activities. He just needs to get accustomed to the way your house runs and find other things to keep himself occupied. By the way, you ought to stop by the mercantile and pick up your pay for my and Petula's keep. I asked the banker to have it ready and that's where he's doing business."

"I appreciate it," said Daisy with embarrassment. "I've allowed myself to be distracted and I didn't get done all I wanted to. So the money really comes in handy." He was such a kind man, but would he prove to be an honest man concerning Abigail? "Thank you."

"You're welcome. Thank you for taking such good care of me and being so good to my sister. I know she's happy here." He gripped the rifle for a moment flexing his fingers and raising his arm. "I'm pretty much mended now."

In the far distance, the sky rumbled and Daisy thought she saw a flash of lightning. A coming storm?

Bass lay the rifle back in his lap and quietly began again. "Any way I can help with Ollie? I wouldn't want to see her take her pranks too far."

"Ever since she learned Thad was here to stay, she's

been trying everybody's patience. Really living up to her heritage," Daisy said.

"I thought the spiders in his blankets was pretty clever." Bass's eyes lit with amusement despite the serious subject. "Gave me gooseflesh. The earthworms in his boots made me check my own before I put them on this morning. Did you ever figure out what sort of creatures crawled out of his mash potatoes at supper?"

Daisy shuddered at the thought. "Looked just like specks of black pepper, didn't they? I should have known when she offered to pour some hot gravy over the potatoes that she was up to something."

"Well, when the pepper started dashing for the edge of his plate, I can tell you I couldn't eat another bite. I don't blame you for sending her to bed without the rest of her meal."

"If I hadn't already promised Myrtle a day off I would have made Ollie stay home today as punishment." Though she'd realized her daughter would have an adjustment period concerning not being the only child in the house, Daisy hadn't expected the viciousness that came from Ollie learning to share.

Teague rode in from his scout position ahead. "Slow the team a little," he ordered. "Everything's clear but we don't want to approach with the horses winded in case we're targeted before we get them stabled."

Daisy complied and reined back, setting a slower pace. Teague resumed his lead into town.

That gave her a moment to glance back at Ollie. Her child was madly scribbling on the list. Why had she brought it with her today? Did she plan on interviewing new men in town?

Daisy turned to look back at the road again, but she caught the blue fathoms of Bass's gaze upon her and forgot what she was doing or going to say. The reins nearly slipped from her hands.

Bass reached out a hand to help her.

"Steady." She exhaled deeply, acting as if she was calming the horses, but she meant the word for herself.

Focusing on her task, memory came back to her. "Do you think you could keep a close eye on Ollie for me today? I don't want her stirring up any hostage situations while I'm running. She's got her daddy list with her. And if the weather changes, I want to make sure she doesn't get scared. I don't know if you remember what she said that first day you met her. She's frightened by lightning."

"I'll do my best, Daisy. I won't let her get hurt." His hand went back to the rifle.

"That's all I can ask." For some reason Ollie had started ignoring Bass if he approached her. She'd stomp off somewhere else when he spoke to her. The two of them clearly had a falling-out. Daisy dared to question him about it. "What's happened between you two?"

"Nothing that won't fix itself." He wouldn't look her in the eye. Which meant he was holding something back, keeping the child's confidence.

Lies, omissions, confidences. The one flaw that might prevent her from trusting Bass and believing it could work between them. Daisy knew she needed to get her suspicions off her mind and quit delaying knowing his reasons.

"Bass, why didn't you tell me you already knew Abigail before she came to town?"

His eyes closed a moment as if fighting off pain, then he exhaled a deep breath. "I met her once. Just once."

"She was with Knox, wasn't she?"

"He'd come to sign the conscription papers and re-

ceive the money. She accompanied him and he introduced her as his wife. I didn't know you were the Daisy
Trumbo I'd sent the memorial money to until the banker
and doctor confirmed your identity."

His eyes opened and met her gaze directly now. He
was telling the truth. Yet the truth hurt deeply. "You
didn't trust me enough to tell me this before, did you?"
she whispered. "You proposed out of obligation only,
but I thought we'd become friends. A friend would never
hide such a secret. How many more are you keeping
from me?"

He shook his head and reached out to her, but she
scooted away, not allowing the touch. Once again, she
wasn't good enough for someone to offer the best of
himself.

"I didn't trust myself," he tried to explain. "I didn't
want to tell you what I suspected because I didn't want
to corrupt the memory you had of Knox. Just like you
won't tell Ollie about her father. And I didn't want you
to think I wanted to gain your favor by default."

Everything he'd been reluctant to tell her seemed, in
his opinion, to be his way to protect her feelings. "A lie
by omission is still a lie," she said quietly. "I can't be
tied again to a man who lies, Bass. I wouldn't survive."

"We'll leave your house as soon as we return from
town and can gather our things," he stated, his voice
deep and holding back an emotion she couldn't comprehend.

She shook her head and felt herself closing off from
him slowly as if she was a wilting flower. "No, Bass,
come home. Get well. Do what's right by Petula and
Teague, then I *trust*—" she stressed the now hurtful
word "—you must go your own way."

Blood rushed from her head, her pulse increasing as

she warred with a stunning realization. She knew she would miss his vibrant presence in her home. The care and concern he'd shown her and Ollie, and now Thad. Most of all, she would miss his friendship and what she'd almost allowed herself to believe could make both their futures worth anticipating. But she'd discovered she wanted more from him.

Maddox had been right and she'd been reluctant to admit it. She'd allowed herself to fall in love with Bass, after all. But she didn't know if she would ever completely count on him again or even know how she would go about rebuilding her faith in him. How could she give her heart to a man who could betray her?

Was she never meant for someone to offer the best of himself? Was there something left lacking within her never to experience true care and devotion? She'd allowed herself to hope, but now she wasn't sure what to feel about herself or Bass.

"I'll never forget my time with all of you here." His hands gripped the rifle as if he were trying to hide his emotions. "It's been life-changing."

No matter her sense of betrayal from him, she couldn't let him go without knowing he wouldn't be forgotten, either. "I'm not sure Ollie will ever get over you, Bass. You sure you don't care to tell me why she's upset with you?"

"Let's just say, she's a lot like her mama. It's her way with no room for compromise." His gaze locked with hers and held. "I'm not sure I care to compromise my own dreams for a woman who can't trust in herself enough to get past her disappointment in me. I'm worth more than that, Daisy. So are you if you'll just let go of the past and look to the future. If you can't, then I'll go and do my best to forget you and the children. Though I don't even know how to begin to do that."

Later as Bass conferred with Maddox and the others about where to meet once Daisy crossed the finish line, his heart was breaking. He knew he should walk away from Daisy. He wasn't what she wanted. He certainly wasn't what she deserved. Most of all, he wasn't good enough for her.

Trouble was, even though he'd told her he would leave, he couldn't live his life without her anymore. He realized that he loved her and had just risked losing what he'd wanted all along—a real home, a family, someone who could love him despite any of his faults. Everything his parents never gave him as a child.

But would Daisy ever believe him when he told her how much he loved her and asked her to let him prove the rest of his life that she was the only woman for him? That he would step up and be the kind of man she needed? That he'd never keep anything from her again?

He knew, given the chance to win her love, with God's help, he could be that man she needed and wanted.

When his cohorts suddenly ventured in different directions, Bass discovered he hadn't heard where they'd decided to meet. Thaddeus elected to stay near him while Ollie stood some distance away yet in sight.

Bass took the boy's hand. He'd just have to stick near the finish line and watch for the others' gathering place. "Let's grab Ollie and see where Daisy's going to line up this time, okay?"

"Okay." Thad's initial enthusiasm to spend the time with him dimmed. "But you reckon we can do something just me and you 'fore we leave town?"

"Sure. After Daisy's done racing and says there's time," Bass agreed. "Is that okay with you?"

Thad echoed Bass's answer. "Sure."

When they turned to get Ollie, Bass didn't like the look of the stranger she had chosen to interview. Moving up, Bass made his presence known to the bowlegged man. Why was he asking her questions concerning the races? She was the interviewer, not him.

"That's enough, Ollie. Let the fellow go about his business." Bass took her arm, but she tried to jerk away. "You need to come with us."

"You her daddy?" The man broadened his stance when she glared at Bass.

"Her guardian for the day." The fact that he had wanted to be so much more pained Bass, gripping him with a deep sense of loss.

"Well, you ain't gonna be my daddy, that's for sure," Ollie countered. "You ain't even on my list anymore."

"Sounds like you got women trouble, mister."

"A lot less than you'll have if you don't back away from my children," Bass warned. "Anything you want to know you ask somewhere else."

Bass kept his attention on the stranger, but his words targeted Thad. "Son, you think you can spot Uncle Maddox and tell him I could use a hand?"

"Sure."

"Then go…right now."

Bass set the boy's hand free. Thad ran off to find Maddox.

"I'll go with him." Ollie tried to shake free.

"That won't be necessary. I got a bead on him." Teague's razor-edged voice echoed from behind the stranger. The Ranger sat his saddle, his rifle fixed steady on the bowlegged man. "Any questions, mister?"

"Guess not." The stranger turned to see who held him at gunpoint. "Mighty unfriendly town."

"Not so much." Teague motioned him on his way with the rifle barrel. "Just when a man's quick to get too friendly with one of our little ones."

"Think I'll head somewhere friendlier, then." The stranger moved past Bass and took out for the Twisted Spur.

"Thanks." Bass nodded to the Ranger, refusing to offer his hand so Ollie wouldn't take advantage.

Teague tipped his hat. "Anytime."

He sheathed his rifle and melted back into the crowd as quickly as he'd come.

"We've got to go get your brother." Bass looked up at the sky, checking the sagging clouds for sign of a readiness to spill their dark weight. Maybe they would hold off long enough to see the race finished. "He could probably give your mother a good run, he let out of here so fast."

"He can't run faster than me. Let me show ya."

Bass wasn't falling for her tactic as she did her best to jerk away. He grabbed her up into his right arm and hefted her against his side, carrying her as he would a watermelon. "You're sticking with me today so you might as well get used to the fact and settle down."

Her struggle proved useless so she decided to make herself deadweight and hung her arms and legs like a wet tarpaulin thrown over something to dry. He had to admit, this was just as hard to manage as if she was a squirming billy goat.

"Okay, if that's the way it's going to be, then we'll see who's the most stubborn. And I've had a few years on you in that particular skill. You care to tell me why that man was asking you about the amount of purse being offered to the winners?"

She shrugged her shoulders then remembered to slump over again. "Don't know. Guess he wants to be in the race. Told him he wouldn't win anyway. Mama's sure to win if nobody shoots her. He asked how long the race was, too."

Bass didn't like what he heard. Asking about money and the length of a race meant the stranger could have something dangerous in mind. That set up all kinds of caution in Bass's thoughts. Something told him that he should have taken a better look at the bowlegged man.

Maybe Ollie could clue him in on other things about the stranger from her notes.

"Why did you choose him to interview? What was it about him that caught your interest?"

"It's hard to talk like this." She started coughing as if she was about to choke. "My belly. You're holding it too hard. Can I get down now?"

Bass eyed her closely. Little Drama Britches was faking. But when she did something, she did it full-out. Her cheeks were flushed. Her sandy lashes batted a mile a minute. Her tongue stuck out as if she was gagging. He couldn't take the chance he was wrong about her antics.

Bass set her down. "Move one inch the wrong way and I'm going to put a lasso on you and tie you to my waist. Understand me?"

Her sigh was half grumble as the back of her hand pressed against her forehead and she looked as if she might imitate Esther Sue Jenkins's so-called funeral fainting.

Thad returned with Maddox and his other uncles.

"You got everything under control now?" Maddox

checked Ollie from head to toe. "Nephew here said you's about to get into it with a one-eared fella."

"One ear." Bass mentally took note of what he hadn't before. "Thanks, Thad. I noticed his bowed legs. The angle of his hat hid his eyes."

Not to be outdone, Ollie joined in. "He's left-handed like me. Carries a pearl-handled pistol, too. Sure is pretty. I was hopin' he'd let me use it if he gets to be my daddy."

That narrowed the field in spotting him among others in the crowd.

"What's all the fuss about him? Want me to beat him back straight-legged for ya?" Maddox grinned. "I'm ready for a good row. How 'bout you, brothers?"

"We're with ya," they replied in unison.

"Did he say anything else you think might be important for us to know?" Bass hoped for some clue as to why every instinct in his body warned the man had targeted Ollie deliberately.

"Nothin' else, 'cept he sure hoped it didn't rain and spoil things. Oh, yeah, he asked me if I had some matches. I told him that I don't smoke."

"Could be he's bet on the race and don't want it called off 'cause of rain." Maddox stated the most logical answer.

"Let's hope you're right about him and that they do call it off." Thunder echoed in the darkening sky, fear beating a steady tempo in Bass's brain. "This is one time I want to be wrong."

As a few raindrops splattered, the race committee decided not to call off the footrace. Too much money had been spent and no one wanted to disappoint the crowd. A disappointed crowd became rowdy. And a rowdy crowd, dangerous. Everyone agreed that only fifteen minutes more was not much to ask of the competitors and they'd probably just get a little wet.

Though Daisy was more than apprehensive, she knew if she didn't participate, she would lose valuable sales because people would be upset with her. And she truly believed she could win the race if she wasn't attacked before she crossed the finish line. So she lined up, ready to get this over with.

Just as the gun sounded the start, lightning flashed and brightened the sky, enhancing the display of the brooding clouds that hovered above. In seconds, echoing thunder warned the rain was certain to drop in earnest any moment and they'd waited too long to begin the competition. She started to count as she ran, matching her footfalls to the seconds between the time of the next thunder clap.

One one-hundred.

Two one-hundred.

Three one-hundred.

Another flash. Another rumble.

Big raindrops struck the bare earth so hard that little puffs of dust rose on impact in their wake.

Fifteen minutes. Three miles, Daisy told herself. *That's all it is. You can do it.* Even though she told herself she could make it, Daisy prayed the downpour would not come before she crossed the line.

A bolt zigzagged across the sky, a bluish-white sizzle that raised the hair on the back of her neck.

One one-hundred.

Two one-hundred.

Thunder came quicker now, warning the storm was moving closer, not away, and clapping so violently that it made her shout. She and the other racers had put themselves in great danger by being out here in the open. All for money and a sense of pride. What a fool she'd been.

The smell of something burning flared her nostrils and she prayed the lightning had not scarred the earth. The solid-packed Texas dirt would need a downpour to drench the ground hard and fast. Otherwise, the rain would simply run off to find softer ground or a gully.

Lightning-scarred earth meant the possibility of setting a wildfire. *Lord, not that. Please not that.*

She didn't know what to do. Turn around and head back into the storm or keep running trying to stay ahead of it. Once she passed the halfway mark, all she could do was head back anyway, try to outrace the danger and warn the townsmen of the strike.

Just ahead the sentinel that had stood watch for so many years lay on its side burning, uprooted now by the fierce bolt that had finally torn it asunder. The flames turned the courageous seedlings into curled ash. Life could be gone in the blink of an eye.

That was a truth bigger than any lie. Any omission. In that moment she realized she couldn't live without Bass Parker and wanted him to stay.

Bass, her heart called out to him. *Keep my children safe. Keep yourself from harm. Be waiting with open arms so I can ask you to forgive my pride.*

Daisy prayed it wasn't too late. After all, she'd said things to him in anger. Could her love be enough to convince him to stay? To guide them to the truth of what they felt for each other?

Chapter Twenty-Three

The team gave him fits, but Bass didn't care. By the time he managed to get the wagon through the crowd without hurting anyone, he suspected Daisy should be somewhere near the halfway point. He didn't know the path she took, but he knew the direction of her return and reined the horses into the storm.

"Hey!" a tiny voice yelled from under the blanket that rolled beneath his feet. "That hurt!"

"I didn't do it, he did," another small voice argued.

Bass couldn't take a chance on stopping. "What are you two doing down there?"

Ollie and Thad peeped from under the blanket he'd borrowed from Junior Pickens. He'd meant it to be for Daisy in case she got drenched. Not for two disobeying children he'd left with Snow and Petula at the mercantile. "You said for us to stick with you," Ollie reminded.

"That was before I told you to stay with your aunt," he growled, wondering how the pair had managed to stow away beneath the driver's box without him noticing. Bass watched for sign of the runners.

God, let me take the right path, he prayed.

"We came to help Miz Daisy." Thad's voice bounced with every rut.

"Grab hold of something and don't let go even if it's each other. You should have stayed back there. I told Daisy I'd keep you safe. Promised her I'd do my best. She'll never trust me with you again. Either of you."

"Then don't get us hurt," Ollie said, partially slipping inside the blanket.

"Olivia Jane Trumbo soon-to-be Parker if I have my way, that's exactly what I intend to do."

Ollie yelled and pointed. "Hey, Bass, look, there's that bowlegged stranger I talked to. He's got a torch! He's bending down and touching the grass."

A thin line of flames raced across the horizon as a trail of smoke drifted in its wake.

"Wildfire!" Bass yelled. "Hang on, children! We've got to find Daisy. We must outrun this."

Thad's forefinger pointed just to the right of where Ollie did. "And look, there's two other men waitin' on him. They're holding a horse for him."

Two shots rang out.

"Get covered, now!" Bass yelled and sent the team into a full gallop.

"One of them's got red hair like the fire," shouted Thad as he did what he was told.

"Winker." Fear filled Ollie's voice as she identified the redhead. "The robbers are after us, Bass. Maybe that other man is one of the gang and I just didn't recognize him. We got to help Mama. She don't know they're comin'."

Lightning flashed and Ollie yelled, "I…I don't like lightnin'. Sorry I screamed, but it's gonna get me."

"Try not to yell again, honey. The robbers will hear you. Let's hope the runners did. I'm not turning back and I'm not leaving Daisy out here. Maybe those men set the fire for another reason, but I can't take a chance that they aren't after Daisy. We've got to reach her before the wildfire or they do."

"If you save my mama, I want—"

"*Our* mama," Thad insisted. "She's my mama now, too, remember?"

"No, she ain't," Ollie argued.

No time to give Ollie a stern talking-to. Bass had to make her understand. "You have everything, honey. All he has in the world is Daisy and you. You're hurting your mother by acting like this."

"*Our* mama," Ollie finally relented, screaming as lightning flashed again. "And I want you and nobody else as my daddy. His, too."

"Then here's one saved mama coming up," Bass tried his best to reassure them.

Another shot rang out.

The sting of a bullet hit his leg. Way too close to the children. Bass gritted his teeth and strengthened his hold on the reins, praying. *Let me keep my word, Lord. They're counting on me and I'm counting on You.*

Torturous minutes later, he found Daisy. She ran like the fire chased her, and it did. Another wind-driven wildfire was eating up the dried grass behind her, getting closer and closer to collide with the one the robbers had set. The rain still took its time working itself into anything but a light patter.

Come on, let it pour, Bass prayed fervently.

He reined up precious moments, jumping down to grab Daisy as she flung herself into his arms.

"Oh, Bass, it's you. Really you. I love you, do you hear me? Truly love you. I've found the man I want to spend the rest of my life with if you'll have me. If you'll forgive me for being so stubborn. I was afraid I wouldn't make it back to tell you."

"I don't have time to kiss you, but I promise I'll do that thoroughly once this is over." He hugged her then nearly hurled her onto the wagon seat.

Jumping onto the driver's box and pushing Daisy on top of the blanket on the floor beneath him, he quickly told her about the robbers. "We've got to rescue the rest of the runners before they're caught between the two fires and warn the townsfolk of the danger if they don't already smell it."

Another shot rang out, pinging off a wagon hub. Ollie and Thad screamed.

"Keep your heads down and hang on tight," Bass commanded.

Daisy groped the bundles beneath the blanket. "What are the children doing—"

"Mama, you're safe!" Ollie screeched.

"Mama, we came to save you." Pride echoed in Thad's voice. "And we did it. Bass and us did it."

The outrage at finding her children here ended in an equally frightened tone. "What are you thinking, bringing them out here with you?" She noticed his leg. "Oh, you're bleeding."

Daisy grabbed the hem of her petticoat and ripped off a piece, tying it around Bass's right leg to stem the flow of blood.

"I'll make it." He flicked the reins and horses into action. "You have the next fifty years to yell at me if you want to. Just trust me."

Fortunately, many of the runners were not that far behind and had already cut across open field toward High Plains. Daisy counted them as quickly as she could.

"That's everyone, I think," Daisy assured him. "You

won't have to stop and pick up any unless the smoke overcomes them. Hurry, Bass. Turn the wagon their way."

Shots rang out.

"Everybody stay down!" he yelled. All he could do was dodge, keeping Daisy and the children safe beneath his legs and praying none of the runners took a bullet in back.

Next thing he knew Teague and another man raced toward him from town. A handful of other riders trailed close behind the lawman. Shots competed with the thunder. The Ranger and his friend returned fire.

Teague motioned the rider closest to him to pass him. "Catch 'em, Newcomb, and see that you don't get burned doing it. I'll be there in a second."

Teague didn't halt but turned and drew up alongside the wagon, keeping pace. "You got the kids? Pet says they're gone."

"Yes."

"I saw the runners just now. You got the widow?"

"I'm here," she announced from beneath Bass.

"You know who's shooting at you?"

"Part of the gang that robbed the bank. They set the fire."

"Winker's one of 'em and that bowlegged man." Ollie peeped from beneath the blanket. "I seen him set it."

"Good." Teague's hand went to his gun. "We've got a witness."

Bass took a long look at the town he'd come to think of as home. "I suspect they mean to keep us busy with fighting the fire so they can pull another robbery."

"No maybe to it. That's exactly what the rest of the gang just tried to do. Maddox has them. Take care of the fire. We'll take care of this." Teague pulled leather and headed in the direction Newcomb had taken.

As the team raced into High Plains, Bass shouted, "Wildfire coming! Two of them. Grab your buckets and shovels! Dig fire paths. Clear the grass so the fire will turn back on itself."

People raced everywhere at the sound of alarm. As soon as Bass reined in, Petula and Snow rushed toward the wagon.

"Get in," he ordered. "You're going with Daisy."

They looked puzzled until Daisy and the children scrambled from beneath his feet and took a proper place in the wagon.

Bass handed Daisy the reins. "If it looks like we can't control the fires," he said as he pulled her close and kissed her gently, "get down to the lake on your property if you spot the flames coming your way."

She moved away slightly. "I'll never tire of looking at you. Come back to me."

He caressed the hair at her temple. "Stay in the water. It's the only place I think you might ride this out. I want you safe."

Daisy kissed him hard, her eyes searching his for assurance. "We don't want to leave you. Ever."

"You've got to. I'll be home in a while. We've got things to talk about. And I owe you a thorough, forever kiss."

Chapter Twenty-Four

It seemed a lifetime ago since Daisy left Bass to battle the fires. The saffron rays of tomorrow crept into the parlor window as she watched for his return.

The heavy downpour she'd prayed would put out the wildfire had come and gone, but had it been too late even though she'd never been forced to head to the lake?

Had Bass survived the fire and leg wound?

All of a sudden, he and her brothers-in-law rode in, trailed by Teague and the man he'd called Newcomb. All looked exhausted and smoke-stained. When Bass dismounted from behind Jonas, she could see his leg had been bandaged properly and he wore a tired smile.

She raced out into his arms, not caring that he reeked of smoke or that a half dozen men looked on as they dismounted.

Bass picked her up and swung her around joyfully.

"Kiss me," she pleaded. "Like you said you would."

"First we talk. Got a lot to tell you." His eyes searched hers, then focused on the Ranger. "Teague, you care to share what happened with the gang? You know more of the details."

Teague started to speak, but Maddox interrupted

him. "Let me tell her our part." He grabbed each brother in a headlock. "We had us one of the best fistfights ever. Part of the gang decided they was goin' to rob the safe at the mercantile, but we didn't let 'em get away with it, did we, boys?"

The two sandy-colored heads shook in response but couldn't get out of their big brother's hold.

Maddox laughed. "Soon as we figured out how many was in on it, we went to cracking heads. Can't say as we didn't get a few innocent bystanders, too, but it was hard tellin' who was being legal and who wasn't at the time."

Everyone laughed. Teague stuffed his single leather glove in his pocket. "The shooters we chased nearly got burned alive. They got caught between the fires and passed out from too much smoke. It was pretty easy for us to haul them in with them begging for their lives. When we told them we had an eyewitness to them setting one of the fires, they—"

"Two. You have two witnesses," Bass corrected. "Both children saw them."

"Two, then." Teague continued, "When we got the whole gang together in a jail cell, the ones the Trumbos took care of said they weren't going to be held responsible for the safecracking, the fire and trying to take you two out as witnesses to the first robbery. Let's just say, every man decided to spill his guts all at once about his own personal role so he'd get the least amount of jail time."

"So they were trying to kill us." Daisy shuddered in Bass's arms.

"But we outran them." Bass hugged her tightly.

"Kiss me," she pleaded, not wanting to wait another moment. They could tell her anything else she needed to know later. She only wanted to know one thing now. Could Bass forgive her? Did he love her?

Blue-violet eyes stared deeply into her own. "Can you accept me as I am? I'll never be perfect, but I'll do my best to learn how to be everything you want and need."

Tears sprang into her eyes as he held her close. "I have my faults, too. I realized I expected far too much of you. Just because I feared you would betray me like Knox did, I was afraid to give you my heart. But as I ran from the fire, I realized that I love you and could never do without you. Letting you go would be the greatest danger of my life, Bass. Will you forgive me?"

"You made me angry," Bass admitted. "It seemed your feelings were the only thing you'd considered or that mattered. I felt pushed to the side as though mine weren't important. Then I discovered it wasn't anger I felt, but fear. Fear that by having lost your trust in me, I had risked all that you had come to mean to me and I didn't even know it until then. I can't live without you, either, Daisy. It wouldn't be living at all."

Her fingers traced his lips and he pressed a gentle kiss against them.

"Looks like we've got all our cards on the table," he whispered. "We can't change the past, but what we can do is start a new course and make our path as smooth as we're able. We're going to have bumps and holes and hurdles, but together we'll reach the finish line."

She laughed, her heart soaring with the promise of their future. "Stay. Never leave me." Daisy savored the moment and the opportunity to give her heart to him for the rest of forever. "I love you."

Say it, she willed him the words.

"I love you, too. You have my heart, lady. Take good care of it."

"Deal," Ollie and Thad spoke in unison as each ran

up to grab his legs. Snow, Petula and Myrtle followed close behind.

Ollie stared at Bass when he winced. "You're gonna be my—" she glanced at Thaddeus "—*our* daddy now. Mama done said so and I tore up all my papers." She dusted her hands as if ridding herself of the matter then leaned in and giggled. "You was the best one anyway. I just got mad at ya for a tiny, bitty bit."

"I told Mama up in Heaven about it," Thad informed. "I can't hear her, 'course, but I think I felt her right here." He touched his heart. "Something all squiggly moved around and made me smile."

Bass let go of Daisy and rustled both of the children's hair. "Then I've got one thing to say to *this* mama."

He patted his vest and grabbed something from the inside pocket. Kneeling down on one knee, he rested beside each child and handed Daisy the gift. "Daisy Trumbo, thank you for making me forget who I was told to be and helping me become the man I wanted to be."

He stood and slipped the ring on her finger. "Will you marry me? Be my bride and make me happy? Make us all a forever family?"

Her simple one word reply blended with the welcome of his urgent kiss, fulfilling the deep yearning they both shared to heal the past and accept the bright future ahead of them.

Daisy raised her arms and laced her fingers through his midnight hair and gave as much as he offered. A sense of belonging left no doubt she was truly loved, and their commitment to make their corner of the world the best it could be would lead them down the perfect path of true love.

* * * * *

Dear Reader,

I'm fascinated with history. I'm ever curious about little-known historical facts. I came across information about The Pedestriennes, women runners in the 1800s, and asked myself why a woman might choose to compete with men in footraces. I also read about the common practice of offering money to someone to take one's place in war. Could a hero do this and have good reason? Would such a couple combine to touch my readers' hearts? Answering that began my interest in writing this story.

Widow Daisy Trumbo is determined to prove she can raise her daughter all by herself. Even if it means earning extra money competing in footraces and making shoes.

Factory baron Bass Parker carries a secret guilt—he knows Daisy Trumbo blames him for offering her husband money to take his place in the war seven years ago and holds him responsible for her child never having met her daddy. Guilt and duty require Bass to finally convince Daisy to accept the funds she's refused since becoming widowed.

Add to that a little matchmaker determined to have two parents and who will go to any length to interview bachelors for her daddy list.

Guilt, obligation, forgiveness and refusing to settle for nothing less than true love are the main themes in *The Daddy List*. I hope you enjoy Bass and Daisy's story.

I'm always excited to hear from my readers, and I can be reached at dewannapace@suddenlink.net or my website, www.dewannapaceonline.com.

Many blessings,

DeWanna Pace

COMING NEXT MONTH FROM
Love Inspired® Historical

Available April 7, 2015

WAGON TRAIN REUNION

Journey West

by Linda Ford

Abigail Bingham is reunited with former flame Benjamin Hewitt when she joins a wagon train headed west. Will the Oregon Trail offer a second chance for the socialite's daughter and a charming cowboy?

AN UNLIKELY LOVE

by Dorothy Clark

Marissa Bradley is drawn to Grant Winston, but his livelihood is to blame for her family's destruction. Can Grant find a way to maintain the family business and to have Marissa as his wife?

FROM BOSS TO BRIDEGROOM

Smoky Mountain Matches

by Karen Kirst

What starts as a strictly professional relationship grows into something more between boss Quinn Darling and his lovely employee, Nicole O'Malley. Until Quinn discovers Nicole's been keeping a secret that could derail their future together.

THE DOCTOR'S UNDOING

by Allie Pleiter

Doctor Daniel Parker doesn't want a fiery nurse telling him how to run his orphanage. But Ida Lee Landway's kindness—and beauty—slowly chip away at his stubborn exterior.

LIHCNM0315

REQUEST YOUR FREE BOOKS

2 FREE INSPIRATIONAL NOVELS
PLUS 2
FREE
MYSTERY GIFTS

Love Inspired
HISTORICAL
INSPIRATIONAL HISTORICAL ROMANCE

YES! Please send me 2 FREE Love Inspired® Historical novels and my 2 FREE mystery gifts (gifts are worth about $10). After receiving them, if I don't wish to receive any more books, I can return the shipping statement marked "cancel." If I don't cancel, I will receive 4 brand-new novels every month and be billed just $4.74 per book in the U.S. or $5.24 per book in Canada. That's a saving of at least 21% off the cover price. It's quite a bargain! Shipping and handling is just 50¢ per book in the U.S. and 75¢ per book in Canada.* I understand that accepting the 2 free books and gifts places me under no obligation to buy anything. I can always return a shipment and cancel at any time. Even if I never buy another book, the two free books and gifts are mine to keep forever.

102/302 IDN F5CN

Name _____ (PLEASE PRINT) _____

Address _____ Apt. # _____

City _____ State/Prov. _____ Zip/Postal Code _____

Signature (if under 18, a parent or guardian must sign)

Mail to the **Harlequin® Reader Service:**
IN U.S.A.: P.O. Box 1867, Buffalo, NY 14240-1867
IN CANADA: P.O. Box 609, Fort Erie, Ontario L2A 5X3

Want to try two free books from another series?
Call 1-800-873-8635 or visit www.ReaderService.com.

* Terms and prices subject to change without notice. Prices do not include applicable taxes. Sales tax applicable in N.Y. Canadian residents will be charged applicable taxes. Offer not valid in Quebec. This offer is limited to one order per household. Not valid for current subscribers to Love Inspired Historical books. All orders subject to credit approval. Credit or debit balances in a customer's account(s) may be offset by any other outstanding balance owed by or to the customer. Please allow 4 to 6 weeks for delivery. Offer available while quantities last.

Your Privacy—The Harlequin® Reader Service is committed to protecting your privacy. Our Privacy Policy is available online at www.ReaderService.com or upon request from the Harlequin Reader Service.

We make a portion of our mailing list available to reputable third parties that offer products we believe may interest you. If you prefer that we not exchange your name with third parties, or if you wish to clarify or modify your communication preferences, please visit us at www.ReaderService.com/consumerschoice or write to us at Harlequin Reader Service Preference Service, P.O. Box 9062, Buffalo, NY 14269. Include your complete name and address.

LIHI3

Benjamin Hewitt stared. It wasn't possible.

The man struggling with his oxen couldn't be Mr. Bingham. He would never subject himself and his wife to the trials of this journey. Why, Mrs. Bingham would look mighty strange fluttering a lace hankie and expecting someone to serve her tea.

The man must have given the wrong command because the oxen jerked hard to the right. The rear wheel broke free. A flurry of smaller items fell out the back. A woman followed, shrieking.

"Mother, are you injured?" A young woman ran toward her mother. She sounded just like Abigail. At least as near as he could recall. He'd succeeded in putting that young woman from his mind many years ago.

She glanced about. "Father, are you safe?"

The sun glowed in her blond hair and he knew without seeing her face that it was Abigail. What was she doing here? She'd not find a fine, big house nor fancy dishes and certainly no servants on this trip.

The bitterness he'd once felt at being rejected because he couldn't provide those things had dissipated, leaving only regret and caution.

She helped her mother to her feet and dusted her skirts off. All the while, the woman—Mrs. Bingham, to be sure—complained, her voice grating with displeasure that made Ben's nerves twitch. He knew all too well that sound. Could recall in sharp detail when the woman had told him he was not a suitable suitor for her daughter. Abigail had agreed, had told him, in a harsh dismissive tone, she would no longer see him.

It all seemed so long ago. Six years to be exact. He'd been a different person back then. Thanks to Abigail, he'd learned not to trust everything a woman said. Nor believe how they acted.

But Binghams or not, a wheel needed to be put on. Ben joined the men hurrying to assist the family.

"Hello." He greeted Mr. Bingham and the man shook his hand. "Ladies." He tipped his hat to them.

"Hello, Ben." Abigail Bingham stood at her mother's side. No, not Bingham. She was Abigail Black now.

Don't miss
WAGON TRAIN REUNION by Linda Ford,
available April 2015 wherever
Love Inspired® Historical books and ebooks are sold.

www.Harlequin.com

LIHEXP0315

*Can Mary find happiness with a secretive stranger who
saves her life?*

*Read on for a sneak preview of the final book in
Patricia Davids's
BRIDES OF AMISH COUNTRY series,
AMISH REDEMPTION.*

Hannah edged closer to her. "I don't like storms."

Mary slipped an arm around her daughter. "Don't
worry. We'll be at Katie's house before the rain catches
us."

It turned out she was wrong. Big raindrops began hit-
ting her windshield. A strong gust of wind shook the
buggy and blew dust across the road. The sky grew
darker by the minute. She urged Tilly to a faster pace. She
should have stayed home.

A red car flew past her with the driver laying on the
horn. Tilly shied and nearly dragged the buggy into the
fence along the side of the road. Mary managed to right
her. "Foolish *Englischers*. We are over as far as we can
get."

The rumble of thunder became a steady roar behind
them. Tilly broke into a run. Hannah began screaming.
Mary glanced back and her heart stopped. A tornado had
dropped from the clouds and was bearing down on them.
Dust and debris flew out from the wide base.

Dear God, help me save my baby. What do I do?

She saw an intersection up ahead.

Bracing her legs against the dash, she pulled back on the lines, trying to slow Tilly enough to make the corner without overturning. The mare seemed to sense the plan. She slowed and made the turn with the buggy tilting on two wheels. Mary grabbed Hannah and held on to her. Swerving wildly behind the horse, the buggy finally came back onto all four wheels. Before the mare could gather speed again, a man jumped into the road waving his arms. He grabbed Tilly's bridle and pulled her to a stop.

Shouting, he pointed toward an abandoned farmhouse. "There's a cellar on the south side."

Mary jumped out of the buggy and pulled Hannah into her arms. The man was already unhitching Tilly, so Mary ran toward the ramshackle structure. The wind threatened to pull her off her feet. The trees and even the grass were straining toward the approaching tornado. She reached the old cellar door, but couldn't lift it against the force of the wind. She was about to lie on the ground on top of Hannah when the man appeared at her side. Together they were able to lift the door.

A second later, she was pushed down the steps into darkness.

Don't miss
AMISH REDEMPTION by Patricia Davids,
available April 2015 wherever
Love Inspired® books and ebooks are sold.

www.Harlequin.com

LIEXP031

SPECIAL EXCERPT FROM

Love Inspired
SUSPENSE

Framed for a crime she didn't commit,
museum curator Lana Gomez must prove her
innocence under the watchful eyes of
Capitol K-9 Unit officer Adam Donovan.

Read on for a sneak preview of
the next exciting installment of the
CAPITOL K-9 UNIT *series,*
DUTY BOUND GUARDIAN
by **Terri Reed.**

K-9 officer Adam Donovan's cell buzzed inside the breast
pocket of his uniform shirt. He halted, staying out of the
rain beneath the overhang covering the entrance to the
E. Barrett Prettyman Federal Courthouse.

"Sit," he murmured to his partner, Ace, a four-year-old,
dark-coated, sleek Doberman pinscher. The dog obedi-
ently sat on his right. Keeping Ace's lead in his left hand,
he answered the call. "Adam Donovan."

By habit Adam scanned the crowds of tourists flood-
ing the National Mall, on alert for any criminal activity.
Not even nighttime or an April drizzle could keep sight-
seers in their hotels. To his right the central dome of the
US Capitol building gleamed with floodlights, postcard
perfect.

"Gavin here" came the deep voice of his boss, Captain
Gavin McCord. "You still at the courthouse?"

Adam had had a late meeting with the DA regarding a case against a drug dealer who'd been selling in and around the metro DC area. The elite Capitol K-9 Unit had been called in to assist the local police during a two-hour manhunt nine months ago. The K-9 unit was often enlisted in various crimes throughout the Washington, DC, area.

Ace had been the one to find the suspect hiding in a construction Dumpster outside of the National Gallery of Art. The suspect took the DA's deal and gave up the names of his associates rather than stand trial, which had been scheduled to begin later this week.

A victory on this rainy spring evening.

"Yes, sir."

"There's been a break-in at the American Museum and two of the museum employees have been assaulted," Gavin stated.

"Injured or dead?" Adam asked, already moving down the steps toward his vehicle with Ace at his heels.

"Injured. The intruder rendered both employees unconscious, but the security guard came to and pulled the fire alarm, scaring off the intruder. Both have been rushed to the hospital on Varnum Street." Gavin's tone intensified. "But the other victim is who I'm interested in. Lana Gomez."

Don't miss
DUTY BOUND GUARDIAN by Terri Reed,
available April 2015 wherever
Love Inspired® Suspense books and ebooks are sold.

www.Harlequin.com